TO

'I'm afraid I'm too dirty to enter the bath. Could you make sure I'm clean enough to go into the water? I think I must be especially dirty down there.' Ping looked back into Sandra's eyes. 'Please.' The trace of Sandra's fingers down her spine sent a light spasm through her flesh. Her loins clenched in anticipation as Sandra's finger pressed against her button then moved forwards between her nether lips. It sank into her sex for a moment, withdrew, found her nub and pressed hard. Ping released a quiet moan deep in her throat and leaned her body forwards to give Sandra better access, then sucked in a sharp breath as Sandra pushed the tip of her soapy wet thumb onto Ping's bumhole. At the same time a finger of her other hand sank into Ping's channel. Ping fell onto her hands and knees and raised her hips towards Sandra, her oil oozing from her quim. She pushed her hips back, forcing Sandra's fingers deep into her twin gates. 'Nnngh!' Ping's arousal began building as the rhythmic pace of Sandra's probing digits quickened.

TOKYO BOUND

Sachi

nexus

This book is a work of fiction.
In real life, make sure you practise safe, sane and consensual sex.

First published in 2006 by
Nexus
Thames Wharf Studios
Rainville Road
London W6 9HA

www.nexus-books.co.uk

Typeset by TW Typesetting, Plymouth, Devon

Printed and bound by
Clays Ltd, St Ives PLC

ISBN 0 352 34019 3
ISBN 9 780352 340191

All characters in this publication are fictitious and any resemblance to real persons, living or dead, is purely coincidental.

You'll notice that we have introduced a set of symbols onto our book jackets, so that you can tell at a glance what fetishes each of our brand new novels contains. Here's the key – enjoy!

cp (traditional)

cp (modern)

spanking

restraint/bondage

rope bondage/hojojutsu

latex/rubber/leather/enclosure

fem dom

willing captivity

medical

period setting

uniforms

sex rituals

One

In shadow, James Burke watches sweat bead on the skin of a young Chinese woman. The light of a bare bulb plays along her glistening flesh as her arms jerk against steel shackles holding her wrists. Her shoulders press against a thin mat. Her back arches.

Wei Xian-xi holds a needle as thin as a human hair. It whips like a reed in the wind as he twirls it between the thumb and index finger of his right hand. His left hand presses into the moist cleft of his disciple. He eases two fingers into her sex, curling them upwards against her G-zone as he strokes her clitoris with his left thumb.

The woman breathes in short bursts of anticipation. Taut cords stand out in her graceful neck as she lifts her head to watch. Arteries throb visibly under the light beige of her flawless skin. Her pale-brown nipples swell with heat and the rush of blood. Muscles knot in her belly, creating narrow furrows for the trickles of her salty fluid.

Wei runs his flat broad tongue across her quim, then he hardens and shoves its point against her throbbing bud until her ejaculation soaks his chin and fingers. He sniffs deeply and rolls her juice over his tongue, drawing air across it as though he were testing a fine wine.

She is ready.

Wei pinches her nubbin hard and pricks the needle lightly and rapidly against its tip. The woman clenches her teeth, hissing as she sucks air between her spread lips.

Her limbs strain against the shackles. Wei flicks the needle faster, just nipping the surface of her flesh. His wrist moves with a drummer's speed but greater agility, teasing the full shaft of her short nub. The woman's shoulders writhe as he works the surface of her quivering organ.

Suddenly he stops.

The woman clenches her stomach and raises her shoulders off the mat. She draws a long slow breath. Before she has filled her lungs, Wei sinks the needle into the core of her sensitivity. She slams her shoulders back against the mat and arches her back high. By sheer will, she holds her hips immobile. A savage groan rumbles out of the depths of her body.

The needle is as flexible as a thread. Wei curves it across her mound and tapes it to her skin. He attaches a wire that is secured at its other end to an electrical transformer, minutely calibrated. He sets the current low at two milliamperes and the potential at two thousand volts. The hair at the woman's crotch dances about her sex, excited by the gentle, teasing current and the high voltage. Her hair lashes across her face as her head thrashes from side to side.

Wei adjusts the amperage at irregular intervals. At each change the woman's moans rise or fall with the electrical fire raging and ebbing through the steel inside her. He reaches a harmony with her passions, bringing her at his will to heights of ecstasy and release. She strains her ankles against the shackles that hold her legs wide, but otherwise keeps her lower body still.

She has been trained to endure pain, exquisite in its application.

Burke mentally recorded each of Wei's actions, every response of the woman. It would be his only lesson in this aspect of Wei's skills. The Chinese master motioned to Burke to step forwards.

'To understand, you must feel,' he told Burke.

'On a man, where do you put the needle?'

'You already have knowledge of the pain and soothing of the needle's prick and sting. To truly know, you must become the needle. Remove your clothes.'

Burke wore only a loose shirt and trousers secured at his waist by a cord. He started to pull the shirt over his head, but Wei stopped him.

'Slowly. Step into the light so she can see you. Her name is Ling-shau. Say it.'

Burke watched her jaw grind and heard her breaths come in shallow pants as he walked towards her. He spoke her name and drew the shirt up, gradually exposing his stomach and chest to her eyes, black with desire.

The single lamp cast the hard outlines of Burke's lean musculature in stark patterns of light and dark. As he untied the cord and slid his trousers downwards, her hot gaze alone made him hard.

Burke stood over Ling-shau, watching her tongue push against her lower lip as her eyes focused on Burke's swelling prick. Her hips twitched, craving the power of his sex. She gasped softly as he let the trousers fall to his ankles and stood naked before her.

'Straddle her, there.' Wei pointed to Ling-shau's face.

Burke put one foot on either side of her head.

'Lower yourself, slowly.'

Centimetre by centimetre, Burke brought his groin closer to Ling-shau's face.

She strained against her bonds and raised her head towards him, ravenous for his touch and taste.

Burke held himself just out of reach and let only his sac brush her nose, cheeks and eyes.

Ling-shau groaned and flung her face against Burke's thigh, biting into his muscles and pushing her tongue against him. She clenched her teeth and jerked her head back, nipping out hair then lapping at his sweat, savouring his taste in her mouth.

'Lower yourself to her chest,' said Wei.

Burke stepped back and sank to his knees, pressing his sac against her breast. He rotated his hips as she forced herself against him, covering him in her softness. He rocked back and forth so the full length of his stiff cock slid along her tender areola and the firm bead at its crest.

'Her belly,' said Wei.

Burke moved along Ling-shau's body, squeezing his hard rod between her stomach and his own until the base of his sex just touched the dark follicles at Ling-shau's mound. He massaged her delicious breasts with his face and hands, raking their sensitive brown summits with his teeth and pinching them just enough to make Ling-shau grimace. He lifted himself off her, kneading the firm flesh of her limbs and pressing his nose and tongue into the acrid musk under her arms, then licked the sweat that pooled at the juncture of her jaw and neck, kissed her eyes and sampled the salt tears that ran down her cheeks. He wanted to know all of her.

Ling-shau's body shivered despite the heat of the night. Her voice quavered at the back of her throat.

'She hungers,' said Wei. 'Let her touch you.'

Burke lowered his groin to Ling-shau's hand, then moved forwards and back to give her full access as she squeezed and stroked his glans and rigid staff. She pressed a fingertip onto the tiny mouth at the tip of his proud prick and eased her fingers deep between the cheeks of his buttocks. He moved to her face and let her take his sac into her mouth. She played her tongue over his heavy balls, along his perineum and even touching the pucker between his cheeks. She sought the tip of his staff, but Burke pulled away and turned to put his face into the sparse fur of her mound. Her subtle bouquet lured his mouth to her folds, slippery with the oil of her excitement. His fingers slid easily past her slick entrance, deep to the silken walls of her channel. As he licked the thick lips of her sex, he lowered his hips to let her take him into her mouth.

Ling-shau eagerly raised her head and spread her jaws wide to admit his girth, then thrust her head up and back and swallowed, milking the full length of his staff with the muscles of her throat. When she felt him tense, she released him and teased the underside of his cock with her tender pouting lips and tongue.

Burke felt his engorged sex on the verge of bursting when he felt Wei's hand on his shoulder. He looked up and the master simply nodded.

Burke rose and stood between Ling-shau's splayed legs as Wei applied a thin conductor to one of the inner lips of her sex, wet with her come, and attached a wire from it to the transformer. When Wei nodded again, Burke lay on Ling-shau and eased himself slowly into her narrow channel. At the moment he penetrated halfway, the first jolt of electricity struck. Burke felt as though his spine had been pierced with slivers of ice. His back arched, and in a fierce spasm he thrust the entire length of his massive cock into Ling-shau. He bucked once more and almost withdrew completely, struggling to control his body against the charges that wracked his frame. His mind fogged as he slammed again and again into Ling-shau.

She pressed the back of her head against the mat and pushed her breasts, belly and cunt against Burke with astonishing strength. Her limbs strained against the shackles as her hips pounded to meet Burke's savage thrusts. A growl rumbled in her chest as she bit into the thick flesh of Burke's shoulder.

He shook free and pressed his palm against her shuddering breast, then gripped her hair with his other hand and forced her head down, kissing her hard on the mouth, pushing his tongue between her yielding lips. The electric current raced over the sweat of their bodies and into the saliva of their new union. Burke lost all sense of being except for the sheer physicality of sex with Ling-shau. He felt unable to breathe as his life force flowed from his body into hers. Then he felt the current wane. The electrical surge became a gentle prickle, like nettles just brushing his skin. He gasped air into his starved lungs and slowed his movements, sliding gracefully in and out of Ling-shau's exquisitely tight hole.

Ling-shau let her body go limp. She took long, deep breaths, filling her lungs. Her head filled with the universal *chi*, which spread through her, cooling her with the sensation of internal goose flesh and making her feel as though her body would float into Burke's.

Burke understood, matching the pace of his breath and the gentle rhythm of his sex with the rise and fall of Ling-shau's lungs.

When their strength was restored, Wei increased the current.

This time Burke was prepared. He felt the charge heighten his sensations of pleasure and pain simultaneously, but he remained in control. He forced his loins to a jackhammer tempo as Wei's current urged him on.

Ling-shau could not keep pace. She opened her body and spirit to receive him, to rejoice in his mastery of her being. His sexual power engulfed her, his driving rod devouring her consciousness.

Burke felt a droplet of semen escape into Ling-shau's charged juices. It was enough to draw the current into the rod of his prick, stinging the tender globes of his sac. His body shuddered.

Wei raised the current higher as the droplet was followed by a rushing river of white-hot seed.

The electrical current raged into the sexual cores of Burke and Ling-shau. Their screams ripped the fabric of the ether and the power of *chi* flowed through them, filling their bodies.

Burke lay still on Ling-shau and slowly withdrew his diminishing staff as Wei released her bonds.

Free now to touch his body, Ling-shau took his head in her hands and kissed his mouth. She kneaded the thick tensors along his spine and embraced his hips with her legs.

Burke rolled onto his back with Ling-shau on top of him. He gripped the firm globes of her arse and ran his hand between its cheeks, teasing her tight sphincter. It brought a giggle from Ling-shau, who tightened her cheeks on his fingers. She laid her head on his chest and hummed deep in her throat as Burke looked up and saw Wei standing over them.

A wisp of a smile softened the master's face. 'Are you enlightened?' he asked.

Burke answered with a single nod, then cocked his head to the side. 'But perhaps not completely.'

Wei laughed. 'Not only is that an honest answer, it is also astute. You have learned that there is a path beyond the one you sought, but you don't yet know the way to that path.'

Burke had come to Wei to learn secrets of acupuncture and electrical stimulation known to very few. The price of admission to Wei's 'university' was knowledge. The master required his disciples to first teach him, but Burke had nothing to offer. Spurned, he went to Japan and trained in shiatsu, aikido and an arcane discipline called *katsugen undo*, which relied on diet and training in *ki*, the Japanese pronunciation of *chi*. In his training, he discovered quite by accident that when two points on the body are pressed while the left wrist is twisted in a certain fashion, the victim's anal sphincters go completely lax and the colon compresses. He had little hope that this would impress Master Wei, but since he found no one who had heard of his technique, he returned to China. When he demonstrated on one of Wei's disciples, the master roared with laughter, despite the poor victim's humiliation. Burke's face burned red. He was sure that Wei's laughter meant the master considered him a fool, but to his surprise the old man expressed deep gratitude.

Wei said many of his patients were elderly and would pay well and regularly for such a service. He immediately called a female disciple and told her to remove her clothes and squat. When he tried the technique himself, and it worked on the woman, he warmly welcomed Burke into his training.

'Come.' Wei called Burke to the transformer. 'There are crude versions of this machine in the torture chambers of despotic governments around the world. They char the flesh and blunt the minds of the victims. What use is a statement from a man subjected to such barbarity? This –' Wei stroked the electronic dials lightly '– is a fine sable-hair brush, and the human body a canvas for a montage of pain – and pleasure.' He smiled at Burke. 'As you know, it is the current, not voltage, that harms the body, although the body does sense the aura of electrons generated by a high potential. Combined with the needle, you can achieve wonderful precision. Would you guess that with you and Ling-shau, I never came near even one ampere?'

Burke had felt like he'd been hit with 200 amps and 10,000 volts. He shook his head.

'There are amateurs who use electrical gadgets for sexual stimulation. Frankly, I don't understand. Such devices and techniques are hopelessly crude. It's like a woman hitting herself with a poleaxe when what she really wants is to be scourged by a sliver of bamboo. It's a dangerous game for amateurs. The brain communicates with the heart by electrical impulses. Even if you keep the amperage low, there is a possibility that the frequency will match that used by the brain and disrupt the signals, causing the heart to fibrillate.'

Burke had long since lost his amazement at Wei's broad knowledge and command of English. The old master had studied Latin as well as terms and techniques of Western medicine that Burke had never heard of.

Ling-shau brought tea. She was still nude and Burke admired the clean muscular lines of her body and her precise movements. Her ebony hair draped straight across one shoulder and to the middle of her back. Her nose made a gracefully high arch between her coy almond eyes and full lips. The fine, sharp features were typical of the people of her region. Her breasts more than filled Burke's big hands, but they rose high and firm on her chest. She stood close enough to Burke for her nipples to just touch him, and lifted a teacup to his lips. As he sipped, Ling-shau touched her fingertips lightly to Burke's lower abdomen, closed her eyes and projected her *chi*. Burke's rod rose hard between her thighs.

'Master Burke,' said Wei, 'you know *ki* as the Japanese know it, but now you are in the land of Lao Tsu, the original master of the Tao, yin and yang, the universal forces. Here we understand *chi* on a very different level. Do you wish to know it as we do?'

'I . . . but,' Burke stammered.

'You have taught me a technique, and I have taught you, so perhaps we are even. However, I believe Ling-shau would like to express her appreciation for your superb performance just now. Since your technique has stimulated my cash flow,' Wei continued, smiling, 'I gladly lend you my apprentice, if you accept her ministrations. Do you?'

Ling-shau set the teacup aside and placed both hands on Burke. His cock seemed to acquire a will of its own as it rose harder against Ling-shau's cleft. He choked back a groan as the sensation of an orgasm struck his groin, but he did not ejaculate. No sooner had it quelled than she brought another. Burke gripped her shoulders to steady himself.

'Your answer, Master Burke? There is much more to learn, more than you could dream, if you have the will.'

The cords had constricted in Burke's throat, but he managed to speak.

'I do.'

Two

A taxi driver swerved and sped down a narrow street to escape Dan Tanner's outstretched arm. The driver muttered a curse against foreigners as he swerved again to avoid a cyclist flitting between pavement and street and a motor scooter skirting a line of parked cars. He braked to a skid at a crossing as a mother heedlessly pushed a baby carriage into the street, then stuck his head out the window and spat as he looked back to see Tanner stumble back to the relative safety of the pavement. He cursed once more and drove away.

Tanner cast an alcohol-addled gaze at signs and street markers written in bastardised characters. Ancient Chinese ideographs, appended to a language they did not suit, were mixed with two sets of syllabic script: *hiragana* to satisfy the need for inflected verbs and *katakana* for words borrowed from foreign languages. They each represented the same pronunciations but were shaped differently to ensure that the theft of Chinese script was not polluted by more recent linguistic larceny of words from England, Portugal or Spain.

He looked in vain for a familiar landmark. Colour codes marked the entrances to subways, but Tanner could not remember the colour of the line that took him to his pay-by-the-week apartment. He wanted to go home, but lacked the cash for an airline ticket. He'd spent nearly all his money moving halfway around the world. Three weeks ago, he'd landed at Narita International with a promise of employment at a salary higher than he could expect from any American company. Two weeks later, Matsunaga Technologies informed him that the department he'd been hired for and his contract had been terminated, effective immediately. 'Thank you very much, you may now leave our country.'

When he got the news, Tanner had enough yen in his pocket for a minor binge. Tokyo bars didn't open until 5.00 or 6.00 p.m. at the earliest, but restaurants began serving beer right after breakfast. He started drinking at noon and was high by 4.30. A youthful skinhead in a hurry bumped his shoulder into Tanner's chest. The American stepped back, banging his head into a wall, then lurched forwards into the grip of a Caucasian man.

'Are you all right?' James Burke gripped Tanner's arm to hold him upright.

'Unnn,' Tanner gurgled. 'No, man, I ain't all right, I've been screwed.'

'Lucky you.' Burke grinned.

'Naw, I'm talking major shaft.' Tanner made a fist and flicked out his middle finger. 'Corporate bullshit.'

'And what corporate would that be?'

'Matsunaga Technologies.'

'They dived, didn't they, and took you with them, jetsam on the sea of nitwit strategies.'

Tanner drew back. 'Who the hell are you, and how do you know so much?'

'James Burke.' Burke smiled and held out his hand.

Tanner shook it and belched. 'Excuse me, Dan Tanner.'

'You look like you could use a coffee.'

'I could use a ticket to the States, but I'm broke.'

Burke gripped Tanner's shoulders as though to steady him. He noted the American was lean and hard-muscled. The man's suit was cheap and dishevelled, but he had an Adonis face. He might have possibility.

'How's your Japanese?' Burke asked.

'Not so good.'

'Perfect. Well, Dan – may I call you Dan?'

'What else would you call me?' Tanner frowned. 'That's my name.'

'Right. As I was about to say, Dan, this could be your lucky day. Are you up for a walk? There's someone who might be able to help you, but I think a long walk would be a good idea. It would be better if you were . . .'

'Stone sober?'

'Mmm.'

'I got a buzz on, but I'm not drunk, and I definitely need help. How far?'

'An hour, I should say.'

The late August heat seemed to radiate out of the concrete maze of Tokyo's trendy west side, where people went to dine and drink and find a mate for the night. The chances were good for all comers, but those with ample cash could do more than find a sex partner: for a night in the right establishment they could be lord of a harem, a subway groper pawing willing young women or a dominatrix grinding stiletto heels into the rumps of frustrated salarymen. Fortunes changed hands by the hour and whether you paid or earned depended on how you played the game.

It was Burke's own fiefdom.

Tanner's shirt was damp from perspiration by the time they stopped at a wooded area on the fringe of Roppongi. Chirps of cicadas nearly drowned the sounds of street traffic. Grass and trees cooled the pine-scented air. Burke told Tanner to smooth his hair and clothes before they turned onto an alley-wide path, paved with brick. Three-storey homes fronted the walkway, overhung by maple, ginkgo and cherry trees. The path was no more than 100 metres uphill, and dead-ended at the entrance to a towering townhouse. The building stood four storeys tall and was topped by a glass-walled room that overlooked the entertainment district below. Flagstones were inlaid in the building's façade and paved the entry grotto that led to high double doors. On the outer wall was a small metal plate embossed with the word EXCALIBUR.

'Here we are,' said Burke.

'Whoa.' Tanner whistled under his breath as he looked over the building. 'You live here?'

'Work.'

Tanner studied the metal name-plate. 'What do you do?'

Burke ignored his question and pressed a button on the intercom.

'Hai,' a woman's voice answered.

'It's me.' Burke waited for the electronic buzz and click of the latch, then swung the doors open. The foyer was paved with the same flagstone. One wall had rows of cubbyholes holding slippers. Burke sat on a wooden bench, took off his shoes and exchanged them for soft leather slip-ons. When Tanner had done the same, Burke led him down a bare-wood hall and knocked at a door.

It was opened by a tall, lithe Japanese woman. She wore a long black dress that draped thinly over her slender hips and lean thighs. It was cut low across her breasts. When she bowed slightly, the pale-pink rim of a nipple peeked out.

Tanner gaped.

'Look what I found.' Burke tilted his head towards the American.

Mai Ito smiled faintly and crossed her arms as she stared back at Tanner. She moved forwards and stood so close that she could feel Tanner's breath on her face. She pushed her hand against his stomach and chest. 'He looks fit.'

Tanner tightened his stomach muscles. 'I was on my university wrestling team.'

'Hmm, not too bad, once you get past the smell of stale beer. What do you plan to do with him?'

'First a shower, then we'll see what we have to work with.' Tanner started to protest, but Burke interrupted. 'Bear with me, Dan. Your lucky day.'

'I need to get cleaned up, but what's going on, James? What is this place?'

'It's a very lovely house, Dan. Mai will show you the way.'

Tanner's misgivings faded at the sight of Mai's round arse shifting under the thin material that clung to her cheeks and the backs of her thighs. The dress was cut so low at the back that Tanner could glimpse the crack of her bottom as the fabric swished at each step.

She opened the door to the bathroom. It was almost as spacious as Tanner's one-room apartment. The tile bath could comfortably accommodate five or six people. A sunken area in front of the tub had a drain in the floor, for bathers to wash or shower. The tub was only for soaking after the wash. It had already been filled with water hot enough to induce prickles of pain until the bather's body adjusted to the heat.

Mai took a basket from under the sink and put it beside Tanner. 'Put your clothes in there. I'll have them cleaned.'

'OK.' Tanner emptied his pockets onto a counter and waited for Mai to leave.

Instead she stayed, drawing her dress up one thigh and sitting her cheek and leg on the edge of the washbasin counter. She stroked the inside of her bare leg with the back of her long, slender fingers and leaned forwards so that the dress dipped to the tips of her lush cream-coloured breasts.

Tanner had not been with a woman for months, and the sight of Mai's breasts only an arm's length away was almost more than he could bear. He saw her eyes fall to the growing bulge in his trousers. He grew harder watching her smoothly tapered fingers caress her inner thigh, pushing the dress closer to her quim at each stroke. She turned her hand and used her fingertips to massage the flesh that ran to the juncture of her sex.

'Dan.' Mai's voice was low and husky. 'I asked you to put your clothes in the basket. Now, if you please.'

Tanner's pulse raced as he took off his coat, tie and shirt, while he watched Mai put her hand under the dress. When Tanner unfastened his belt, she sucked in a sharp breath and pushed her hand hard between her legs. The brownish-pink lip of her sex was just visible as the side of her palm slid over it. Tanner dropped his trousers in the basket and put his thumbs in the band of his shorts, but she stopped him with a gesture and beckoned him to her.

Mai rubbed Tanner's straining organ through the thin cotton of his briefs then squeezed the whole of his sex in a firm regular rhythm. Her fingers slid under the band at his crotch, felt for the head of his cock then pushed between his balls and the underside of the rod that strained to stand erect. Her skin absorbed the sweat and musk of Tanner's groin, then she pulled her hand away and dug a finger into her own sex. After stroking herself slowly, she lifted her hand, held it to her face and breathed deeply. Then she rubbed her fingertips across Tanner's lips.

Tanner let her slide her fingers into his mouth and over his tongue. He tasted his own acrid essence mingled with Mai's faintly bitter oil. One strap of her dress fell from her shoulder. Tanner gripped the exposed breast with one hand and pulled Mai to him with the other. Her lips parted as his mouth covered hers, and their tongues reached into the hollows, sliding over and under one another, until Mai pushed away.

'In there,' she said.

The last of Tanner's clothes fell into the basket. His prick, finally rid of its constraint, stood stiff and free.

Mai knelt before him and took his rod between her lips, teasing it with her tongue. She gripped the staff in both hands as she pumped her mouth over the bulbous tip. She felt Tanner's hands on the back of her head, trying to force more of himself into her, but she resisted and moved her mouth to lick the underside of his cock and his sac, then raised herself again and took the other strap from her shoulder.

Tanner had never seen skin of such beauty. It was almost translucent in its lightness. Her nipples were the pale pink of plum blossoms. Strands of pure ebony hair fell in vivid contrast across her shoulders and breasts. The dress Mai was taking off had been contoured to her svelte body and its waist hung snugly at her hips. Tanner knelt and tugged it down gradually over her lower belly and pubic mound. As she stepped free of it Tanner reached for the pinkish swell of her sex lips, but she stepped away.

'We'll bathe now,' she said.

They sat on low stools. Tanner flinched when Mai poured a small bucket of hot water on his back. She scrubbed him with lavender soap and a spiny natural sponge that scraped away dead skin like a rasp.

Tanner felt like his body was covered with tiny scratches. The hot water Mai poured over him to rinse his skin was salt in the wounds of a thousand pinpricks. He shuddered.

When she was done, Mai said, 'Wash me.'

Gently, Tanner stroked the sponge across Mai's precious skin.

'Harder.'

Tanner pressed more firmly and increased the tempo of his strokes.

'Harder!' Mai looked over her shoulder and scowled.

Tanner bore down so forcefully that Mai slipped forwards on her stool. He reached around to steady her and cupped her breast in his hand.

'Don't touch me with your hands.' Mai stood to give Tanner full access to her body. 'Use the sponge.'

He raked the coarse fibre across the globes of her buttocks and down her legs. She turned to face him. As he worked up her legs his hand pressed into her sex. She pushed it away and pointed to the sponge. Tanner scraped it between her thighs and pressed between the labia to the nub of her clit. Mai closed her eyes, threw her head back and groaned at the back of her throat as he raked the sponge over the tiny organ. As he moved farther up her body, scraping the sponge across her abdomen and breasts and neck, she stared into his eyes. He took the bucket and filled it from the tub. The water burned his hand, but Mai stood still as the scorching liquid poured over her scoured flesh.

Mai took Tanner's hand and stepped into the bath.

Tanner sat and grew faint in the scalding heat. He started to rise, but Mai wrapped her legs around his hips and held him to her. He felt her reach under him and massage his wilting cock, her hot sex pressing against his belly. He took the softness of her breasts into his mouth. As she moved against him, his staff grew stiff despite the water's heat. Guided by Mai's hand, his prick, fully hard again, slid into her. The water roiled as Mai pushed herself onto his pole. He raised his hips to meet her and slipped on the tub's slick surface. His head sank underwater. He tried to rise, but Mai pressed her hands to his throat and bore down with her full weight as she pummelled his cock with her hips. Tanner strained against her, but he could not gain purchase in the bath. His body thrashed wildly in its craving for oxygen, but he could not escape Mai's lock on his groin and neck. He thought he would drown, and had opened his mouth to breathe water when Mai released her grip on his throat. She threw her body back in a spasm of ecstasy. Tanner's head broke the surface. His mouth gulped air as he gagged from the water. Coughs wracked his body, still crushed in the vice of Mai's thighs.

Mai held his eyes in a feral glare, her teeth bared as she plunged onto his cock a final time. Then she stood and helped Tanner to his feet. They emerged from the bath with scarlet flesh, their skin agonisingly sensitive even to the slightest vibration in the air. Mai grabbed the base of Tanner's still-erect cock in one hand and shoved it between her legs.

'Did you like my pussy? Is that what you want, mama's boy?'

Tanner's mind reeled from his near-death experience and Mai's attack on his person and his honour. He staggered back as she jerked his rod, then grabbed her wrists, but she stiffened her elbows and dipped from her hips towards him, her upper body erect. Tanner kept his grip, but his shoulders lurched downwards. As he moved, Mai whipped her arms in a circle and pinned Tanner's forearms against her sides with the powerful muscles of her back. He screamed and fell back against a wall, only for her to slam her face into his chest and sink her teeth into his nipple. With the wall as a brace, Tanner put his hands on her chest and shoved with all the strength of his arms, belly and legs.

Mai bounced off the sink counter and fell to the floor, sucking back a line of saliva that had begun to drop from her mouth. Her belly contracted rhythmically in the after-throes of her passion. She kept her eyes on Tanner as she gripped the counter and pulled herself to her feet. She went to a cabinet, took out two packages and ripped off the plastic coverings, then laid them on the counter. With her back to Tanner, she spread her legs and bent forwards at her hips. She looked over her shoulder, but Tanner only stared. She picked up one of the packages and flung it at Tanner's chest. He caught it.

'Come on, mama's boy. Do you know what that is?'

Tanner looked at what he held in his hands. It was a bladder of liquid, with a slender nine-centimetre nipple attached. He nodded, then positioned himself behind Mai, spread her arse cheeks and pushed the nipple into her bumhole. He squeezed the bladder, forcing the liquid into Mai. When it was empty, he tossed it aside.

'More!'

Tanner used the other bladder as Mai clenched her jaws and her ring. He had to press hard to insert the other nipple.

Mai mumbled unintelligibly as her head and body swayed against the urge to release the pressure. She raised her arse as Tanner pressed himself against her and squeezed her tits. Her mind focused on the inner and outer sphincters of her colon and rectum. When she could bear it no longer, she took Tanner's wrist and opened the door to an enclosed toilet. She sat on the porcelain throne and embraced his hips with her arms, crushing his sex against her face as she voided her colon in a violent splash, again and again, until the splashes became trickles and the spasms of her abdomen worked against nothing. She turned on a fount of water to clean herself and flushed the toilet.

Tanner backed away when she stood, and followed her to the counter of the washbasin. She resumed her position and looked back at him, her lip curling as she ordered, 'Fuck me.' He slipped the tip of his staff into the entrance to her sex.

She jerked away and spun to face him. Her hands shot to his nipples. She pinched hard and twisted, then turned back around. When Tanner's cock touched the folds of her sex again, she hammered the back of her fist into his chest. 'Stay away from my pussy. I said "fuck me", mama's boy.'

In a cloud of rage and indignation, Tanner raised his hand high and twisted his shoulders and hips into the blow as he slammed his palm against Mai's bare buttocks. His hand burned and left its red outline on her arse as her blood welled to the surface. He seized the back of her neck and forced her down as he flailed at her arse with his bare hand. When his right arm tired, he struck with his left until Mai's arse cheeks were a mass of red and white welts.

She held her face in her hands, sobbing, as rivulets of come ran down her thighs. 'Fuck me, Dan.' Her voice was low and hoarse. '*Onegai*, please, fuck me.'

Tanner grabbed a packet of lubricant, tore it open and rubbed in onto his cock. He entered the pink pucker of her arse, slowly penetrating one sphincter then the other. He felt their squeeze as he gradually sped the pace of his thrusts. Mai's cheeks bucked against him. Inside her, the rings of her anus and colon tightened and relaxed until they had milked gushes of sap from Tanner's stiff rod. He withdrew from Mai's body and stepped away from her. His face reddened in revulsion at his own violence. He had never struck a woman. He touched Mai's tear-dampened cheek gently.

'I'm sorry for hurting you. I lost . . .'

Mai turned around and shoved her knee into Tanner's crotch. 'Don't spoil the mood, lover. Come on.' She started for the door.

'My clothes . . .'

'. . . are dirty. Let's go and see James.'

Naked, they walked down the hall to the room Mai used as an office. Burke was waiting for them.

'How'd it go?'

Mai turned to show him her streaked buttocks.

Burke raised his eyebrows and dropped the corners of his mouth in admiration. 'Good man.'

'He apologised later,' Mai said.

'Still, I'd say that's a respectable start.'

'Needed encouragement, a lot of encouragement.'

'But there is potential, is there not?'

Mai touched Tanner's flaccid tool. In a limp state, it

was scarcely a modest handful, but he had used what he had well. 'Mmm-hmm, I believe there is.'

'Well done, then. I expect your troubles are over, Dan.'

Tanner's face reddened. 'Potential for what?' he demanded.

'All things in time. Let's find you something to wear.' Burke started for the door then turned back. 'Can you do without me tonight, Mai?'

'Hirano-san has made a reservation. She likes you.'

'She also likes your Argentine gaucho, Rafael. Is there anything I can do that he can't?'

Mai lowed her chin coquettishly and smiled. 'You know there is.'

'Ah, but Hirano-san doesn't. Until tomorrow, then.'

Burke found suitable clothes for Tanner and stood by as he dressed. 'Are you ready for another stroll, a short one this time, about fifteen minutes? There's a small club down the hill, which could be interesting for you.'

'I'm broke.'

'No worry. It's on me or Mai or whoever.'

'Any more surprises like here? I could do without being drowned.'

'I think we're safe on that account.'

The evening air was tepid with the waning heat of late summer. They cut through a park heavy with the fragrance of night-blooming gardenias from a private garden. It was only a brief respite from the city's clamour. Soon they were at a broad street that led to Roppongi Crossing, a nexus for a bizarre blend of humanity. Women wore long satiny dresses, micro skirts that scarcely covered bums and shorts that didn't. Polka-dot bras showed through sheer blouses. Long net trousers exposed legs and hips covered only by thong knickers. Hair shades ranged from bright orange through bleach blonde to mellow brown. Makeup ran from garish to none. Men wore sleeveless

T-shirts revealing tattoos, zoot suits dragging the ground and finely tailored sharkskins with silk ties. Hawkers from Africa, the Middle East and South Asia urged passers-by into a richly creative array of pleasure dens and jazz bars.

None of that, however, was adequate preparation for the Bound Maiden.

Burke pushed open the door and led the way into a swirl of soft light that emanated from the walls in pastel shades merging to white at the centre of the room. It illuminated a young woman hanging by her wrists from a beam in the ceiling. She wore a red silk robe designed as an undergarment for a kimono. It was trimmed in white. Her toes just touched the floor. A man wearing only a *fundoshi*, a Japanese loincloth, had tied a rope around her waist and was lacing it down the length of one leg in diamond patterns of knots. When he reached her ankle, he threaded the rope through a pulley and hoisted the woman's leg into the air. Her other leg dangled free. The man pulled her kimono back as though unveiling a statue. Except for the silk robe hanging from the back of her shoulders, she was nude.

Murmurs of admiration buzzed through the audience, who showed their appreciation of the graceful arc of the woman's bound arms and leg. A woman noted how the draped kimono complemented the subject's dangling leg. A man praised the contrast of the rope's symmetrical weave against the overall asymmetry of only one bound leg and a coil of rope at her wrists. When the rope master demonstrated the utility of the design by inviting a man from the audience to kiss the helpless woman's small breasts and fondle her sex, a light smattering of applause ran through the audience.

As the customer turned to go to his seat, a small spotlight focused on the obvious bulge in his trousers. He clasped his hands together and held them over his head like a victorious prize-fighter.

'Are you surprised yet?' Burke smiled.

'Yeah. You sure there's no drowning pool?'

'The only water is in the drinks.'

A waitress came to take their order. Like the other waitresses, she wore only a length of rope fashioned in an intricate design on her torso. One strand between her legs disappeared into the depths of her labia and arse cheeks.

'Mineral water.' Burke ordered first. 'And you, Dan?'

'Tea.'

The waitress spoke too fast for Tanner to follow. Burke held up one hand and ticked off his fingers as he translated. 'Hot, iced, lemon, milk, black, Japanese cha or Chinese oolong?'

'Iced, black, no sugar.'

'The lad knows his teas, doesn't he?' A woman sitting alone at the next table grinned at Burke and made a wanking motion with her fist when she said 'teas'. She had strawberry-blonde hair and a freckled face that was farm-girl fresh. Her cheeks and bare arms looked smooth and as soft as down.

Tanner scowled. After his experience with Mai, he was in no mood for more abuse from women.

'No offence, I didn't mean to say you were a wanker or anything like that.'

'What's a "wanker"?' Tanner asked.

Burke imitated the woman's gesture.

Tanner glowered.

'Ooh my, we do have a sensitive friend, don't we?'

Burke held his hands up palms out. 'We've just met.'

'You're not –' she rocked one hand back and forth '– are you?'

'No, not yet anyway.'

Tanner recoiled from Burke and the woman.

'Joke, Dan.' He turned to the woman. 'He's had a difficult day.'

The woman grimaced as though to say she'd had one herself.

'Would you care to join us?' Burke asked.

'You buying?'

'Are you selling?'

The woman stiffened and fixed her gaze on Burke's eyes. 'I meant drinks. Anyway, I'm no good at sales, probably end up giving away the store.'

'I know what you meant, and yes I am buying.' Burke pulled out a chair, which the woman accepted. Burke introduced himself and Tanner.

'I'm Sandra Callie,' the woman said.

'Let's hurry through the expat routine, then. Where are you from, and what are you doing here?'

'Born in Wales, escaped to London when I was sixteen, worked as a roadie a couple of years, ended up with a bond trader, or some such, in the City. After a couple of years I escaped from him. Now I teach kindergarten at a private English academy.'

'You don't look like a kindergarten teacher.' Tanner's voice was harsh.

'Cheeky! I guess you'd better see me in bifocals and my hair in a bun, hadn't you.'

Burke took her hand in his own, with his thumb at the juncture of her index finger and thumb. 'What are you doing in this club, Sandra?'

'Same as you, I guess.' Her eyes widened suddenly as a tingle from Burke's thumb ran through her arm. She squeezed back at his hand.

'I'm here because I enjoy the show. I also enjoy the play. Same as you?'

'Yeah, I've done a little. The bond trader I lived with liked it, spanking too. At first I thought, "What have I been missing," but it was always the same with him. Every night, or whenever we did it, it was tie me up, tie me down, wham bam thank you ma'am. Routine as washing dishes. "Sometimes, let me do you," I said, but he wouldn't have it, so I left.'

'The pain, Sandra – do you like being spanked?'

'If it's bare hand, it can be a rush. I wouldn't like a cane. I want to feel skin, not wood. Especially . . .'

'Especially what, Sandra?'

'Es–' The word choked in her throat as another tingle flashed through her arm, stronger this time. She felt it through her spine.

'If . . . if I'm rubbing myself or someone's rubbing me. It's like sensory overload, everything going on at once. You want to run away and run towards it all at the same time. It's like . . .'

'Is it like this?' Burke turned Sandra's wrist up and touched it lightly with his fingers. The tingle she'd felt before became an electric jolt, and she was unconsciously rocking her body back and forth when Burke pressed his thumb with all his strength into the joint at the base of her hand.

Her explosive gasp attracted stares from the club's patrons and staff alike. 'I . . . I've wet myself.'

'I'm sorry,' said Burke. 'We can find a change.'

'No, it's all right. I don't mean wet myself that way, I mean the other. How?'

'Who are you?' Tanner and Sandra spoke in unison.

'James Burke, born in Singapore to English parents. Reared mostly in Hong Kong. Lived in Malaysia a while, and attended university in Tokyo. For the most part, I've been here ever since. The only time I've seen England is on vacation.'

'You didn't learn that in any Tokyo university,' Tanner said.

Burke let the implied question lie as he watched the waitress approach the table with another woman. The woman wore a black kimono undergarment similar to the robe worn by the earlier bondage subject. The waitress asked Burke's permission for the woman to speak, then left. Burke remained seated as the woman bowed deeply. She told him that the rope master had seen him touch Sandra and asked if he would be gracious enough to touch her after she was bound.

'I would not touch you to please someone else,' Burke said.

She bowed again and spoke with her eyes cast downwards. 'My name is Sayuri. Sayuri desires your touch. *Onegai itashimasu* – I entreat you.'

'Then I shall touch Sayuri-san.'

She thanked Burke, formally. When she straightened, her eyes were bright with anticipation and only briefly met Burke's before she hurried to the centre of the room. She stood erect as the rope master unfastened the sash that held her robe and used it to blindfold her. He stood behind her and traced the lines of her belly and breasts with his hands as he parted the robe and let it fall to the floor. Sayuri stood naked and blind as the master tightly cinched her arms behind her with coarse hemp. He wound the cord three times above and below her breasts, then tied it at the front of her chest and hoisted her off the floor with a pulley. At each ankle he tied lengths of rope and lifted her splayed legs into the air. He adjusted the three ropes until Sayuri was suspended with her spread V at the height of his hips. The rope master then stepped away and bowed slightly towards Burke.

As promised, Burke went to Sayuri and ran his fingers lightly along her inner thighs to her sex. She was already moist. He eased his hand between her cheeks and pushed the tip of his index finger into the tight orifice between them. His thumb slid into her slippery tunnel, while his other hand found her nub. The manual stimulation of her nether zone caused Sayuri's body to tense in ways that Burke carefully noted, measuring the flows of energy that she herself produced.

Burke closed his eyes and breathed slowly. A full two minutes passed before he had filled his lungs with a single breath and charged his spirit with the universal *chi*. Slowly, he exhaled and let the power flow gradually from him through Sayuri's natural channels of energy.

Her head fell back, her mouth wide, as her back and legs brought her hips closer to Burke. The intensity of her spasms rose steadily until, in a violent shout, Burke released the last of his charge through her. Sayuri screamed, her eyes wide and wild, the veins of her neck and arms swollen under her skin. Come cascaded from her quim and flowed to the floor. At last, her body hung limp, swaying from the ropes.

There was no sound in the room save Sayuri's gentle rhythmic moans.

The rope master bowed deeply to Burke. As the Englishman returned to his seat, his eyes met those of two men at a table near the stage. One was a Caucasian dressed in a poorly cut suit of coarse material. The other was a broad-shouldered Japanese with closely cropped hair. Burke saw the Japanese give a waitress a thick envelope and gesture towards the rope master. The back of the man's hand bore a scorpion tattoo.

The master took the envelope and quickly estimated its contents at 500,000 yen, equivalent to more than 3,000 pounds. He held it in both hands and raised it to his face as he bowed slightly to his benefactor. Then he left the stage.

The Japanese walked to Sayuri's crotch, unfastened his belt and let his trousers fall to the floor. He was already stiffly erect. When he impaled the girl, she did not respond, even as he swung her in short arcs along his girth. As he fucked her, he stared directly at Burke. For 500,000 yen, he expected more than a public fuck with a rag doll.

Three

Tanner's ego tried to tell him that if he'd had anywhere else to go, he would never have returned. But even as he mulled over those thoughts, his id knew they were lies. Even if he had commanded a fortune, he would have come back, drawn like a parched man to a poisoned pond. Never had he dreamed that sex, the primal force of life, could be anything more than a quest for vaginal intercourse with a girl you swore eternal fidelity to for the rights of procreation. Then, 2.2 kids later came the drought, masturbating in the shower, timid daydreams of women at the office, prowling the Internet for images that raised more guilt than excitement. He'd never married, but he'd seen it in friends and his own parents, who for as long as he could remember had slept in separate rooms. His id knew that if Dan Tanner were to walk the Earth as a man, it would be as a man of the Excalibur. It also knew there was a long way to go. He pressed the button to the intercom.

'Hai.' Mai's voice.

'It's Dan.' The buzzer sounded. He pushed open the double doors, walked down the hall to Mai's office and knocked.

Burke opened the door.

Tanner stepped forwards like a public school ne'er-do-well facing the headmaster.

Mai sat behind a desk. 'He's back.' She swivelled her chair to face him. 'Are you sure about our pretty boy here, James?'

Tanner bristled at the epithet, but at least she had dropped the word 'mama'.

Burke folded his arms across his chest. 'I see things, Mai. Sense them in our lad, maybe even more than Dan himself. He has my vote.'

'He needs two votes, though, doesn't he?' Mai propped her leg on the edge of her desk. 'It's been a long day. My feet are tired. Do you know how to massage a woman's foot, Dan?'

Burke opened a drawer in Mai's desk, took out five 10,000-yen notes and fanned them like a hand of poker. 'If you're still with us at the end of the night, these are yours. It might be enough for your air ticket home. If you pass the first test, the second will be to see if you stay of your own accord. This is only the beginning of your trials, Dan, and your opportunities. There is much to learn and much to endure. Most recruits don't make it. Now you are a toy, but if you eventually become one of us, you can spend this much on a tie pin.' He shifted his eyes towards Mai's foot.

Tanner pressed his thumbs into the soles. He was surprised at the velvety texture of her skin, even at these extremities. He'd begun kneading her toes when she told him to stop, turn around and put his hands behind him. A thong of braided leather was wrapped around his wrists and pulled tight. When Mai told him to continue, he tried to back towards her.

'Turn around,' she said. Tanner looked confused. 'Use your imagination, pretty boy.' She licked her lips.

Tanner turned, knelt and kissed the whole of her foot, pushing his tongue and lips against her pliant skin. He heard Mai purr as he took her toes into his mouth, sucked each slowly and forced his tongue between them. At Mai's command, he stood and walked to her. Her hands teased his nipples, unbuttoned his shirt and pushed it back over his shoulders. A surge welled in his groin as she unfastened his trousers and pulled them off him. The ball of her foot pressed into his scrotum and her toes tickled the base of his swelling prick. Tanner rubbed the length of his staff against her until he ached for release.

Mai drew away, stood and guided Tanner to the floor. He lay on his back with his hips resting on his bound hands. She straddled him and lowered herself as she reached under her dress and pulled her nylon shield to the side, guiding him into her. She leaned her face close to Tanner's and rocked her hips slowly and smoothly, raising the tempo steadily until she saw him grimace. She slid off before he came. 'Save your energy for our guests.'

'Get dressed, Mr Tanner. I'll show you around a bit.' Burke untied Tanner's hands and led him to the Excalibur's main room. The ceiling was two storeys high and crossed with two heavy exposed beams that supported metal arms attached to hinges. A railed terrace around the second-floor level had a variety of chairs and sofas that provided views of the main floor below. At one side of the room was a small stage surrounded by sofas and low tables. 'Would you like something to drink while we wait for the lads? I recommend mineral water or fruit juice, at least until the guests arrive.'

'How many "lads" are there?'

'Counting you and me, nine. It's quite a place for only nine, but we're a select outfit. Like I said, yesterday was your lucky day.'

'What does the "select outfit" do?'

'I thought you would have guessed by now.'

'I mean specifically.'

'We cater to a highly exclusive clientele. Specifically how depends on the client. I assure you, you will not be disappointed in any of the guests. Mai is quite discerning in that regard. No old biddies –' Burke rubbed his thumb and index fingers together '– and no cheapskates. But of course that means we cannot disappoint the clients, doesn't it?'

The buzzer sounded at the front door and the seven other hosts began arriving. Burke introduced Rafael, the Argentine; Dirk, an Austrian; Marcel, a Frenchman; Lazarus, an American; Sergio, a Brazilian; Giovanni, an Italian; and Lars, a Dane. They were all from their mid-20s to late 30s, fit, friendly and impeccably dressed.

'There are no Japanese,' Tanner pointed out.

'That would spoil the atmosphere. We are exotica. There is an expression in Japanese, "*Tabi no haji wa kaki sute*", which means throw away your shame when you travel, particularly when you travel abroad. When a guest enters the Excalibur, she goes abroad. There is no shame here. Besides, all the clients have travelled and speak foreign languages. They enjoy using their skills – linguistic and otherwise. Don't be shy and don't be aggressive. If a guest is interested in talking to you, she'll let you know. Beyond that, remember what you've seen and done since yesterday, and I'm sure you'll do fine.'

The first guest came alone. She wore stiletto heels and a short skirt that was slit to her hips on either side. Her blouse was loose and opened to the edge of a lacy pale-blue bra that peeked out with the slightest movement of her shoulders. It scarcely covered the nipples of her ample breasts. She appeared to be in her mid-30s, and her skin had a sheen that spoke of hours in beauty salons. The tone and grace of her body attested to strenuous workouts in aerobics and weights.

Burke was the first to greet her. 'Reina-san, it's been too long. We've missed you.' He bowed then took her hand and kissed the inside of her wrist.

'You're a tease, James. I was here last week.' Her voice had a trace of a California accent, but she spoke with clear diction. She accepted greetings from the other hosts as though she were a star, offering her hand or cheek to each for a kiss. When she came to Tanner, she stopped. 'Who's this young fellow?'

'Dan Tanner.'

'What do you do, Dan?' When Tanner appeared confused, she looked at Burke.

'He's an apprentice.' Burke smiled. 'But I believe he has some skill with his open palm and a taste for a well-turned foot.'

'Well, he's gorgeous. I want first dibs.'

'First dibs on what?' A woman in her mid-40s walked in, grabbed Giovanni's arse and squeezed it hard.

'Kazuko-san,' said Burke. 'I'm sorry I missed you yesterday. I was occupied with a new recruit.'

Kazuko Hirano sneered at his apology and started to put her hand down the front of Tanner's trousers.

'Uh-uh, Kazuko. Reina has already claimed first rights.'

'You owe me, James. I was greatly disappointed last night. If this young man is the reason for that, then he should be mine.'

'I saw him first,' Reina protested.

'You both have valid claims. Let me take this to Mai. I'm sure she'll think of an entertaining way to settle it.' By the time Burke had returned with Mai, several other clients had arrived and were seated around the stage. 'We've reached a decision. There shall be a *janken* contest.' He noticed Tanner's frown. 'A game of stone, scissors, paper. The loser of each round will remove an article of clothing until she has nothing left to remove.'

'Boring!' said a heckler in the audience.

Burke ignored the complaint. 'In addition to the young Mr Tanner, the loser will also belong to the victor. Furthermore, the winner will exact her satisfaction here on the stage. Does either of you ladies wish to forfeit in advance? Once you agree, there is no turning back.' A murmur of anticipation rippled through the guests and hosts. Burke waited for one of the women to speak, but standing down now would entail a loss of face that neither client would be willing to endure. 'Then it's settled.'

The women faced each other as the audience began a rhythmic clapping. The contestants pumped their fists three times then extended their arms. Kazuko kept her fist closed as a rock, while Reina spread her hand wide as paper.

'Paper covers rock,' said Burke. 'Mr Tanner, do the honours. The article of clothing is your choice.'

Kazuko scowled as Tanner knelt in front of her and removed her shoes. 'Boring!' The heckler this time was Reina. She sneered as she spoke.

The next round, each woman repeated the same gesture. Kazuko lost again. Tanner could remove her stockings or her dress. The 'boring' rebuke had stung, so he turned Kazuko around, unzipped her and peeled off the dress that had disguised her figure. She was nearly a Rubens nymph, her lush flesh enticingly feminine in contrast to her harsh character. Tanner pitied her for not realising her own beauty. The dress was too large, concealing too much, while her undergarments were too small, revealing too much. Her bust bulged against a bra that should have been a cup size larger, and her knickers were too narrow to fully cover the rich thatch of her sex. Only her stockings, held by garters high on her thighs, fitted perfectly.

Kazuko's face turned red in anger and embarrassment. Reina had thrown paper twice in a row. Surely she would not expect Kazuko to repeat rock, so that narrowed her choices to scissors or rock. After all, no one would throw the same sign three times in a row. No one, that is, except a trickster bitch like Reina. Kazuko threw scissors and won.

Determined not to be boring, Tanner moved behind Reina so that his crotch pressed against her bum. He reached in front of her and slid his fingers along her thighs as he lifted her skirt to the boundary of her sheer knickers, before he released the skirt's zip, then he slid his hands across her rump and pubic mound as he pushed down the skirt.

Kazuko shouted a curse when Reina won the next round by throwing paper for the fourth time in a row. Tanner felt a trickle of moisture seep through her knickers, despite her humiliation, when he let his hand linger between her legs as he freed her stockings from their garters. Lust burned through her angry eyes. Tanner saw in them a craving that excited and frightened him in ways he had never experienced. He probably wouldn't know the truth of her yearnings tonight. She was losing and unnerved by the game.

Who could tell what Reina would throw next? She had proved herself to be unpredictable. The only way for Kazuko to come back would be to stop guessing and take control. As they pumped their fists to prepare for the next throw, Kazuko let the fire of her anger sparkle in her eyes, and grinned as though she could see into Reina's mind. Her own telepathic message said, 'Go ahead and throw five papers in a row, you bitch. Scissors will win.' She looked sure of herself as doubt clouded Reina's eyes. Reina threw rock to break scissors, but Kazuko had thrown paper. She won.

Tanner gripped the crotch of Reina's knickers and pressed his knuckles into her cleft until they were damp with her oil. He pulled the knickers down and off and tossed them into the crowd. After Kazuko won the next round, Tanner removed Reina's shoes. Kazuko won again and leered as Tanner pushed his palms and forearms into Reina's breasts. When he'd removed her blouse Kazuko snatched it and tossed it to the crowd.

Nude except for her low-cut bra, Reina turned her back and breathed deep to regain her composure. This time, as they faced each other, Reina's eyes shined more brightly. She watched Kazuko throw paper a split second before her scissors.

'No contest,' said Burke. 'Throw again.'

Reina bowed in apology, but she had achieved her objective. Kazuko's rhythm had been disrupted. She also knew that Kazuko wouldn't throw paper again. That sign was bad karma now. Rock would either win or tie. She threw rock and won.

Tanner nipped the back of Kazuko's knickers in his teeth and pushed his face into her ample bottom. His nose found the button between the cheeks, and he sniffed loudly before he pulled the knickers down.

The women in the audience giggled. Kazuko's face reddened at their ridicule, yet still she could not control her passion. Tanner's lips, teeth and tongue in her crotch sent a hot rush of lust through her belly even as anger filled her mind. She scowled as Tanner twirled her knickers on his finger and flung them to a host, who held them to his nose and imitated Tanner's loud sniff.

The only thing now between defeat and victory for either woman was a bra. Burke called a recess in the game. Reina and Kazuko sat in chairs apart from each other. They were attended by hosts, massaging their shoulders and the backs of their necks, until Burke called them back to the floor.

Both women had used all the psychological wiles they had. The final throw would come down to luck. The audience clapped rhythmically as the contestants pumped their fists and threw the same sign once, twice, three times. The hosts and women watching took sides and shouted the combatant's names as the foes threw the same sign a fourth and fifth time. They pumped their fists for the sixth trial.

Just before the throw, Kazuko let go a powerful shout. Her rock crushed Reina's scissors. She didn't celebrate. She simply stared at Tanner and Reina. A grim smile crept across her lips.

Burke led the applause. 'How shall you be satisfied, Kazuko-san?'

Only he could hear her soft reply. He relayed it to two hosts, who left to make preparations. 'Will you have Mr Tanner as he is?'

'No, I will not.' Kazuko unzipped Tanner's trousers and freed his erect shaft. 'Look at me. Do you know what you've done? You've humiliated me.' She slapped his offending prick with each hand. 'Take off your shoes. I don't want to touch them.' She made him undress himself and swatted his shaft after each article of clothing was removed.

Tanner tried to will the spirit out of his cock, but it was no good. He had revelled in Kazuko's and Reina's willingness to suffer humiliation just to have him. His prick had soared with his pride, one of the seven deadly sins, the sin that goeth before a fall, but his prick would not fall. It stood ever stiffer with each swat of Kazuko's slapping hands. She stepped back with her fists defiantly on her hips. Tanner could not help but admire her spirit.

At Kazuko's command, Rafael tied Tanner's and Renia's hands to ropes hanging from two metal arms attached to ceiling rafters and pulled them above the floor. Lars brought Kazuko a tray with a wide selection of lashes and canes. Kazuko took her time examining the display and checking Reina's eyes as she handled each instrument. She chose the riding crop when she saw it induced the greatest terror.

Tanner revealed no fear as Kazuko pushed the crop against his phallus and smacked his sac lightly. She gripped his hard cock in one hand and slapped the crop into its spongy head. He was more curious than afraid at these new sensations. The gaze of the female guests on his abused member excited him. He felt their rising passion and wanted Kazuko to do more, to push him to his limit. He thrilled at the sight of her arm slashing the crop towards his thigh and at the merciless pain that seared his flesh, but above all he thrilled at the collective gasp from the women entranced by his torment. Tanner gnashed his teeth as the crop fell at the same spot again and again. A welt rose white and red. He swallowed a scream when the crop struck once more. He had taken only four shots, but already doubted whether he could endure any more. He felt guilt at his relief when Kazuko transferred her attention to Reina.

'*Yame*!' The terrified woman pleaded for Kazuko to stop before she'd even begun. Kazuko spun her halfway around so her beautifully sculpted arse faced the audience, then drew back the crop and struck Reina with such force that her right breast was jolted from its encasement. Reina's high-pitched squeal filled the room. Kazuko struck her other cheek and the back of one thigh, making a triangular pattern of welts, then stepped back to examine her work. The crop was an interesting beginning, but too blunt for Reina's lithe frame. Kazuko admired the woman's beauty in spite of herself. She lashed the leather through the air to test her aim, then snapped the tip, just grazing Tanner's rod. He gasped and tried to jerk away, but it was useless. Kazuko slashed his thighs just below his sac.

Tanner winced, but did not cry out. As the quirt stung its way down his thighs, he watched the rapt eyes of the women looking at him. Some had their hand in the crotch of the host next to them. Others had begun to rub themselves, but Tanner knew their thoughts were with him. Each woman's eyes shone with lust when they met his, each grateful for a moment of his attention. He was sorry when the lashes stopped.

Kazuko did not use the quirt again on Reina, selecting instead a sliver of bamboo. The first slash cut across Reina's back, leaving a thread-thin streak. Kazuko's bra had become an encumbrance to her swing, so she removed it and continued the slashes along Reina's back, each marking a parallel line to the first. There were no more squeals from Reina, but she made low moans at the back of her throat each time the switch fell. When she reached Reina's arse, she changed the angle and whipped the bamboo into the backs of her legs, until Reina's body was a fine pattern of hash marks accented by three round welts. When Kazuko stopped, she saw a trickle of come on the inside of Reina's thigh. Kazuko dipped her finger in it and proudly showed it to the audience.

Tanner gritted his teeth when the bamboo sliced across his thighs and singed the surface of his tender glans. He looked down at his shaft as Kazuko's expert hands whipped the lash, just brushing its tip before searing his abdomen. His confidence had been building until the attacks on his cock and balls. How far would this angry woman go? When he saw Kazuko replace the sliver with a bamboo sword, of the type used in Japanese fencing, fear made an oily sweat bead on his forehead. Kazuko held the instrument in both hands and swung it into Tanner's abdomen with a loud thwack, just missing his phallus. He was relieved when she turned him around and used the sword on his strong buttocks and back. He could no longer see the women, but he could hear their soft moans and whispered gasps. He sensed their heat as he endured the pain.

Kazuko left him and turned Reina to face the audience, then selected a cat-o'-nine-tails made of braided leather. The lashes began at Reina's feet and rose up her legs to her pubic mound. Kazuko lingered at her sex, slapping her again and again with the cat. Reina flinched at each blow, her face reddening as the cat stung her belly. Kazuko paused before delivering the final blows across the woman's quivering breasts. The trickle of come now flowed freely, and Kazuko cupped her hand against Reina's quim until her palm was wet. Then she turned Tanner around and rubbed Reina's oil into his stiff rod. The metal bars swung on their hinges as Kazuko pushed Tanner and Reina around to face each other.

Tanner stared at Reina. The cat had left a mottled array of red and white streaks across the front of her body. He wondered at her strength: she had endured as much as he had. They swung so closely together that Reina's sharp breaths kissed his face, the musk of her fear, pain and lust filling him. His loins ached as Burke and Rafael tied ropes just above Reina's knees and lifted her legs up and apart. For the first time since his trial had begun, a loud groan erupted from Tanner when Kazuko gripped his staff and guided it into the liquid haven of Reina's sex. The hosts secured the ropes at Reina's knees behind Tanner's back, and Kazuko bound them together with straps at their waists and chests. A fiery lust burned through Tanner as he felt the strain of heart and lungs, the spasms of the woman's sex as he helplessly impaled her.

Kazuko found two lashes with horsehair tufts. The hair would have been barely noticeable on normal skin, but on scourged flesh the lashes were biting razors. She struck Reina and then Tanner, lashing at one then the other in a clean, constant rhythm. Reina's vaginal muscles undulated on Tanner's cock at each blow. Kazuko worked across their bodies, slapping the tufts between their legs, urging their passions higher. Reina bit into Tanner's shoulder, muffling her scream of release, then threw her head back, gasping air. She was spent.

Tanner remained hard even as Kazuko stopped her ministrations. In his frustration, he tried to pump his cock into Reina, but the ropes held him fast. Kazuko untied them and pushed them apart. Tanner's cock bobbed in spasms. Frustrated by his unfulfilled desire, he could not bring himself to look at the women. His head hung low, but Kazuko was not finished. She flashed a horsehair lash into the underside of his prick.

Tanner sucked in a sharp breath. She struck again in a slow, steady tempo. Restored by the aphrodisiac of anticipation, Tanner raised his head and saw that the women watching had begun to undress. Breasts were bared; knickers were pushed down splayed legs. The scent of animal ardour overpowered the faint fragrances of costly perfumes and filled the room. Kazuko flicked her wrists faster and faster still, sweat streaking her skin as she drummed a frenzied tattoo against Tanner's cock. A keening 'nnnn' sounded in his throat as he finally came, his tortured cock spurting out semen. A woman near the stage caught the first gush in her hand and put it to her lips. Kazuko fell to her knees and gulped Tanner's pole into her mouth, while she pressed the horsehair lash hard against her clit and gave it a few quick strokes.

She came hard, a shudder running through her body.

A rush of satisfaction swept through Tanner. He had lasted the trial and seen to the needs of not one but two of the customers. He had overcome humiliation – or so he thought, until he saw the woman standing next to Burke. When their eyes met, Sandra Callie shook her head at him and sneered.

Burke walked towards Tanner, but instead of congratulating him he helped his Japanese tormentor to her feet. He held her face in his hands. 'You were magnificent, Kazuko.'

The contractions of her ebbing orgasm clutched at her womb as she embraced Burke. 'Thank you, James. Thank you so much.'

Rafael lowered Reina to the floor and untied her wrists. She went to Kazuko and kissed her passionately in a naked embrace. 'You're the master, Kazuko-sama, a true artist.'

Kazuko smiled and turned to Rafael. 'Medicinal oils, and a private room, please.'

'Of course.' He led the women away.

Burke stood next to Tanner. 'Ladies, if there are any among you who would personally like to welcome Mr Dan Tanner to the Excalibur, you may do so now.'

The first to accept the offer was the woman who had sampled Tanner's seed. She applied her bare hand to his backside then selected a paddle. Its sting was feeble compared to Kazuko's work, and Tanner was too excited to concentrate on it. Now each woman in the club came forwards and either stroked him, struck him or both. In time, he would have them all.

Mai was the last. She ordered Lazarus to lower the rope that held Tanner aloft, then unbound him and kissed his raw wrists. 'Well done, Mr Tanner.' Mai whispered the words close to his ear. Her breath stirred his craving. He crushed her against him and gripped her arse hard in his hand. She whispered in his ear, 'You've had me, sir, and I've had you. Would you not pleasure another?'

Burke noted the gleam in Tanner's eyes. 'Whoa, tiger, I don't think you're injured, but let's get some salve on you. Speed the healing. You remember Sandra, don't you, Mr Tanner?'

'If he doesn't, I do.' Yuri Koike bowed slightly to Burke. 'I was at the Bound Maiden last night: very impressive, James. I've heard of technique such as yours, but I didn't believe the stories were true. You must show me sometime.'

'If the circumstances are right, Yuri-san, I would be delighted.'

'How much, to make them right?'

'Never a charge, and I would not accept a gift. It is a covenant I made with my teacher. But as I say, the circumstances must be right.'

'I hope that covers only its application. I wasn't the only one impressed. Do you remember the man who had the bound woman after you left her limp? He paid five-hundred thousand yen for that small privilege, primarily to gain your attention. He is my acquaintance. I told him I knew you, and he asked me to make you an offer to teach him. He can pay handsomely: five-hundred thousand yen would not even be a token.'

'I'm flattered, Yuri-san, but please tell your friend I am compelled to decline. There is the covenant. There is also a danger. The techniques can be misused. I'm sure your friend would never do so, but he might be tempted to teach others who could be less trustworthy.'

'I see, but I must say that my acquaintance can be very persistent.'

'And I can be very stubborn. My answer is respectful, but firm.' Burke bowed deeply. 'I had better see to Mr Tanner's care.'

Yuri returned Burke's bow with a shallow dip of her head. A wan smile crossed her lips as she turned to leave.

'As I was saying, you need some salve. Sandra is my guest tonight, but since she has some experience in this regard, we might put her to work. Would you mind, Sandra?'

'Hmm, why not? Someone needs to take care of little Fauntleroy.' She flicked the tip of his cock with her finger.

'Perfect; he needs to be fit for tomorrow. After tonight's performance, it was only fair to offer Reina a special request. She wants to meet you on a train platform tomorrow morning, early. I believe it's the thick of rush hour. I'll write down the details for you.'

Sergio started to lead them to a private room.

'Oh, and Mr Tanner,' said Burke, 'be sure to wear boxer shorts.'

Tanner turned around with a puzzled look.

'She was very specific about that.'

Four

The city was teeming again after the end of the *Obon* season, when metropolitan émigrés returned to their hometowns and villages by the hundreds of thousands to honour the spirits of their ancestors. Tanner shouldered his way to the designated car and door number on a train platform at Yokohama station. The platform led to the Tokaido line, an express that ran eight to ten minutes between stops to Tokyo. He was early and hung at the back of the line until he felt someone's hand push into his back.

'Board now.' It was Reina's voice. 'When you get through the train doors, turn around and back in.'

Tanner did as he was told.

Reina shoved him into a wall of bodies. She wore a light cotton frock that buttoned down the front. From the jiggle of her breasts through the thin fabric, it was evident she was braless. She pressed against him and shifted to the side to let her hand slip into his groin. He slid his hand between two buttons on her dress just before the doors closed and a mass of commuters crushed them together. Not only was she braless, but she wasn't wearing any knickers either. Tanner strained to twist his hand so it cupped her mound, and found her black moss growing quickly damp from the dew of her passion. Tanner's finger found her cleft and entered her channel, the base of his knuckle pressing her clit hard in the crush of humanity around them.

His other hand lay at his side against the tender leg of a stranger. At each sway of the railcar, the stranger's body shifted involuntarily, ever so slightly, so his hand inched closer to the inside of her thigh. He could feel her heat as her breast moved, against her will, to press against his arm. Tiny spots of sweat showed through her clothes. She was wearing a T-shirt and thin bra to cope with the late summer heat. The crowd surged against her as the train rounded a curve. The full front of her mound now pressed against the edge of Tanner's hand. He turned it only a few degrees so the fleshly muscle at the base of his thumb pressed against her short, thin skirt, pushing into her cleft. She deliberately pushed her face against his shoulder. As the train slowed for a stop at Shinagawa station, she ground her pelvis against Tanner and lingered there as she let others push past her for the exit. A new crowd on the platform began to enter. At the last moment, she kept her face down and left the car.

Tanner and Reina stayed pressed together, but in their brief freedom of movement he unfastened one button on her dress for better access before the crush returned. As he did so he felt a pull on his zip and Reina's hand in his trousers. People surged in. Reina discreetly took Tanner's cock from his trousers and brought it into her open dress, then pushed it down, squeezing the shaft as it pointed between her bare legs. Tanner's hand rubbed hers as he pushed his thumb against her nubbin.

An intoxicating wave of lust swept over Tanner as the crowd around him undulated in the sway of the train. Unknown to individuals hard against his back and side, touching him rear to rear and breast to back, his hand was kneading Reina's hot sex. His stiff cock, in turn, was being massaged by her expert hands. He ached to enter her, but his hips were too high. Still, she was able to push his rod against her clit and force her pelvis against him. As she did so, Tanner dipped one shoulder and eased two fingers into her tunnel, rubbing against her G-zone. He saw the muscles and vessels of her neck stand out as she held back a cry of ecstasy.

A woman who had been standing shoulder to shoulder beside him had managed to turn so she faced his side. She made no pretence of being at the mercy of the crush, but had shoved her hips to push away a man next to her so she could press her mound into Tanner's hand, lying at his side. At each sway of the railcar, she stroked her pubis along his hand and pressed her breast against his arm. She stared into his face, her mouth open and her nostrils flared, to let him know that she was in control, even in the core of this crowd, exulting in the primal urges that flowed through it.

Reina turned her head to look at the woman. The two were eye to eye when the train came to a too-sudden stop at Shimbashi station. The quick halt caused the crowd to surge. Reina stumbled and the woman moved in front of Tanner. His freed cock slapped her belly. She grasped it and ran her fingers over his glans as she pushed it into his trousers and zipped them up.

'*Ki-o-tsuke na.*' She smiled slyly at Reina and Tanner, and then left the train.

'What did she say?' asked Tanner as they followed her off.

'It means be careful.' Reina led the way towards the ticket barriers. They were just a few paces behind the accentuated swish of the woman's hips. 'What is the English expression for what we Japanese call "three piece"?'

'Ménage à trios, but that's French, and it's a euphemism.'

'Explain later.' Reina looked at Tanner and raised an eyebrow. 'What do you think?'

Tanner had kept his hands in front of his crotch until he went limp, but now he felt himself about to harden again just at the idea of three-way sex. 'I like it. You don't mind?'

'Are you kidding? She's beautiful. Stay behind me. I'll talk to her.'

Reina caught up with the woman and spoke as they continued walking. Tanner followed a few paces back. They hadn't gone far when the women stopped. Tanner stopped too, but Reina motioned him to come forwards. 'This is Natsuko. She thinks you're cute. She is also curious about foreign men. So, her answer is "yes". Shall we go?'

Reina suggested a rather famous and glitzy love hotel, but Natsuko had been there and found the service poor. She knew a Japanese inn and hot springs just outside the city and suggested that Tanner might find that more interesting. When he agreed that he would, Reina flagged a taxi for the one-hour ride.

The inn was in forested hills that provided a view of Mt Fuji. It was built of traditional post and beam construction, with a gently sloping roof. A narrow wood terrace ran across the front of the building. Hawks and sparrows graced the air in place of the crows and pigeons of the city. Scents of cedar and pine and the rich humus of the earth replaced the acrid odour of traffic fumes. A gravel path led through a fastidiously landscaped garden.

Natsuko slid open the front door and stepped into a foyer. '*Gomen kudasai*,' she called to the proprietress.

A middle-aged woman padded down a long hallway to greet them. She wore a dark-brown kimono dappled with yellow and gold thread. '*Irasshaimase*.' She bowed deeply and asked only Natsuko's name before she led them to a room then left to prepare refreshments.

Natsuko pushed open a panel that concealed access to a private garden. The fragrance of lilac wafted into the room, blending with the fresh-mown essence of new *tatami*. At a low table, she knelt with her legs tucked beneath her and was joined by Reina and Tanner. Soon the proprietress brought sweet cakes to eat with bitter green tea and rice crackers to eat with bitter beer.

Tanner sampled the crackers and beer and left the cakes and tea to the women.

After they had slaked their thirst, Natsuko stood. 'I've invited you, and I thank you for coming. Let us continue our adventure.' She unfastened the button and zip that held her skirt and pushed it down her legs, then deftly removed her blouse. She reached for Tanner's hand, drew him to his feet and nipped his neck teasingly hard. Then she turned for him to unfasten her bra and slid off her knickers.

Reina's muscular physique was svelte, but in comparison Natsuko was willowy. In contrast to her vamp's manner, her boyish figure sported modest breasts and slender hips. She slid open the doors to a closet that contained bedding, took out two foam-rubber mats and spread them on the floor. Rays of the late-morning sun angled in through the garden and highlighted the fine sparse hairs on Natsuko's body. Her muscles snaked under her taut skin as she topped the mats with cotton futon and linen sheets.

Tanner's unfulfilled arousal had nagged at him since the train. That ache grew stronger as Natsuko lay on her back on the futon and stretched her arms over her head. Her stomach became a valley between her chest and thighs, the bones of her hips and mound rising above it. He began stripping away his clothes.

Despite his haste, he was slower than Reina. In a trice, she had unbuttoned her only garment and tossed it aside. He looked on as Reina straddled Natsuko's hips and slowly rocked her labia over the thinly furred pubis until musky oil anointed Natsuko's mound. Reina leaned back and shifted her leg under Natsuko's so their lower lips kissed.

Tanner knelt beside them and massaged the breasts of both women before sliding his hands down their bellies and pressing his fingers to each nub. He pushed against the wet lips and dipped inside their sheaths, then let his fingers slide from clit to cunt, from one girl to the other, in a steady rhythm. He felt Natsuko's hand grip his pole and pull him towards her eager mouth, and let her impale her face on his cock, squeezing him with cheeks and tongue. Tanner gave a low whimper as Reina massaged his balls and teased his arsehole. His sac was suddenly warmed by her mouth, as she gently rolled the balls from side to side with her lips, until Tanner felt sure he would erupt. His hips bucked involuntarily as Reina ran her tongue along his perineum and stabbed it between his arse cheeks.

Reina sensed his urgency, holding his hips away from Natsuko and pushing him onto his back. Her mouth found his organ, and her expert tongue and lips brought Tanner to the verge of release repeatedly. But each time, just before he came, she stopped exciting him and squeezed the base of his prick and sac to prevent his ejaculation.

Happily for Tanner, Natsuko had no such need to stay her orgasm. She had planted her quim on his eager mouth, and her delicious juices washed over his face in a flood of ecstasy as she rocked her cleft back and forth along his lips and tongue. Her head fell back as a moan rattled deep in her throat. The pressure of her loins was now too great for him, and he pulled his lips back and pushed his tongue between her labia as her nub ground against his teeth. Natsuko's head fell back and her hips shimmied from side to side. Tanner relished the taste of her delicious oil. In quick spasms her stomach tensed in sync with her sharp breaths, and Tanner, sensing how close she was, pushed against her clit until a rush of her nectar wet his face. Her body bucked, once, twice, then she fell away onto her back, panting.

Tanner had focused on Natsuko while Reina continued to minister to his cock. But now that Natsuko had come, he turned his attention to the other woman.

He had been her toy long enough. Now he would have this finely toned woman his own way. He gripped her hips and stabbed his prick into her uplifted sex. His sensations were muted by the earlier pain of Reina's grip on his bollocks, and even though she rode him fast and hard, she came long before he himself was ready. When her final tremors had subsided, he withdrew and saw Natsuko watching him.

Her fingers, wet with her own juice, were in her mouth. There was a basket of *yukata* robes, with sashes to hold them. He took two sashes and rolled Natsuko onto her stomach, then tied her wrists to her knees so that her shins and shoulders were on the futon, with her arse held high. He took his time entering her quim from behind, first coating his rod with her oil. Never had he experienced so tight a fit as the gate between Natsuko's narrow hips. Her vaginal muscles clenched around his pole, restoring its sensitivity.

If her cunt could be so tight, what delights could there be within the bud that winked above it? Tanner withdrew his greasy cock and pressed its soft head against her button, but he could not enter. He wet his finger in her quim and exercised her bumhole until it loosened. She grimaced as his finger entered to its full length. 'It's just a prelude,' Tanner whispered to Natsuko. Again, he pressed his pole to her sphincter. This time the head slid into her. As he pushed deeper, he felt as though his modest cock had become a harpoon rending Natsuko's narrow passage. She bit her mouth into the futon to stifle her cry. Tanner slid out and plunged in again, ignoring her tears and muted sobs in his desire to drive deep inside her. His sac slapped against her labia as he slammed into her, driving her forwards. Finally, the sensation of hot tightness was too much, and he emptied his balls into her. When he had recovered, he eased his diminishing rod from her rear and untied her.

She clenched the cheeks of her arse and rolled onto her back. Her eyes were closed and she was moaning softly.

Even as Reina kissed the tears from her cheeks and stroked her breasts, Natsuko was smiling. 'I've never . . . thank you. It was new for me.'

Tanner kissed her gently and slid down her body to her sparse thatch. His mouth and tongue teased her until she came again, this time quietly. Afterwards her head slowly rocked from side to side in her exhaustion.

'*Yasahii ko*. You are a sweet dear,' said Reina. 'If you have the will, we can take you to heights you have never dreamed of. We should leave now. Are you coming with us?' When Natsuko said she would stay, Reina laid a card beside her. 'This is the number to a private club. It is rather expensive, but you would be welcome as my guest. If you forget my name, it's written on the back. Call us.'

Natsuko scarcely stirred when Reina and Tanner kissed her goodbye.

Shortly after they left, a dark-skinned man, tall and lean, entered Natsuko's room. He was pleased that even though she watched him come in, she made no effort to cover her nudity. The corners of his mouth dipped in a smug smile when he saw the Excalibur card lying on a pillow. He punched a number into a mobile phone. 'This is Mousavi. Mission accomplished.'

He put the phone back into his pocket. The hand that held it bore a scorpion tattoo.

Five

Go Ishido looked at the array of instruments in front of him: picks, drills, vices, pincers, electrodes, screws, bludgeons, scrapers and a coffin. He also had sun-lamps and speakers for sensory overload, as well as dark rooms and saltwater chambers for sensory deprivation. He was a master at his craft. There was no one he could not break, but a broken man, or woman, was not quite as valuable as one who was whole. Inevitably errors crept into interviews. Subjects ended up saying what they thought you wanted to hear. He would always be left to sort fact from fiction, much as he was in the initial inquisitions. If he did not enjoy his work so much, it would hardly be worth the effort.

Years ago, Ishido had sought out the master Wei Xian-xi to gain his knowledge of the universal forces. With the power of *chi*, he could bypass the flesh and directly touch a subject's mind to deliver pain or pleasure at will. There would be no need for these crude instruments, but the proud Chinese had refused. Ishido had given up until he saw Burke at the Bound Maiden. Such technique could only have come from Wei. The Chinese master had rejected Ishido's fortune in gold, but had trained an English fop who displayed his precious gifts like a circus clown. Burke too had refused a fortune to teach. Why? Ishido would know soon enough. Through Burke's American protégé, the woman Natsuko had gained access to Excalibur. It was only a matter of time.

Burke chuckled at the bruise on Tanner's neck. 'Did Reina get rough with you?'

'It wasn't Reina. It was someone you couldn't believe.' Tanner paced and gestured broadly as he told Burke and Mai about his and Reina's experience with Natsuko. 'I swear, she had absolutely the tightest pussy I've ever been in, but her little button . . .' Tanner made a small circle with his thumb and index finger and peered at Burke through it. 'She was an ass virgin. You couldn't imagine.'

Mai made a show of crossing her arms and pouting, but Tanner didn't notice.

'You've got to try her, James. Reina gave her the club's card and invited her as a guest. I'm sure she'll come. If she was tight for me . . .'

In an erect state, Burke had five or six centimetres on Tanner in length and another centimetre or two in girth.

'Good point, I hope she does call.'

'Harrumph!' Mai commanded the attention that she could not get through gestures. 'Mr Tanner, have you completely lost your manners? This is the Excalibur. You do not wax eloquent about a woman's ASS-ets in front of another woman, perhaps especially if that woman happens to own the club. James, what have you been teaching this boy?'

Burke lowered his eyes and bowed.

'Did you ever get the rod at school?' Mai stood and walked to the front of her desk. Tanner remained silent. 'I thought not. Then there's a lot to make up for, isn't there? Drop your trousers and assume the position. Now!'

Tanner bared his arse and leaned across Mai's desk.

'What do you think, James? He's still marked up a bit from last night, but we can't let this go.' She accepted a heavy wooden paddle from Burke. The device had holes drilled in the flat end and a leather thong wrapped around the handle. Mai gripped it in two hands, stepped back and took a running swing at Tanner.

Thwack! He hadn't anticipated such a thundering blow and jerked his head around at the sound and the pain.

'Who told you to look back? Eyes front, or I'll shove this up your arse.' She took two more swings. 'I guess that's enough of that, don't want to damage this pup. Besides, I believe he likes it. Still, I don't think he's learned his lesson. We'll have to try something else.' Mai slipped her hand between Tanner's legs and began massaging his prick. She did the same to Burke, making rustling sounds along the fabric of his trousers. When Tanner's rod swelled, Mai pulled it down between his legs. 'See that, James? I believe he's as hard as you are. We'll see how long that lasts.'

Mai quickly and noisily unzipped Burke's trousers, and his body stiffened in surprise. She winked and pointed to a rubber butt-plug. Burke handed it to her. 'Now then, one for the money –' she swatted Tanner's arse with her free hand '– two for the show –' another swat '– and he's all yours, James.' Mai hooked her ankle inside Tanner's to spread his legs, then rammed the plug home.

Tanner grunted in rage, braced his hands on the desk and spun around. He was breathing hard.

Burke faced him with his arms folded, slowly shaking his head. 'To each man his own, I always say, but we aren't that kind of club, Dan.'

Tanner started to reach for the plug, but Mai stopped him. 'But we are a club of discipline. That stays until I take it out. You must understand the seriousness of your breach of conduct. Not only that, but there's also a likely possibility that you were wrong. I believe that you require a demonstration.' Mai squeezed Tanner's cock to attention and lubricated it only lightly. She lifted her dress, dropped her knickers and bent over. 'Do you need an illustrated manual, Mr Tanner?' She opened her mouth and breathed deeply to relax her nether hole for his prick.

Tanner easily slipped into her and pushed in and out comfortably. She wasn't even as tight as she had been at their first encounter. If she thought she could compare to Natsuko, someone must have been too free with his compliments. Tanner wondered what to say, if she asked him later. As he pushed deeper into her, he felt a constriction around his rod that eased his worry somewhat. Perhaps he wouldn't have to tell such a big lie after all. The constrictions got stronger, so much so that he had to put more muscle into his thrusts. Suddenly, Mai forced him to a dead stop. He could neither enter further nor withdraw. The harder he tried, the tighter Mai strangled his prick. He felt like he was bound with steel bands. Despite his intention not to be bested in what was rapidly proving a contest of wills, his moans grew louder.

Efforts to will his cord to flaccidity were useless. Mai's sphincters stopped the flow of blood out of his engorged organ. She looked over her shoulder at his grimaces and straightened to increase the pressure. As suddenly as she had clamped down, she relaxed and sent Tanner stumbling with a push of her hips. 'What were you saying about Natsuko-san's tight bum?'

Tanner pulled up his trousers. 'I get your point. I apologise.'

'Accepted. However, contrary to what I said earlier, you should know you got off lucky because you behaved as you did in front of the club's owner. If it had been a paying client, the punishment would have been much harsher. Just to help you remember today's lesson, let's keep the plug in for a while, shall we?'

Tanner walked out of Mai's office mumbling to himself.

'What do you think about Dan's new friend, Natsuko?' Mai asked Burke.

'Like he said, someone I couldn't imagine. I sense things, Mai. The event on the train strikes me as a bit too odd. It might be paranoia, but I've been on edge since Yuri spoke to you about her "persistent" friend from the Bound Maiden. I am curious about Natsuko, but for reasons Dan would not understand. I have a class at the dojo tomorrow. Some day soon, I believe I'll take Dan to train. It might be a good idea for him to learn other forms of discipline.'

'Why are you giving the young Mr Tanner special treatment, James?'

'He needs a keeper. He's also out to prove himself, and he's in debt to me. That could make him a good ally. Apart from me, he's the only host here who's not in it for the money.' Burke frowned at Mai's cynical snigger. 'Fair enough, I take what comes my way, but I don't chase it.'

'I know. That's one of the reasons you and I are allies, isn't it?'

'In any case, something about this bothers me, but I'm not sure what it is. I want to talk to Reina to see if her perspective was any different. I also wouldn't mind meeting Natsuko, just to test how persuasive I can be in getting a woman to talk.'

With his butt-plug still firmly in place, Tanner walked into the main room to see Sandra cleaning it. 'What are you doing here?' he asked.

'I'm the new chambermaid: kindergarten in the morning and the Excalibur at night. It makes for a fascinating day.' A knowing smile crossed Sandra's lips when she saw Tanner's stride, which was at once bowlegged and mincing. 'What's that, Dan? Did you sprain something? Your back? A little lower, maybe?' She raised her shoulders and squinted in mock sympathy. 'Ooh, must be a terrible pain. You poor, poor lad.' She scrunched her bum cheeks tight and imitated his walk, before her guffaw turned Tanner's face scarlet.

Six

A woman dressed in aikido's white jacket and black *hakama* held a thick stick high. She was poised before a curved wooden drum two and a half metres in diameter at its centre and four metres long. The instrument sat on a stand of wooden posts lashed together with rope. At a sign from the *sensei*, she struck it once. The drum's deep groan rumbled through the vast room as though the Earth itself had spoken. The martial arts dojo, set among Kamakura's forests and temples, was built in the ancient style. Massive pillars along the outer walls held the high, sloping roof aloft. Canvas mats lay across the floor, which was unobstructed by supports except at the outer walls.

About twenty aikido students bowed to the teacher. It was an all-woman class, including Okabe-sensei. At her invitation, Burke was attending as a guest instructor for special-techniques training. After stretching and rolling to warm up, Burke was paired with Okabe's assistant, Kei, for preliminary techniques. He punched at her head and was swept in a broad circle as the woman grabbed his wrist and spun him away, redirecting his force along a harmless path. Still holding his wrist, she pushed down, reversed her movement and threw Burke onto his back. She pulled his arm straight, at the same time rolling him onto his stomach. To complete the pin, she planted her knee into his armpit and pushed down on his elbow. Burke patted his hand on the side of his leg in submission.

The students imitated the movement and a chorus of eerie *kiai*s filled the training hall as the women shouted at moments of maximum exertion.

Kei let loose her own cry, arcing her arm over her head and chopping the edge of her hand towards Burke's face.

He stepped to the side and spun so they were shoulder to shoulder, facing the same direction. He followed her momentum, grabbed her wrist with his outside hand and locked her elbow with the hand closest to her. She fell headfirst as Burke pushed down. He scissored his legs around her arm and fell onto his back with her elbow locked against his groin. She took her time patting the mat to acknowledge defeat.

After several attack and defend exercises, Burke had to admit Kei's technique was superior to his. He'd had to rely more than once on his muscular strength to complete a throw. They went through only a few more techniques before Okabe stopped them.

'Are you ready?' They both nodded. '*Yame*!' Okabe called a stop to the exercises and addressed her students. 'Today, we will have a reality drill. It might get rough, so if you don't want to participate, you don't have to. But if you get through it, you will be able to protect yourselves against attack from real-life perverts.' Okabe held her hands several centimetres apart between her legs. 'Even big foreign guys, like him.' Nervous laughter tittered through the hall. 'Kei-san, you will go first, to demonstrate.' Okabe told Burke to attack Kei from behind. Burke stepped in with his knee between her legs to restrict her mobility, and wrapped his arm around her shoulders.

Kei started to react, but Okabe stopped the exercise.

'Has anyone here actually encountered a pervert?' More than half the women raised their hands. 'How many of you were wearing your training jacket?' All hands went down.

Kei unfastened her belt and took off her jacket. She wore a white T-shirt underneath, but the brown crowns of her breasts showed clearly through the sweat-dampened material.

'Now, how did you grab her, Mr Burke?'

Burke put his arm around Kei's shoulders.

'Stop. Of those of you who have been attacked, how many were grabbed by the shoulders?'

No one raised her hand.

'I didn't think so. Where did they grab you?' The women spoke in unison, '*Oppai, oshiri, asoko*.' Okabe-sensei continued, 'We don't seem to have encountered any shy perverts, Mr Burke. At first, you grabbed her shoulders. That isn't real life. You have three choices: tits, bum and "down there".' She pointed to her crotch. 'Try again.'

Burke stood close behind Kei. She was big for a Japanese woman, only half a head shorter than Burke. He watched the hairs on the back of her neck stand out as her skin tightened in anticipation. Her body exuded an acrid odour of fear, even though she herself was dangerous. He blew on the back of her neck to disrupt her concentration, then thrust his arm between her legs and clasped her breast from behind. He tried to push forwards and lift with the arm in her crotch, but she anticipated the move and dropped into a semi-squat. With the resistance in front of him gone, Burke's upper body went forwards, off balance.

Kei's stance was solid. She reached both hands back and grabbed Burke's collar. A simple crunch of her stomach muscles sent Burke over her shoulders and onto his back in front of her. She grabbed his wrist and fell with his elbow locked under one of her knees and his throat pinned under her other leg.

'Excellent,' said Okabe. She pointed to another student.

The woman was bouncing on the balls of her feet when Burke dipped low and wrapped his arms around her stomach, pinning both of her forearms while he reached in front and cupped her mound with his other hand. She could not free her arms, but she could push them together in front of her. She gripped Burke's little finger in both hands and pulled. He wrenched away before she broke it.

Burke rubbed his finger. If the women were playing this seriously, it was time for him to get into the spirit of the training. The next student was tall and rangy, with small breasts but a world-class bum. The target was obvious. The problem was how to hold her down while he fondled it. He walked around to her front and feinted to her breast. She tried to grab his wrist and shift her arse into him for a hip throw, but he had already pulled his hand away and hooked his leg behind hers. The blow broke her stance, causing one shoulder to dip.

Burke added pressure to her shoulder and pushed her to the mat on her belly. He pressed his legs on top of her arms and straddled her back as he faced her arse. She could do little but squirm as Burke pushed his hand under her trousers and knickers and squeezed her naked cheeks. She bucked as he pushed his thumb against her sphincter. Her violence could not dislodge Burke, but she freed her arms and brought her elbows under her chest, then spread her legs so she could get leverage from her knees as well as her elbows. When she did so, Burke slid his hand into her cleft. It was a fatal move, as the distraction lost him his concentration on holding her down.

She pushed and lifted Burke just enough for her to flip onto her back, raise her knee and kick him under the chin. He drew back quickly to avoid a blow from her other foot.

Okabe paced back and forth like a boxing referee. 'Yes! That's it. Forget technique, just fight.' She clapped her hands. 'You.'

Another student jumped up, feet spread, knees bent, arms loose at her sides. The target on her was also obvious. Her breasts were velvety cones, heaving their pink knobs against her cotton camisole. It was cut low under her arms, exposing the sides of her luscious chest.

Burke took off his jacket and walked slowly around her. From behind, he simply put his arm over her shoulder and grabbed her bosom. The arm was merely bait. Like a bass snapping at a fly, she grabbed Burke's wrist for a shoulder throw, but he had already shoved his knee into the back of hers. With no leverage she was easy prey. Burke fell onto his back, bringing the woman with him. He wrapped his legs around her waist to hold her and clamped one arm around her neck in a headlock. As she tugged at the arm at her throat, Burke slipped his free hand under the camisole and kneaded her breast at leisure. She tried to grab the little finger on the hand at her throat, but Burke's fist was too tight. He pushed his arm across her right cone and fondled the left. Her efforts to pull that arm away were useless. Burke pushed his hand down towards her quim. To reach it, he forced his heels between her legs and pulled them apart. He had just cupped her mound and slid his finger between its lips when she arched her back in a wrestler's bridge, driving Burke's finger inside her.

The move opened a gap between her pelvis and Burke's groin. She stabbed her hand between his legs and grabbed his flaccid cock and balls. It was more than a handful for her, but she gripped as hard as she could.

Burke grunted in pain and pushed her off.

She stood and turned to face the other students with her hand palm-up and fingers spread. Her mouth was open in an 'O' shape, her eyes wide.

From that point on, the game changed. The women readily let Burke grab whatever his target was just so they could use the same defensive measure. A few even managed to slip a hand inside Burke's trousers to grab raw flesh. Okabe-sensei seemed oblivious to the new objectives. She just paced and shouted, prodding them to fight.

At the end of the session, Burke's skin was a mass of mat burns and his prick and balls throbbed painfully. The scents of the women's fear, aggression and lust clung to him. The feel of their flesh was fresh in his mind; the pain of his falls and scrapes had only intensified the experience. He returned to the Excalibur in grand humour.

Mai was waiting for him. 'Reina arrived several minutes ago. Natsuko is meeting her here later. What's your strategy?'

'Wit, charm and . . .' Burke closed his eyes and inhaled slowly. He put his fingertips to Mai's temples and heard her sigh as he released the power.

'If she's a woman, James, there's no problem.'

In the main room, Reina was being entertained by Lazarus. Burke took his place. 'Dan told me about your train encounter. I'd like to hear your version.' Except for minor differences, she verified Tanner's story. She admitted that the meeting with Natsuko was improbable. However, until Burke asked, she hadn't considered it anything but serendipitous. Frankly, she still didn't, and couldn't see how it could be anything else. After all, she had been the one to chase Natsuko, not the other way around.

'Good point,' said Burke. 'Though I must say, Dan roused my interest. If she accepts, I would like to have a private session with her tonight.' Reina started to protest. 'You and she will be my guests for the evening. I promise to do all I can to ensure she comes back, if you wish it.'

Reina pouted. 'All right, James, on one condition: the next time I come, I get the private session, and you use your fabulous needles.'

'Done, and thank you. Is she as lovely as Dan said?' Burke got his answer from Natsuko herself, as Dirk escorted her into the room. She wore a sleeveless white linen dress, cut low under her arms. It was cinched at the waist by a wide belt and fell to just below her knees. When she stepped in front of the lights shining on the stage, the material became translucent, showing that she wore only a bra and knickers under the dress. Her black hair had a bluish sheen in the light, and framed her oval face in a soft flow to a ribbon that held it back with casual elegance. Finely arched eyebrows swept up and back, giving her almond eyes a wild, carefree air. Her nose was slightly too wide at its bridge, the imperfection that ensured memorable beauty. Dark-red gloss accented her finest asset, lush pouting lips.

When Reina introduced her, Burke took her hand in both of his and kissed her palm and wrist. 'Welcome to the Excalibur.' He bowed and offered her a seat. The reason for Tanner's enthusiasm was clear. The mere thought of buggering this slender fawn sent a twitch through Burke's loins. But that happy event might have to wait. Tonight he had other priorities. They sipped wine and nibbled hors-d'oeuvres while more customers arrived. Tanner came to greet them and lingered as though waiting for an invitation to sit. Instead, Burke pointed out a guest who needed attention.

At climactic points of his retelling Reina's story of the train, he interjected praise for Natsuko's adventurous spirit. He also described some of the impromptu games that were played in the main room. Tonight, Natsuko would be welcome to observe or participate as she liked, but after all was done, it would be a wasted evening if she did not visit a private room.

'I would be delighted, if you would show me,' she said in Japanese.

Reina butted in with, 'A bit later. Look, that's Aya.'

One of the hosts directed a stage light to the second-level terrace. Aya was slowly removing her clothes and tossing each garment down to the floor of the main room. She had large breasts and broad hips, but her stomach was flat. Her knickers were the last item of clothing to fall. When she had tossed them down, she kept one hand on her mound and walked out onto a wide beam. She stood there, her legs spread, snatched off her wig and raised both arms over her head. There was not a hair on her body. Even her pate had been shaved clean.

'Bravo!' shouted Rafael as murmurs of praise rose from the audience.

Lars was up in the beams and tied her wrists behind her. Next, he shackled her ankles to the ends of a pole about a metre long. A chain ran through rings on each end of the pole to a pulley secured in the ceiling. He laid her down on the beam she had stood on, pulled her into the air and slowly lowered her head-first to the stage, where Giovanni, the most hirsute of the hosts, waited. His dark-brown ponytail fell to his waist and his body hair glistened in the stage lights. He had been stripped nude and stroked to arousal by two female guests. He reached for Aya as Lars let her down until her face was at Giovanni's hips. She took his cock in her mouth.

'Would you like to join in?' Burke posed the question to both Reina and Natsuko.

'How?' Natsuko asked.

Reina took her hand and led her to the stage. She selected four thin bamboo switches and gave two to Natsuko. Reina struck first, scoring Giovanni's backside.

Natsuko lashed Aya, looking Reina in the eye as they synchronised their cadence. The tempo of their rhythm sped until both women began to perspire.

Giovanni's arse twitched at each bite of a switch, driving his cock deep into Aya's throat. He put his face between her legs and lapped at her smooth, hairless quim, slipping his tongue into her moist channel where it quickly found her hard bud. He sensed that Aya was near orgasm, when Reina's hand gripped his hair and pulled him back.

Aya felt the lash of Natsuko's switches flick between her legs. Their thrilling stings spurred her greed for Giovanni's cock. She put her hands on his hips and pushed herself back and forth along his rod, taking its full length into her throat. Her body shuddered as the exquisite nips of pain, now lashing around her clit itself, brought her to orgasm. She buried Giovanni's cock within her mouth and swallowed the white lava that erupted from his loins. When she had licked the tip clean, Rafael lifted her in his arms and Lazarus unshackled her ankles from the bar. He untied her hands, only to secure them to the chain. Lars pulled her up so her hips were level with the groins of the two hosts.

Aya watched hungrily as they stripped. The two men embraced her, caressing and kissing her. Rafael's nibbling at her breasts stirred light spasms in her womb, and pride swelled within her as she saw his prick harden in desire and felt Lazarus's erect phallus against her cheeks. She wrapped her legs around Rafael's hips and drew him inside her, savouring the power of his sex. Meanwhile, Lazarus's oiled rod eased into the pink pucker between her arse cheeks. She writhed on the chain as the two vigorous men pumped inside her, one in her bumhole and the other in her oiled vagina. They quickened their pace in and out of sync, pumping their cocks into her with powerful thrusts. Their pounding carried her into the sky, filling her. The chain that bound her meant that she could only buck against the cocks as she felt her orgasm build until she came with a shiver. The men carried on fucking her, groaning as her muscles spasmed on their cocks, until Lazarus's seed spilled inside her, moments before Rafael's grimace.

Aya hung limp as the muscles of her sex and colon clutched at the men's softening cocks in receding waves of spent passion, then the men pulled out and she felt their seed running down her legs as her muscles closed on air.

Burke traced his fingertips along Natsuko's thigh and pushed them towards her V. From her heat, he sensed that she had become aroused either from lashing Aya or watching the three-way union. He put his mouth next to her ear. 'There's more to see.'

Natsuko followed Burke as though entranced. After the show, she was alive with anticipation as he held her hand lightly and guided her to the glass room on the townhouse roof. Lights of coloured neon, street lamps and the full moon filtered through the tinted glass and washed gently over Natsuko's white summer dress. Burke removed her belt and held her against him as he slid the zip down her back. He lifted the dress off her delicately boned shoulders and lowered it for her to step out. A few strands of black fleece showed above the band of her tiny knickers. She pushed them down over her prominent mound, revealing a dark wavy V, then bent at the hips as she lowered the fragile garment to her ankles, stood and left it on the floor. Burke unfastened her bra, but she crossed her arms over her bosom and removed it herself. Her modest breasts appeared incongruously large on her thin frame.

A shimmer of delight coursed through her as Burke touched his palm to the tip of her nipple and ran it slowly back and forth. She reached for his face and found his skin warm in her hand. Early dew began trickling in her canal at his kiss to her wrist, its nerves stimulated by his lips and tongue. The tingle of that caress seemed to run through her entire body as Burke's fingers ran lightly over her. She ached to clutch him to her but stood stone still as her desire soared.

Despite the effects on Natsuko of his ministrations, Burke was dispassionate as he noted her energy flow along the twelve horizontal *kei* and twelve vertical *raku*, as well as the eight multidirectional *kikei* ranges. Those highways follow the same general routes in all humans but have slight variations in each individual that must be charted for maximum efficacy. When he was satisfied that he understood her personal *chi*, he led her to a four-poster bed, where he bound her wrists and ankles to the posts with silk scarves.

He pressed his hands against her breasts and ran them down her abdomen to her pubis and cleft, then down her thigh. His thumb found a hollow on the inside of her knee and pressed hard against the nerve that crossed it.

Natsuko flinched. 'Are you going to hurt me? You won't, will you?' There was a teasing quality to her plea.

'Who sent you, Natsuko?'

She looked embarrassed at the question and stammered before she responded. 'What do you mean? No one, I . . . Reina invited me.' Sweat beaded on her upper lip. 'They didn't send me.'

'Who is "they"?'

'No one!'

'Sorry, love, you've given yourself away. I don't believe you. As I'm sure you know,' said Burke, 'there is joy in the sting of the lash. It tells us we are alive. When it is combined in proper doses with sexual thrill, there is no greater rapture in the physical world.' Burke's face was solemn as he looked into Natsuko's eyes. 'This will not be like that.'

He removed his clothes and stood with his back to her. His arms swept slowly above his head as he inhaled a single breath, then stepped forwards with his left foot and lowered his arms. After repeating the exercise several times, he knelt in Zen meditation. When his mind was clear of distraction, he knelt between her legs, touched his fingers to the base of her throat and unleashed a bolt of universal power.

Her body stiffened so fiercely she couldn't breathe. Her pristine face contorted in a pain that wracked the mind more savagely than any physical assault. An abyss of torture, black in its misery, enveloped her in fear. She fought impotently to open her eyes and see the physical world, to escape the madness that was rending the essence of her humanity.

The pain stopped.

She gasped air in great gulps. Her eyes wide with terror, she flailed at her restraints in a futile effort to escape Burke. There was no trace of teasing in her supplications. 'No more, please.'

'Stage two,' said Burke. He entered her tight sheath and arched his back until he was just touching her with his hips. He channelled the energy to his rod and released it in easy pulses into the core of Natsuko's sex.

Her eyes half closed as the pleasure engulfed her in security and warmth. It nourished her spirit as a mother's womb nourishes a babe. Tremors of carefree delight rolled through her loins. She felt her body sing as it rocked against Burke's hard pole. Her head thrashed as the intensity of the waves neared a crescendo. Her heels dug into the mattress and an explosive groan began to rumble out of her lungs.

'Stage three,' said Burke. He withdrew from her sex and touched her neck.

Coils of pain and terror strangled Natsuko's groan. The nurturing womb became a suffocating oppression. She felt she would drown in its wet folds. Mucus ran from her nose and spittle from her mouth, choking her. She could not cough as her own muscles crushed her lungs.

'Stage four.' He sank his phallus into her to its full length.

A nova of ecstasy exploded within Natsuko. Of their own volition, her hips thrust against Burke. Rivulets of her juices soaked his prick and ran down her cleft, as her body bucked in her excitement.

'Stage five.' Burke started to withdraw.

'Nooo!' Natsuko lifted her hips to keep him away from her throat, to hold his cock deep inside her. Tears ran freely down her cheeks, as her head rolled from side to side. 'Stay inside me. Stay in me.'

He lay upon her, belly to belly, caressing her hair and wiping the tears from her face. 'Who sent you, Natsuko?' Fear shone in her eyes and echoed in her silence. He had only to touch the base of her throat and lift his hips away from her loins to force a response.

Her pubis pushed against him. '*Sasori*.'

As Natsuko opened up, Burke's pelvis took on a languid rhythm. His voice was low and gentle. '*Sasori*? A scorpion sent you?'

A hum sounded deep in her throat as Burke slid slowly through her sex. 'Untie me,' she said. His cock pushed in to its base as he reached for one of the scarves holding Natsuko's wrist. She showed him the back of her freed hand. 'A tattoo, here.'

'The man who had the girl at the Bound Maiden had a scorpion tattoo. Do you know about the night he saw me?'

'No. There is more than one – a few, maybe many. Foreigners too.' She spread her hand over her nether lips so she could feel Burke's cock with her fingers as he fucked her. 'I'm afraid, James. If they find out I've told you . . .'

'What would they do?'

Natsuko was silent.

'Who is the one who sent you? Where do I find him?'

'Untie me.'

Burke felt her stiffen for an instant as his finger brushed near her throat. 'Will you tell me, if I do?' When she nodded, Burke released her wrist and ankles. Her arms reached for him, her thighs embracing his hips as he entered her. 'Where?'

'The inn; Reina knows.'

She was crying again. Burke kissed her eyes, his lips

absorbing their salty droplets. 'Who or what are the Scorpions?'

Natsuko gripped Burke's hair, pushed her face against his chest and shook her head. 'I don't know. Truly I don't. I was a hostess. They gave me money, a great deal, to help them.'

He pushed himself away. 'To do what?'

'Find this place.'

'Why? What do they want?'

'You.' She stared into his uncomprehending eyes. 'Your power.'

'Not to please women?' Burke asked.

Natsuko didn't respond, but Burke saw the answer in her eyes. 'This?' He had only to place his finger on her neck.

Her voice caught in her throat. She nodded her head vigorously.

'They seek only the power of pain.' Burke's expression turned grim. 'I expect they shall not have it.'

'I'm afraid of them. They are strong.' She crushed Burke in an embrace that sought peace.

As quickly as the glowering cloud had descended on Burke, it dissipated. He kissed Natsuko's breasts and lips, then touched the base of her throat again, only this time he brought her pleasure. Undulations of *chi* flowed through him, flooding her body.

'Stop.' Natsuko grasped Burke's arse, pushing his hips towards her. 'Don't use that power. Just you, James.' Her voice was husky with lust. 'Just you.'

Seven

Burke straddled more than 200 horses as he revved his Harley touring bike along a highway out of Tokyo. The throaty roar of the 1450 cc engine streaked through the night. His session with Natsuko had ended with her giving him and Mai detailed directions to the inn where she had engaged Tanner and Reina. The sky was clear. The light of the full moon low on the horizon above Mt Fuji guided him. Images of a dark-skinned man and scorpion tattoos filled his mind. It was just past 3 a.m. when he pulled the bike into a thicket of cedar trees. The inn lay about a hundred metres ahead.

He swapped his helmet for a black balaclava and his boots for rubber-soled slip-ons. From the bike's box, he took out a belt with loops or pockets for lock picks, throwing knives and a short metal bar with a curved tong just above the hasp. It also carried pepper spray, a packet of chloroform and a homemade flash grenade filled with magnesium powder. He looped a coil of rope over his shoulder and slipped a garrotte and a long thin metal strip into pockets on the sides of his trousers. Hard plastic protected his shins, knees, forearms and elbows. His gloves were pliable, but reinforced with steel across the knuckles, the outside ridge and the base of the palm. Each item was securely fastened so it would not make a sound.

As quiet as mist, he moved among the trees towards the inn. When he reached the clearing that surrounded it, he lay flat on the ground and pushed himself forwards with one leg. A terrace ran along two sides of the building. He rolled under it and crawled to the front entrance. The door had a high-security lock, each of the five pins bearing a head like a nail. When Burke raised any of them and twisted the turning tool, there would be a slight give, which made it hard to tell when a pin was in position. The silence of the night magnified the pick's metallic clicks and scrapes, and Burke was sweating heavily by the time he got the main door open.

From Natsuko's descriptions, Burke found the Scorpion's room. It had a sliding door that was secured by a wooden latch from the inside. The door was built to be loose in its grooves and allow easy sliding when the wood swelled or warped in the rainy season. It was generally dry this time of year, so there was a lot of give. Burke bent a slight curve in the metal strip, inserted it between the door and the jamb and pushed it up to lift the latch. Slowly, he slid open the door.

The room was small, the futon askew and empty. The window was open and there was nowhere to hide except the small futon closet, which had a shelf running across its middle. He doubted the Scorpion would leave himself vulnerable by crouching inside it. Either he had gone out the window, or . . .

A fist slammed into the back of Burke's head. For an instant, the blow stunned him, and his knees started to buckle. Acting on instinct, his body pitched forwards and rolled away from the attack. He fumbled for the pepper spray, but his attacker kicked it out of his hand. He rolled away from a second kick aimed at his head and pulled a knife from his belt. The Scorpion gripped his wrist in a flash and dropped his knee into Burke's ribs, forcing air out of his lungs in an explosive rush, then twisted Burke's wrist and wrested the knife out of his hand. The Scorpion stabbed the blade towards Burke's neck, and he punched up to block the blow. The knife sliced through the skin of his upper arm but missed the vital arteries of his throat. He grabbed the Scorpion's knife arm in both hands, brought his knee to his chest and kicked his heel into his attacker's armpit. The Scorpion turned to break the lock, and the move gave Burke room to snap his foot into the Scorpion's groin. The man stumbled back. Burke sprang to his feet and pulled another knife from his belt as the Scorpion lunged towards him. He threw the small blade under-handed into the Scorpion's thigh. The man didn't fall, but his leg stalled for a heartbeat, enough time for Burke to kick the ball of his foot into the man's solar plexus. The Scorpion's stomach was oak hard, but the blow slowed him enough for Burke to pull the chloroform packet from his belt. He clamped it over the Scorpion's mouth and nose. With his next breath, the man crumpled like a half-empty sandbag.

Burke ripped a *yukata* into strips and used them to stanch the blood from the cut in his arm. He then tied the Scorpion to immobilise him and bound the wound in his leg. He put both knives back in his belt and retrieved the pepper spray. The chloroform packet had fallen to the floor. Burke put it over the Scorpion's mouth and tied it in place, so he would get a mix of fumes and oxygen. He hoisted the man onto his shoulders in a fireman's lift and walked out of the inn. When he got to the tree line, he looked back. No one followed. Either the fight had been too quiet or too short to wake anyone at that hour of deep sleep, or else anyone who had awoken was too afraid to do anything.

The Scorpion was still unconscious when Burke slung him onto the back of the big Harley. He started the engine and rode slowly through the forest. In a particularly dense patch, he stopped and pulled the man onto the ground. He unfastened the rope, cut off a short piece and used it to tie his arms behind him at the elbows. There was just enough rope left to cut it in half and tie his legs to two low tree limbs. Burke had to pull his legs up close to the limbs. When he had finished, the Scorpion was bound spread-eagled with his legs in the air and his hips off the ground. Burke untied the strap holding the chloroform packet, sat down and waited.

When the Scorpion came to, he saw Burke sitting cross-legged and staring into his face. 'Who are you?'

'I think you already know.' Burke took a knife and began cutting away the Scorpion's bedclothes.

The man tried to sit up, but he was helpless with his arse in the air. 'What are you doing?' He twisted his body against the ropes.

'I'd be still if I were you.' Burke slapped the flat of the knife against the Scorpion's thigh wound. 'Don't want to get cut again. Who are the Scorpions?' His question drew no response. Burke cut away the man's pyjama trousers and started on his shirt. 'From your features and the quality of your speech, I would guess you come from the Levant, or close to it.' Silence. Burke picked up the rags and put them in his motorcycle box. The Scorpion lay naked on the ground. 'This is the way you work, isn't it?' Burke took the metal bar from his belt. 'Strip a man or woman naked, complete access to their bodies, brutal.' He rapped the bar into the Scorpion's kneecap, hard enough to inflict tear-welling pain in most people.

The man barely flinched.

Burke struck the sole of the Scorpion's foot. 'Your name.' He pushed the metal bar to the man's anus, and returned his glare. 'I wouldn't dirty my tools on you.' He cracked the bar against the man's shin. 'Your name.' He struck again in the same place. 'Who are the Scorpions? Shall I break this worthless twig?' Burke slammed the bar into the man's shin a third time. The crack echoed through the forest.

The Scorpion's jaw clenched in response.

Burke shook his head. 'Are you on to me, Scorpion? I won't hurt you, not really. Is that what you think?' Burke slapped the bar into the man's groin and watched him suck in a sharp breath as he jerked his head towards his chest. 'I'm a poor imitation of you, aren't I? But we have time. Maybe I'll improve. What's your name?' Burke struck the arch of the man's foot. 'Who are the Scorpions?' He struck again.

The Scorpion sneered and spat.

Burke squatted next to the man's head and leaned forwards, so their faces were only centimetres apart. He laughed aloud. 'Well done, chum. You take your own medicine, don't you, like a mighty strong bloke?'

The man didn't respond.

'Your name.' Silence. 'The Scorpions – who are they?' Silence. 'Well, then.' Burke turned his back to the man and raised his face to the sky as he drew in a slow, long breath. He drew another and then another, then turned and squatted next to the man. 'Your endurance is well noted.' Burke knelt with his shins on the ground and his arse on his heels, in the fashion of Zen meditation. 'You're a strong man, Scorpion, but from this point on, strength will do you no good.'

Burke closed his eyes and placed the fingers of both hands on the base of the Scorpion's throat.

Eight

'You left him tied up in the forest?' Mai laced surgical thread through the wound to Burke's upper left arm. The only acknowledgement he gave to the pain was a slight twitch of his eyelid each time she pierced his skin.

'I expect he'll free himself. It won't be easy, but he'll make it.'

'What did he tell you?'

'Everything he knows; unfortunately that's not much. His name is Mousavi, and he's a professional torturer. There's a society of those animals. They hire out to governments, criminal syndicates, sometimes a corporation. The "Scorpions" is the elite group. It's set up in cells like the old communist underground. The tattoo marks them. It's an ID card, if one needs help or training. They don't use names, except among cell members, usually only three or four people.'

Mai finished sewing up Burke's wound and gently pushed him face-down on the bed. She straddled his arse as she started working her hands into his neck and shoulders. 'What's he doing here?'

'He said he hadn't been told yet. As far as Natsuko goes, he was just a messenger assigned to handle her. She doesn't know anything about the true nature of the Scorpions, except that they are very scary. She thought they were some sort of yakuza.' Burke revelled in the complex orchestration of Mai's tender loving care. Her thumbs, fingertips, palms and elbows sought out the traumas of combat and purged them from his body. 'I was simply a target of opportunity, not his real objective. The man Mousavi described as his contact sounds like the Japanese at the Bound Maiden, Yuri's friend. Mousavi thinks his name is Ishido. I need to talk to her.'

'She hasn't been back since that night.' Mai pressed the heels of her hands along the muscles on either side of Burke's spine. 'I don't know how to find her. All our clients need are cash and an introduction, no real names, addresses or phone numbers unless they're volunteered.' Her labia pressed against his leg as she moved down and used her elbows on the hard muscles of his arse. 'You know, James, the Scorpions will figure out what happened between you and Mousavi. When they do, they'll know that he talked.'

'Yes, and when they do that . . .' A soft moan of tranquil pleasure stopped Burke's speech as Mai rubbed her nether lips along the sole of his foot, while she pressed her thumb into the *tsubo* pressure point at the centre of his thigh.

'Mousavi would be better off dead.' Mai finished his sentence.

'He, and the world as well, would have been better off if he had become a doctor or a taxi driver.'

Mai switched legs and pressed the heel of her hand into the hip joint just below Burke's gluteus. 'They still want you, James, but now more than ever, and for more than one reason. You know about them. They might even come here.'

'If they do, don't buzz the lock for them.' Burke ended the conversation by turning over and covering Mai's mouth with his own.

'Are you sure you're ready for this?' Mai was on top, her lips straddling Burke's rod.

'I'm tired, Mai. You know what that means.'

'Mmm hmm, it takes you longer.' Mai inserted Burke's prick into her, just up to its most sensitive area, below the head. She slid on and off the tip as she watched Burke's eyes. She knew he wanted to impale her, but she pulled away whenever he moved his hips. 'Be still, James. Let me work the magic.' She took half his length inside her and undulated her vaginal muscles along his length, at once soothing and stimulating him. Then she put his hand to her breast and guided it lightly over its surface. Her hips crept down slowly, steadily, as though time itself had stopped to watch their union. She nibbled at his nipples, his neck, his ear. They were innocent youths, discovering each other for the first time, finding joy in a hesitant kiss. Her hair brushed his chest. Its shadow fell at a sharp angle in the light of the early-morning sun. It would be high in the sky before they were done.

'Where's James?' Tanner had the expression of a lost urchin.

'He has the day off, Mr Tanner.' Mai looked up from her desk. 'Does that meet your disapproval?'

'Of course, I mean no, I . . .'

'Feel like the lost puppy that you are? Hang with Rafael, if you aren't sure what to do in a game. He's sort of the sergeant-major of the place.' She waited for a response that was not forthcoming. 'You may hang with him now, Mr Tanner. I'm going to take a nap soon.'

Tanner backed out of the doorway and went to the main room. Guests had not yet arrived. Sandra was dusting tabletops.

She stood with her hands on her hips and tilted her chin up, like a proud actress on the stage. 'Guess what, Danny boy – some of the ladies said they liked my looks, so tonight I get to play.' She lowered her chin, her eyes vampish under her light eyebrows. 'You'll be here to see, you lucky lad.' She moved closer to Tanner. 'To see –' she stood on tiptoe, her breast pressed against his chest as she whispered in his ear '– and maybe to join.'

Her vanilla fragrance assailed his senses. Tanner cursed his own weakness. The disdain he had felt for this woman evaporated in the heat of his lust, too easily aroused. His throat was dry. 'Good for you.' His voice cracked.

Sergio walked in with a large shopping bag. 'Sandra, I have purchased your requirements.'

'Then I should be getting ready. Thank you, Sergio.' She kissed his cheek and waved to Tanner over her shoulder.

Aya was the first guest to arrive. After her formal greeting from each of the hosts, she took off her wig and handed it to Tanner. 'See to my things, please, ah . . .'

'Dan Tanner.'

'Yes, Dan. When you come back, sit with me. Bring a Campari, some fruit and whatever you're having.'

When he returned, coloured lights lit the stage in desert tan and oasis green. Small plates of olives, dates and figs had been served to each guest. Aromas of spice graced the air. The thin jangle of a tambourine sounded from a speaker in one corner of the room, then shifted to another speaker and then another as the plaintive wail of song sounded from above. Middle-Eastern lutes, flutes and drums rose gradually in volume, but the tempo remained an *adagio assai* of languid leisure. Into the corona of light at the stage stepped Sandra, a gold chain encircling her forehead. A transparent turquoise veil draped her face just below her eyes, shining brilliantly against painted black shadow. Layers of sheer multicoloured fabric swathed her body. Her bracelets and anklets were adorned with small cymbals that rang with her steps and the twists of her wrists. A gold band cinched her throat.

She was Salome, come to dance.

With her back to the audience she looked seductively over her shoulder and dipped down on one knee. Fabric fell away from the other leg, extended straight to her side. Her skin was milky white, delicately mottled in strawberry-tan freckles. Her musculature was round, firm and feminine. She turned forwards, and the fabric opened along the side of her hips, revealing a luscious portion of her arse cheek. One arm rose as she flicked the cymbals on her wrist in rhythm to the recorded drums. Her eyes met Tanner's as she reached back and pushed away the fabric to let light shine on the full half-moon of one cheek.

Tanner's pulse raced. He stroked Aya's leg and pushed his fingers along the inside of her thigh, but in his mind the flesh he felt was Sandra's.

She stood, lifted her knee and extended her leg, supple as a ballerina, straight up in front of her. As she pivoted on her toe the fabric flowed, with her not quite exposing the wondrous charm between her thighs. Her leg came down hard, stamping the floor, jangling the cymbals. Arms high, wrists twisting, hip thrusting from side to side, she sidled towards Marcel. He loosened the outer veil and pulled it from her.

Sandra pivoted slowly back to stage centre and swayed her hips and shoulders along opposing paths as the tempo ever so slightly hastened from *adagio assai* to *adagio*. She arched backwards, entwining her arms, letting her head fall back. The muscles of her neck strained against the gold band, and she shifted her shoulders and hips in unison as she walked straight to Dirk. He relieved her of another veil and draped it across the guest next to him. With both arms extended towards Dirk, and the cymbals jingling, Sandra walked backwards onto the stage.

She beckoned to Giovanni. When he stood before her, she danced around him, not quite touching him.

She faced him and urged him to join her. He tried to match her rhythm, but he was too fast. '*A poco, a poco*, Giovanni,' Sandra chastised. Her hands went to his hips to slow him down. She slid her palms up over his hard stomach and chest and gripped his shoulders, moving them forwards and back in proper time. The third veil fastened at her shoulder. She placed his hand on its soft knot and pivoted away, leaving the veil in his grasp. He bowed and left the stage.

A smouldering heat welled up in Tanner, fired by desire and jealousy at the sight of Sandra's hands on the Italian. In the Excalibur, jealousy was a fatal emotion. It was one he vowed to control.

The tempo sped to *andante*. Sandra gestured towards Sergio, who tossed her a tambourine. She strutted across the stage, slapping the instrument against her hip, then twirled again and again, in a vivid circle of colour. The veils flared, baring her legs to the top of her thighs. She stopped with her back to the audience and her arms over her head, tapping the tambourine against the heel of her hand. 'Lars!' The host went forwards and removed the fourth veil.

Andantino, Sandra undulated the muscles of her stomach and hips. Her arms stretched out to her sides. The cymbals and tambourine jingled as she pivoted on the ball of her left foot. In the stage lights, accents of her body, her nipples, pubis and arse cleft showed dimly through the remaining veils. She stopped cold, slammed the tambourine against her hip and flung it to a far wall. 'Lazarus!'

He went to her and reached for the fourth veil, but she slapped his hand away. As her hips gyrated in time to the music, she grasped his arm and bit into his wrist. She took his finger into her mouth and flexed her head from side to side to the rhythm. Her hands gripped the sides of his head and pulled his mouth to the knot at her shoulder. His teeth nipped the veil, and she spun away, abandoning the fabric to the American. The remaining veils spun in a kaleidoscope of colour, revealing brief glimpses of bum and fleece and bosom.

Tanner battled his emotions. Most who apprentice at the Excalibur don't make the grade. That admonition from Mai and Burke echoed in his head, but he could not ignore his jealousy. His only thought was that there were two veils left and three hosts. Would she call him?

Allegro assai, Sandra grinned and bared her teeth. Her wrists flicked, her feet stamping a fevered rhythm. Through the thin veils, even her fine body hairs were visible. She spun and twirled as a whirling dervish, swirling the fabric high. Her arse and pubis gleamed with sweat. She called out, 'Rafael!'

The Argentinian was a Latin dancer. He jumped to the stage and matched her fiery pace.

Tanner was helpless with lust. All he could think about was that when she was finished with Rafael, there would only be one veil left. Would she choose Sergio or him? He gritted his teeth into his cheek and felt the pain of his own bite.

Sandra gripped Rafael's face in her hands and kissed his mouth, all the while switching her hips and shoulders to the torrid rhythm. Her hand dipped to his crotch. She felt his hands running over her breasts, and stabbing under the veils to her hot sex. She looked at the audience and met Tanner eye to eye. Her hands slammed into Rafael's chest, forcing them apart. She took the tip of the sixth veil and handed it to him, and he held it as she stepped slowly away.

All that was left was one veil, transparent against the light. Her body was exquisite beneath it.

Sandra rushed to the edge of the stage. Her foot pushed off the rim as she leapt up, tucking her knees against her chest, arcing high. She nailed the landing on the table in front of Tanner and Aya. Her arms rose to her sides, sweat shining through the sheer fabric. 'The last veil, Dan Tanner, is yours.'

Tanner's hands trembled as he reached for the knot of the final veil. He pulled it away and Sandra Callie stood naked before him. 'Have you nothing to say?' she asked.

The heat of Tanner's passion turned to an icy chill. He swallowed the sand in his throat. Before he could regain his composure, Sandra stepped down and walked back to the stage. She turned to her side and raised her right arm towards him. then looked down it like a bowman sighting an arrow.

'Bring me the head of John the Baptist.'

Two guests led Tanner to the stage. Sandra embraced him, pushing her naked body against his clothes. 'You are John, are you not?'

Tanner was willing to agree to anything. He nodded his head.

A wry smile crossed Sandra's lips. She unzipped Tanner's trousers and took out his steely rod. She pushed it down and released it. It sprang back like an iron tine. She crossed her arms as she stared down. 'If I know my Johns –' Sandra looked into the audience and lowered her voice in a conspiratorial tone '– and I believe I do.' She knelt on one knee, squeezed Tanner's rod and sniffed its head. 'This fellow is not the Baptist at all. It's Little John himself, or maybe his quarter-staff.' She stood, held her thumb and forefinger a couple of centimetres apart and winked. 'Couldn't be his full staff now, could it?' She swept her arm towards the audience. 'Away!'

'Bravo!' Rafael led a chorus of shouts and applause for Sandra's performance. She curtsied graciously, then turned and curtsied again, giving her admirers a clear view of the golden gossamer framing her quim.

'Huh!' A gust expelled from Tanner's lungs before two guests led him back to his seat. In shock and rage, he fumbled to hide his hard rod in his trousers, but the female guests urged him to leave himself exposed. He obeyed, his humble being following the noble standard of his prick, standing stiff before him for all to see. He reached his seat and sat down.

'You're a sport, Dan, and so is your quarterstaff.' Aya nuzzled her cheek against his and patted his prick. 'That's plenty for me. I quite like it.'

Tanner scowled. His body tensed, but when he caught a sharp glare from Rafael, he instantly relaxed and kissed Aya's glamorously bare head. 'Thank you.'

She purred and squeezed Tanner's cock as the show went on.

Sandra beckoned to a guest, who eagerly went to centre stage.

'I am Hikari,' the woman said, then bowed. She had a deep tan complexion and broad features. A shyness in her manner contrasted with her rugged frame. She was broad-shouldered and slightly thick in the waist, but her breasts were vast cushions of delight. She smiled happily when Sandra buried her face in the cleavage, exposed by the low scoop of her dress. Hikari stroked Sandra's hair and 'oohed' in surprise at its silky texture. Emboldened, she combed Sandra's golden bush with her fingers, then whispered to her, and when Sandra nodded, she plucked out a curly strand and ran it over her lips and tongue. Then her finger dipped to Sandra's quim and absorbed her dew and sweat; that too went to Hikari's tongue.

Sandra undressed her, leaving her bra for last. It was a dainty garment, but performed its splendid task well, moulding the pliant flesh into perfect orbs. Sandra unfastened the hook at the front and traced her hands across Hikari's skin to the dark-brown nipples. She sucked on each, a tremor running through her as Hikari cupped her arse cheeks and slipped her finger into the bud between them. She lay on the stage and spread her knees, inviting Hikari to explore her further. Her eyes narrowed at the multitude of sensations, with Hikari's fingers in her arse and cunt and her tongue now caressing her clit to orgasmic heights.

Straight before her was Dan Tanner. Through half-closed lids she stared into his eyes. Did she see hunger in them? For her or for Aya? He had wanted her earlier, but he was young and would want any woman. How could she compare to the exotic, ravishing Aya? His hand was on her leg, in her crotch, but his eyes were on her. He was beautiful, an unsure boy, but she sensed strength in him that he himself did not realise. Someday he would know his power and beauty, and when that time came, he would not want her.

Her parents had treated her like an inconvenient pest, so she'd run away as soon as she was able to. As a roadie, she'd found love in buses and backstage, fifteen minutes of bliss. A one-night stand was an eternity. If that was all she could find, she'd take it. She'd had nearly two years with the bond trader. In her mind, he had been the first person to truly love her, but he had thrown her out when he grew bored. She'd tried to turn the table with lies, telling people she was the one who walked away bored. She would not be hurt again. She would piss on Tanner's ego and walk away. By the time he understood her callousness, his desire would turn to apathy, and she would be gone.

The wretched bitch. Tanner had ached for the wanton kindergarten teacher, the bold chambermaid, only to be played for a fool. She had abased him in a mockery of his manhood, used him as a foil when she needed a convenient buffoon as a target for her wit. Now she stared at him as Hikari pleasured her. Why did she look only at him? There was no ridicule in her eyes, only lust. He could not dispel his carnal longing for Sandra, but he could end the stupid jealousy. He kissed Aya in a sudden, powerful embrace and forced her onto her back. He spread her legs, pulled her knickers aside and stabbed his phallus into her. His hips rose high and slammed back. With barbaric fury, he gripped her shoulders and crushed her body between the vice of his hands and his driving loins.

Aya screamed in surprise and delight when Tanner entered her. Her wide eyes looked into Rafael's shocked face, but she waved him away when he started towards them. Her arms enveloped Tanner, her heels, locked against his buttocks, adding her own strength to the pounding of his cock. Within a minute they had come together. Primal shouts and the odour of rutting lust overwhelmed the room's tinkling cymbals and fragile spice scents.

Tanner stared into Aya's eyes as the spasms of her sheath milked the last of his semen. He looked at nothing else, but as he listened to the vacuous silence of the room, he knew everything had stopped. Even Hikari had abandoned Sandra's quim to watch. In the quietness, he knew that she had not been satisfied.

The club's gaiety died in the overpowering display of passion. Rafael was too stunned to respond. Sandra stood, helped Hikari to her feet and held her hand as they bowed together. There was light applause.

Rafael finally came around. He stepped onto the stage and addressed the performers. 'You've driven our man wild.' He drew nervous laughter, as a spotlight fell on Tanner and Aya. With the spell of the show broken, the guests began leaving with hosts and with each other to private rooms. As an apprentice, Tanner was not allowed to serve a client privately. Soon he was the only person in the main room, save one.

'Not many things perplex me.' Mai spoke from her seat. 'This does. I would prefer not to have the club's ambience disturbed. However, Aya told me on her way out that one minute and thirty seconds with you was more intense than her hour on the stage with three other hosts, and by all reckoning, Mr Tanner, "intense" is a lame word to describe that three-on-one show. My inclination is to have you tossed out on your ear. If you had been the first to pull that scene, that's probably what I'd do, but it's happened once before.'

Tanner frowned.

'It was James. He explained it away later. "You have to shake people up every now and again," he said, "just to keep things really interesting." Maybe that's true.' Mai stood and walked to the door. She turned around. 'Maybe it's bollocks. Do you know what really saved both you and James?' She waited for a response that didn't come. 'I hope someday, someone will handle me like that. It hasn't happened yet. Good night, Mr Tanner.'

Nine

There are two ways to hide – deep in shadow or camouflaged in plain sight. The Scorpions had chosen a bit of both. Burke watched the entrance to the Devil's Island Café. It wasn't really a café, and it wasn't Devil's Island. It was simply a prison-themed restaurant at the border of low-rent Yurakucho and sky-high Ginza, Tokyo's traditional pleasure quarters. Mousavi had told Burke about the restaurant in his interrogation; and now the torturer was being led inside by the Japanese and Caucasian men Burke had seen at the Bound Maiden. He gave them 30 seconds then followed.

The entrance was up one floor, accessible by an elevator that opened onto a dimly lit square. In front of the elevator was a door covered by metal bars, while the walls on either side were black. While Burke was trying to figure out how to get in, a young couple exited the elevator. The man pressed a red button. An alarm sounded and a red light flashed, then the bars slid open. Burke followed them inside. The couple were greeted by a waitress dressed in striped pyjamas, cut short and tattered to reveal skin at her midriff, arse and the fringe of her breasts. Black grease paint was smeared on bared skin to complete the effect of dirt and hardship. She handcuffed them together and led them to a table.

The waitress who met Burke looked confused at the single diner. She paused, then handcuffed Burke to herself. When their skin touched, an unfamiliar but pleasant tingle ran through her arm. Her reaction was scarcely noticeable, but it was enough to let Burke know he'd made contact with her animal nature. She led him to a small, low table. Seating was on the floor, and each dining area was sectioned off by burlap drapery, which meant a diner could move along aisles without being noticed by other diners. At Burke's request, the waitress knelt beside him and helped him with the menu's Japanese script. Their skin touched again when she removed the handcuffs. The waitress intentionally made casual contact as they pointed to menu items. She let her knee touch Burke's thigh briefly and was rewarded with a stronger rush of *chi*. After Burke made his selections, she repeated the order twice before she left.

The aisles between the burlap curtains were narrow. Burke could see shapes pass along them, but it was not possible to identify faces. When the waitress returned, Burke asked her about emergency exits. A restaurant with a barred door didn't seem like a safe place to be in a fire or earthquake. There were two emergency exits marked in English and Japanese, she told him. To ease his concern, she led him to each door. Burke noted the size and layout of the restaurant and asked for the toilet. The waitress led him to it and opened the door for him. There was only one for both sexes, so be sure to lock the door, she advised.

Burke did, for reasons of his own. The irregular divisions of the restaurant's panels and the burlap curtains made it confusing, but the position of the toilet didn't seem right. The room was about two metres square. He struck the left and back walls with his fist just solidly enough to create a reverberation. From the feel and sound, they were part of the building's exterior face. He hit the right wall at the farthest point from the door, then continued striking it again at one-foot intervals. The reverberation was greatest for about the first metre, then there was a joist. The wall was more solid from the joist to the door. That wall fronted two different areas – the restaurant and empty space. Why would anyone waste space in a very expensive and crowded city?

At his table, Burke sketched out the layout. There was a metre-wide passage from the toilet to the front of the restaurant that was unaccounted for. On his way out, he checked the front entrance. To the right of the main door, the wall's surface was covered with black facing. He ran his hands along it and found hinges. Under a flap was a four-code lock that opened a concealed door.

Waiting for the Scorpions to act against him would be suicide. They knew about the Excalibur. If he ran, they would look for him, and even now anyone associated with the club was in danger. He had to take the fight to them. He needed a plan and an ally, someone with not much to lose and a drive to prove himself. It was time for a long chat with Dan Tanner.

Mousavi had not escaped from the forest. If he had, he would have run and rid himself of the Scorpion tattoo, even if it meant cutting off his own hand. Burke had not taken him far enough away. When they discovered that he was missing from the inn, they searched and found him, bound and helpless. They had brought him to the concrete Devil's Island, where truth is suspect and lies are expected. He had willingly told all truthfully, except for the one thing they wanted most to know – the identity of his attacker. If Go Ishido knew that, he would know that Mousavi had been broken.

The society of Scorpions had existed for centuries, unknown to outsiders and thus invisible, until now. Requests for their services were channelled through go-betweens who made the transactions with unseen men. In ancient times they had been made with a man whose face was masked and whose hands were gloved. No voice was ever heard. Messages were written in the air and memorised letter by letter. Today, electronics had made the process much more efficient and profitable.

The drug that had made Mousavi docile was wearing off. The torment that was about to begin would not last days or weeks. It would last years. They would keep him alive and in agony, immobilised, sleepless, assailed by sound and darkness and drugs that induced horrors in the mind. He was strapped to an iron cross. He had only moments before he lost his final weapon. Soon they would pull his teeth.

Mousavi gnashed through his tongue, threw his head back and commanded his larynx to open. He suffocated in his own gore.

'Make a circle with your thumb and forefinger,' Burke demonstrated. 'I'll try to pull them apart.'

'Doesn't sound like much of a trick to me.' Tanner imitated Burke's gesture. Muscle and veins stood out as he gripped. Burke put his index fingers through the ring and easily pulled it apart. 'Your back and arms are stronger than two of my fingers. Should I be impressed?' Tanner asked.

'You held your other fingers in a fist and concentrated on the muscles of your arm. You have to hold the ring closed with power beyond your body.'

Tanner looked at Burke as though he'd just described a sexual encounter with an alien.

'Close your eyes.' Burke knelt in front of Tanner in a *tatami*-floored room in the Excalibur. 'Clear your mind. Focus on a point five centimetres below your navel and inside your body. Do not think. Inhale as slowly as you can. Breathe as though you were pulling the air to the back of your head. You will feel the power of *chi* enter through your eyes. Relax and remain peaceful. Let it flow through you and out. You will feel a tingle that will begin in your shoulders and arms and travel down your torso to your hips. When you exhale the tingle will continue through your hips and legs.' He watched Tanner breathe. 'Slower.' After three breaths, Burke told Tanner to hold out his right arm and make the circle. 'Extend your other fingers. Keep the circle firm, but don't grip with your forearm. If your muscle is too tense, it will stop the flow. Close your eyes and inhale.' Burke again put his index fingers through the ring. He pulled it apart, but with much greater effort. 'Do you see?'

Tanner's disdain turned to doubt. 'You didn't pull as hard.'

'I pulled harder. You try. Pull smoothly, don't jerk.' Burke made the same circle.

Tanner pulled with all his strength, but his efforts were in vain until he realised the lesson applied both ways. He closed his eyes and inhaled as he willed Burke's fingers to part. The ring broke slightly and held. When it did, Tanner felt a surge of *chi* that seemed to weld his hands to Burke. He let go. Doubt had turned to confusion. 'I told you I wrestled in university, but did I tell you I won state championship in my weight division?' Tanner shrugged. 'This doesn't make sense. I can break a full nelson, but I couldn't get your fingers apart until I felt the *chi*. It was easier than I thought.'

'Think of it as the "physics" in "metaphysics",' Burke said. 'And it isn't as easy as it seems at first. That was a simple trick. Do you know the eighty–twenty rule?'

Tanner shook his head.

'Twenty per cent of effort gives you eighty per cent of results. To attain the last twenty per cent requires eighty per cent of effort. Businessmen like to use that phrase to avoid work in the name of efficiency. Learning *chi* is a bit different: one hundred per cent of effort in normal training only gives you ninety-nine per cent of result.

The last one per cent requires a paradigm shift, a very special technique for study that few people know. The nature of the last one per cent is also quite different. It opens the door to infinity.'

'I guess you're one of the few who know the last one per cent.'

Burke picked up a book. 'Right now, I would put you at zed-point-one per cent. Here's something to study.' He handed Tanner a collection of anatomical charts showing the body's 365 *tsubo* or pressure points, and the organs they affect. 'That was made for shiatsu, finger pressure. It's crude, but a good place to start. Are you sure you're ready for this, Dan?'

'What happened to "Mr Tanner"?'

'At the Excalibur, you'll be Mr Tanner until Mai, in her odd wisdom, knights you Sir Dan. The Excalibur is a world of games. This is not a game. It's a path that could come to a quick and literal dead-end. Are you still willing?'

Tanner nodded.

Burke had not told him everything he knew about the Scorpions. That would come later. He had said only enough for Tanner to know that the society wanted the ultimate power of *chi* and were likely to kill or torture to gain it. They were a threat not only to Burke himself, but also to anyone who knew him. If he ran, they could destroy the Excalibur and everyone associated with it. Besides, they were a scourge on humanity.

Tanner had remembered the chilling eyes of the Japanese man at the Bound Maiden as he had stared at Burke. He was willing to fight to defend his new life, Mai and her guests.

'It hasn't been long, Dan, but have you figured out the Excalibur yet?'

'The reed that bends . . .'

Burke laughed. '. . . "is stronger than the oak that resists". Lao-tsu, the master of my master, etcetera, etcetera. That's part of it; what does it mean?'

'The analogy describes a gale. It's OK to be an oak at times, but when the pressure is greatest, become the reed. It survives.'

'Yes,' said Burke. 'But for this?'

Tanner exhaled through pursed lips. 'We become the wind.'

Ten

In the cool mountain air, steam rose off the baths in languid swirls of mist, pirouetting whispers on a gentle breeze. The girl who called herself Ping dipped her toe into the hot spring. Her linen *yukata* was pale blue like the summer sky, and striped in yellow and white. It was long and revealed only the graceful contours of her ankle and foot swishing through the water. 'Sometimes monkeys come here to play and bathe in winter. In summer and autumn, they are too busy stealing fruit to have time for play.' A dimple at the corner of her lips accented her smile with an air of youthful innocence.

Burke, stretched out in the shallow water, made no attempt to hide himself from Ping's curious eyes. 'I'll have to come again when it's cold.'

She nodded and sat on a stone at the edge of the pool. Her *yukata* parted to her knees as she dangled her legs to mid-calf in the water. Burke's unabashed gaze warmed her as much as the heat of the volcanic spring. She held her legs straight and kicked them in a scissors motion that opened the robe higher on her thighs. At nineteen, she knew she was a woman, but she was a mountain girl and often felt childish, unsure of herself. It pleased her to have a worldly man watch her with hungry eyes. His desire made her feel strong. She leaned forwards, scooped water into her hands and splashed it on her face. As it ran down her neck, she loosened the *yukata* and rubbed water onto her upper chest. She kept her eyes on Burke and leaned forwards again. The robe draped open, exposing the faint beige of her breasts. They swayed in the rhythm of her arms, dipping into the pool and splashing water onto her calves, face and chest. She took a fistful of water and trickled it along her thigh. Her hair was damp around her face, the robe askew at her shoulders and open along her legs. 'I'm a mess. I must look like a monkey.'

Burke shook his head. 'Don't run away to steal fruit.'

Ping traced his body with her eyes and gazed openly at his groin. Earlier, his ample sex had drooped between his legs. Now it floated upwards towards his belly. She thought it looked larger and watched it as she spoke. 'What shall I do, then?'

'Stay and play.'

Dimples deepened at the corners of her smile. Her face flushed, and she looked away. As she kicked her legs in the water, the sole of her foot brushed across a large pebble. She pushed her leg towards it to pull it to her. As she did so, she reached too far and slid down her stone seat. Its rough surface caught the linen fabric of her *yukata* and held it as her body slipped, pulling it up to her waist. Her thighs, hips and pubis were on full view. 'Ah!' She clasped her hands in front of her mound and sank into the water. She dipped her chin and peered shyly at Burke. 'I'm really a monkey now, a wet one.'

Burke's voice was deep and husky. 'Monkeys don't wear robes.' He glided through the water towards her and untied the sash that held her *yukata*, then grasped her waist and pulled her against him as she slipped her arms free. His hand slid down her back, gripped her bottom and pulled her higher on his body. His lips met hers and opened, inviting her tongue to respond. Lust hardened his rod as she eagerly thrust into his mouth. His leg pushed between her thighs to the hot tissue of her sex.

The taut muscle of Burke's thigh between her legs ignited a fire of craving in the girl. Ping ground her nether lips and nub against his flesh in youthful abandon, then arched her back and reached for his phallus. Its feel in her hand thrilled her. She stroked its length, pushing down and kneading his balls. Her ravenous hands pressed into the hard muscles of his stomach, chest and back. She gripped his arse and straddled his staff, sliding her slippery lips along its sensitive underside.

Burke pressed back. He tried to slide low enough to enter her, but she moved with him, keeping him away from her gate. He pressed his face into her firm breasts. They were full and round, but their points were girlish pips on small circles of pink. He felt her hips quicken as his tongue teased her breasts' sensitivity, and the sensation of her grinding her clit along his staff made his balls tighten in anticipation of filling her. Her kittenish moans grew sharper and deeper in his ear, held in the vice of her teeth. Her pants became a quick steady rhythm as she brought herself near orgasm on the ridge of his prick. He ached to be inside her, but she deftly avoided his penetration, concentrating on reaching her own peak. He felt as though his ear would be severed by the pearl-white razors that held it as Ping's body trembled in the throes of orgasmic rapture.

He lifted his body out of the water as she slid quickly down to his hips and took the tip of his cock into her mouth. He felt he would be torn apart by the pull of her young passion. Her hand pumped the base of his staff at a savage pace, and almost immediately he erupted into her.

'James!' A powerful voice rolled through the hills.

'The master.' Burke's milk spilled from Ping's mouth as she spoke. She snatched her *yukata* and sash from the pool and scurried naked down a hill, out of sight.

A thin white stream ran through the water, as spasms in Burke's loins squeezed out the last of his ejaculation.

'There you are. I should have known you'd find the baths.' Koyanagi stripped off his robe and stepped in to join Burke. The old man was wrinkled, but his robust body was hard with muscle. 'Sorry about last night.' Koyanagi had insisted on food and sake before talking to Burke about the favour he sought. By the time they were done reminiscing, they'd gone through nearly two litres of rice wine and the old man had passed out. 'I can't drink like I used to.'

Burke shook his head. Koyanagi could still hold his drink better than most men.

'You know you shouldn't be out here alone; not safe. One of my maids might have found you. Hah!' Koyanagi slapped Burke on the shoulder. The old man had spent his formative years in China and lacked the reticence of most Japanese.

'I think one did.'

Koyanagi raised an eyebrow, but didn't pursue it. Instead, he got to the point of Burke's visit. 'So who is Natsuko, and what can I do for her?'

Koyanagi had been born in Taiwan when it was a Japanese colony before the war. He knew the island's local dialect as well as Mandarin, which he spoke with the soft 'R's of a Taiwanese accent. Burke had first met him at a temple in China where he was studying *qi gong* breathing exercises. It was Koyanagi who had told Burke about Wei Xian-xi, the greatest *qi gong* master in China.

Burke explained that Natsuko needed a safe house, but he did not name or describe the Scorpions to Koyanagi. He told the old man that there was danger, but instead of worrying him it made him even more willing to help.

'She can stay as long as she likes.' Koyanagi winked. 'She's a beauty.'

'For now, it would be better for her safety if she stayed whether she wants to or not.'

Koyanagi nodded solemnly and led Burke back to the house. Natsuko was waiting. She bowed deeply and thanked Koyanagi for his offer to let her stay. Burke told her that the old man had some skill in *chi* similar to his own. Natsuko's pupils widened. She smiled coyly and said she would strive to repay his kindness.

Burke said goodbye. As Koyanagi led him out, they met Ping. Burke grinned. 'Your maid?'

Ping stiffened and looked hard at Burke.

'Maid! You don't remember little Ping? My youngest daughter. Last time you saw her she didn't come up to here.' Koyanagi held his hand waist-high. 'I worry about this one, though. Nineteen years old and still a virgin.'

'Ah.' A flash of understanding crossed Burke's face as Ping blushed. He turned to leave. Technically, Koyanagi-san, only technically, he thought with a smile.

Eleven

'The "physics" in "metaphysics".' Tanner thought about what Burke had said as he practised breathing exercises in one of the Excalibur's private rooms. The tingles were there, but they could be caused by getting more oxygen into his system instead of magical mystery power. Becoming one with some kind of universal force was a bigger mental leap than Tanner was ready for. Still, there was no denying that he hadn't been able to pull Burke's fingers apart with muscular strength.

Physics of the mind. The tingles stopped. Don't think; just breathe. He focused on his navel – no, two inches *below* the navel. He tried again. No good. The physics puzzle was insidious. It worried his brain. He gave up trying not to think and went to the main room.

Sandra was there. She'd lost her sassy tease and was instead aloof, greeting Tanner with a cool, 'Good evening.' The Dan Tanner of a week ago would have apologised to her for spoiling her show and then would have fretted about whether or not he'd been sincere enough. Tonight, he let it go with a simple, 'Hi.'

Rafael was less casual than normal. He was friendly, but there was a wariness in his manner that hadn't been there before.

According to Excalibur etiquette, hosts stood until they were invited by a guest to sit. As he waited, Tanner practised *qi gong* breathing. He found it easier to void his mind among people than when he was alone. He closed his eyes and felt the tingle as soon as he began the slow inhalation.

'Look at this. The boy's asleep.' The lushly fleshed Kazuko poked her finger into Tanner's stomach. When he opened his eyes, she sneered. 'Did you miss your nap time, puppy?'

'Good evening, Kazuko.' Tanner kissed her hand.

'Bring me a teacup – no tea, just a cup.' When Tanner returned, she led him to the toilet. 'You first.' Kazuko followed Tanner inside. 'Strip.'

Tanner hesitated. 'I'm not yet allowed to serve guests in private rooms.'

'This is not a private room. It's a public toilet. Strip.'

Tanner stripped down to his briefs and waited for Kazuko to indicate whether or not she wanted him to continue. She did. When he was naked, she grasped his phallus and led him to the urinal.

Kazuko held the teacup under his flaccid cock. 'In there. I'll tell you when to stop.'

He bristled at her commands and the act she wanted him to perform.

'Shall I turn on the water tap for you? Sometimes that helps little puppies who are too shy to pee.' Despite her cold manner, her loins swelled with anticipation when Tanner closed his eyes and tried to relax his lower body. She touched herself as his liquid streamed into the cup. 'Stop!' It was half full. Kazuko swirled the cup under her nose and sniffed. 'Pungent with ammonia. You could clean linoleum with this, if it weren't piss. I'll pass it around for the ladies later.' She set the cup on the wash counter and turned her back to Tanner. 'Undo me.' Her spine shivered as Tanner pressed the zip down the back of her dress. She stepped out of it, turned to face him and held up her arms.

Tanner brushed his hands along her skin as he lifted her slip over her head. Her face was lovely. He sensed that her harsh demeanour was a cover for her insecurity. She felt her body too lavish, but she could not deny her sensuality. She came to the Excalibur so that she could command what she feared she could not receive freely. Her manner grated on Tanner, but still he pitied her for not being able to see her own pillowy beauty. What sort of woman would she be, if she could know her true self? Tanner knelt and slid off her knickers. Her loins smelled sweetly of talc and gardenia perfume. Their intoxicating aroma and sensuous lines sparked Tanner's passion, and with it his rod began to swell. When he stood, his burgeoning prick drew a longing glance from Kazuko. He reached around her to unfasten her bra. Even without their support, her breasts were firm and round.

The tender look in Kazuko's eyes was brief; their cold glint soon returned. 'Your paws are dirty, puppy. We have to wash them.' Tanner reached for the tap. 'Not there.' She took Tanner's rod and led him to the throne, where she sat and ordered him to kneel before her. She spread her legs. 'Here.' She pointed to her crotch.

Tanner put his hands under her and rubbed them together in the warm rush of her water. The command to do what he would never think of himself freed him to enjoy this vile pastime without self-recrimination. His cock grew harder, but he felt it was betraying him yet again. Anger at his own submissiveness welled within him even as he grew hot with lust.

'Lick your fingers dry, puppy.' Kazuko's face darkened when Tanner hesitated. 'Do it!'

Tanner touched the tips of his fingers to his lips and tongue. The twin energies of sexuality and rage wrestled within him as he broke the foul taboo. His scowl met Kazuko's hot gaze, and he yearned to ravage the passion that burned in her eyes, craved to break her hard spirit and free the womanly confidence she kept chained. In a flash, he forced open Kazuko's mouth and pushed his fingers inside, forcing her to taste her own brine. He wiped his hands across her lips.

Kazuko's wide eyes were red with rage. She slapped Tanner across the face, in a jolting blow with one hand and again with the other.

He took each blow and accepted the raining slaps that followed as he pushed his fingers between Kazuko's teeth and cheeks. He stood still, unmoved by her blows, his rock-hard rod challenging her. She turned her attention to his cock, flailing at it until Tanner grabbed her wrists and pulled her to her feet. He took her place on the throne and forced her across his knees, then smacked his palm into her rich round bottom. The feathery cushions of her buns grew quickly red in the siege of his blows. He held down her struggling body and ignored her demands, her requests, her pleas for him to stop. Finally she lay still, sobbing quietly as he continued to belabour her arse and thighs. When he had struck Mai, he had lost control; he had only reacted in embarrassment and anger at her taunts. Now he acted with purpose and pleasure in the feel of Kazuko's sumptuous skin growing hot under his hand. He struck the inside of her thigh, and found it liquid with her come. He stood and pushed her in front of the mirror at the washbasin. 'Look at yourself.'

Kazuko put her hands over her face.

He jerked them away. 'Look and see what I see.' He cupped a magnificent breast in his hand.

'Why?' She crossed her arms across her chest. 'Do you hate me so?'

Tanner pulled her arms back to expose her lush breasts to her own eyes, and put her hand on his stony phallus. 'Does that feel like hate, Kazuko-san?' He pushed her forwards to open her oily lips to his shaft, and pulled her head back so she would see her own face as he slid into her. When she twisted her head away, Tanner slapped the outside of her thigh again and again until she watched and could see the pleasure she brought to him. He reached for her chest and kneaded the wondrously soft globes, and was rewarded as he felt her breath catch in a spasm of passion and saw a glint of joy in her eyes. 'Do you understand, Kazuko?'

Her mouth twisted down in a smile. A tear clouded her vision as delight filled her spirit. She hadn't dared believe, but he was there inside her, having her because he wanted her. Even more, he demanded that she know he wanted her. She cried openly now, her smile wide and carefree. Her hand pressed against Tanner's, pushing it down over the luxurious belly that had caused her shame. The squeeze of his fingers thrilled her emotions, while his rhythmically pumping staff inflamed her lust.

Tanner smiled gently as their eyes met in the mirror.

A guest's complaint about the locked door to the loo had reached Mai. She hesitated to intrude on one of the club's best paying clients, but she was waiting outside when Tanner and Kazuko came out. Mai's stern countenance softened immediately when she saw Kazuko's face. She was as radiant as a virgin on her wedding night. 'Kazuko, dear, may I have the very briefest of moments with your escort?'

Kazuko stepped away from Tanner as though in a trance.

'Step closer, Mr Tanner.' Mai lowered her voice. 'Your breaches of conduct are exceeded only by your successes with my clients. There was Aya and now Kazuko. James saw something in you that I have to confess has eluded me, even though, as I said, "I've had you, and you've had me." If the equation of success ever shifts, and your breaches exceed your successes, I will have you again, Mr Tanner – but next time, I'll have you for lunch. Is that understood?'

Tanner nodded. The rebuke had little sting. Tanner believed he would soon become Mai's protector, whether she knew it or not.

'James is back in Tokyo after a short journey. He wants you to meet him tomorrow. Before you leave, stop in my office. I'll give you details. Now, if you please, see to our guests.'

Tanner turned towards the main room.

'Oh and Da– I mean Mr Tanner.' A hint of a smile softened Mai's face. 'I don't know what went on in the toilet, but I never dreamed I would see a look like that on Kazuko-san's face. If anyone asks you about it, don't say anything. A young buck like you could use a little mystique.'

Twelve

'Wrestling, was it?' Okabe-sensei held up a judo jacket to test its size on Tanner. 'Then I guess we won't be needing this.' She tossed it aside. 'Mr Burke, are you sure he's old enough for this training?'

'He shaves.'

Okabe nodded. 'In the age of samurai, a duel in Japan meant someone died. They were true warriors then. Today it is only play. What does it take to win a judo match? One good throw. Karate? Two clean hits. I teach women to be warriors. How can I create Amazons in today's society, if there is no true risk in a fight? I agree that death is too severe, but there must be an incentive beyond a trophy for victory and a risk beyond the disappointment of defeat. Sit.' Okabe called in two of her students from another room.

Burke and Tanner knelt on the floor as the women faced off.

'*Kamaete*!' Okabe ordered the women to fight. One leapt back quick as a spider as the other lunged low like a black panther. The spider jumped high, tucking her knees against her chest as the panther aimed a leg sweep at her feet. But the panther came around too far and exposed her back. While she was still in the air, the spider flicked a kick into the panther's side. The panther made her sweep into a full circle and threw a back-fist at the spider's head, only for the spider to catch it on her forearm. The spider snapped a side-kick into the panther's ribs, sending the woman staggering back, then moved in with a front kick to the midsection, but the panther caught her foot and twisted. The spider fell face down. The panther sprang, but the spider rolled away and grazed the back of the panther's head with a kick, forcing her face into the mat.

The spider leapt for the panther's back. She pushed her knee into the panther's crotch to restrain her lower body and wrenched one arm behind her opponent's back. With her free hand, she twisted the panther's belt around and untied it, then looped it around the panther's arm, pulled the other arm behind her and tied them together. The panther wore nothing under her jacket, and her bare breasts pressed into the rough canvas of the mats as the spider pulled the panther's jacket off her shoulders, bunching it up behind her. The spider reached under the panther's belly and untied the string that held her trousers, then pushed them down to her thighs, exposing the panther's taut round cheeks. The woman squirmed as the spider retied the string tightly around her legs. With the panther's arms bound, and her legs constrained by her own trousers, the spider rolled her onto her back. Her breasts rose high above the ridges of muscle in her torso, her cleft exposed below the black wavy V that covered her mound.

The spider removed her own belt and used it to bind the panther's legs more securely, then stood over her victim and took off her trousers, showing the hard-wired muscle of her legs. She opened her jacket and let it fall from her shoulders, a living statue of chiselled marble. There was no softness to her; even her breasts were small caps on her tautly defined pectorals.

She straddled the panther's hips and pressed her quim against her defeated opponent, leaning forwards to push the panther's shoulders into the mat as she worked her nub into the furred pad of the panther's mound.

The panther pushed her hips up, trying in vain to stimulate her own tightly bound sensitivity against the spider's body. She struggled to scissor her legs so she could enjoy the friction of her own thighs, but the bindings prevented even that minor pleasure.

The spider left a glistening trail of oil on the panther's skin as she ground her clit against the hard ridges of the panther's hip-bone then moved up her body to her breasts. She reached between her legs and parted her lips so they enfolded one breast's brown tip.

The panther's eyes closed as her nipple entered the spider's warm softness. She tensed her back to push herself against the spider's rocking hips, teasing the maximum pleasure from her globe's sensuous crown.

A tremor of delight rushed through the spider as the panther's breast spread against her quim, bottom cheeks and upper thighs, its hard brown tip pushing inside her. She would have lingered there if it had not been for the panther's quiet mewing. She was the victor; the pleasure belonged to her, not to the defeated woman beneath her. She moved up and straddled the panther's face, pushing her swollen nub into her opponent's chin and lips. When the panther's mouth opened to taste the ooze of her passion, the spider moved higher still, raking her nub at a furious pace along the bony ridge of the panther's nose. Her thick nether lips covered the panther's nostrils and mouth, and the sensation of the panther's head thrashing, gasping for air, thrilled the spider as her hips drove against the woman's face. She reached back and clawed at the panther's pubic thatch, gripping and in a shout of rapture ripping away hair then thrusting up her arm as though brandishing a vanquished warrior's severed head.

The room was quiet save for the panther's ravenous gulps of air. Her face was liquid with the spider's come, her breasts and belly red from friction on the mat, her mound stinging in denuded spots. Still her hips twitched, and her thighs worked against one another, her face contorted in frustrated desire.

Burke looked at Okabe. When she nodded, he walked to the panther.

Her eyes widened in expectation. When he knelt beside her, she quickly pulled her knees to her chest, exposing her quim and button to him. She drew a sharp breath and tensed her back as Burke pressed the tip of his thumb into the pucker between her cheeks and slid two fingers into her wet channel. Her soft wail ebbed and flowed like a siren as waves of *chi* undulated through her sex. Her cry became a high-pitched keening as Burke strengthened the power flowing from his hands. At her moment of ecstasy, the cords and veins in her neck rose thick under her skin. The back of her head pressed into the mat and a scream exploded silently in her mind.

Burke started to untie her restraints but Okabe stopped him. The panther was still at the mercy of the victor. The spider had stood by, watching, wondering at what she saw and deciding that if she met this man again, she might choose to lose. Still naked, she untied the panther's bonds and left the room.

'Are you shocked?' Okabe asked Tanner.

'I would have been before I met James, not now.'

'In that case, are you prepared for a challenge?'

Tanner looked confused.

'A fight,' said Burke. 'You've seen the stakes. Are you ready?'

Tanner snapped his head from left to right to look around the room. 'Not you!'

Burke shook his head.

'Who with?' Tanner asked the *sensei*.

Okabe clapped her hands. 'Kei.'

Her assistant walked into the training room and bowed to Okabe then to Burke and Tanner.

'A woman.' Tanner's voice lost its nervous edge. He was eager for the contest.

‘That’s woman with a capital “W”. I’ve faced her a few times, and more than once I was afraid she’d break my elbow. Those two you just saw, she could take them both at the same time.’

Tanner leered. ‘If what I just saw is the punishment, I don’t think I’d mind losing.’

Burke’s face was grim. ‘If she wins, that might not be what she has in mind for you.’

Okabe motioned for Tanner to stand and face Kei. ‘You’re a wrestler, freestyle amateur?’ Tanner nodded. ‘We don’t have any of those cute little suits that you wear. Take off your shirt.’ When he had tossed his shirt into a corner, she ordered him to remove his socks and trousers. He was left only with his briefs. ‘Now you.’ She nodded towards her disciple.

Kei untied her belt, folded it carefully and laid it on the floor. She did the same with her jacket and trousers. She wore nothing at all underneath.

Okabe glanced at Kei’s naked bush and then at Tanner’s briefs.

As he stepped out of them, he was already growing hard with anticipation of touching Kei’s body. For a woman, especially, it takes great sacrifice to develop the thin skin and muscle definition of the spider. There was nothing like that about Kei. She had a solid build that exuded strength, but apart from a somewhat thick neck and a notable width to her shoulders, her proportions were classically feminine. Her breasts were full and bounced when she moved. The muscles of her back tapered to a narrow waist and flared to smoothly rounded hips. As she stood, ankles together, her thighs just touched below her sparsely furred cleft, as did her knees and calves.

‘*Hajime*!’ Okabe shouted for them to begin.

Tanner was unsure how much power to exert against his delicious opponent. He didn’t want to lose, but he didn’t want to look like a bully either. He circled Kei with his knees and hips bent and his arms held out at shoulder width. It would be best to take her down at the knees. She would end up on her back with him lying between her legs. He started to drop, but Kei had already closed the distance to less than an arm's length.

She slammed the heel of her left hand into Tanner's nose. When his head snapped back, she twisted her hips and flashed the ball of her foot into his naked groin.

The breath went out of Tanner, his hands dropping to his crotch. He felt he would suffocate from the pain, until Kei's roundhouse kick struck the side of his head. He dropped unconscious.

The fight had lasted thirteen seconds.

Kei reached between Tanner's legs, gripped his cock and balls in one hand and waited for him to come to. When he stirred, she pressed her hand into the back of his neck. 'Stay down.'

When he regained full consciousness, Tanner tried to push himself up, but Kei's hand on his neck and her tight grip on his sex stopped him.

'I said stay down. Now, bark.'

Tanner tried to twist his head to look at Kei.

She squeezed his balls in a steel grip and twisted. 'Bark! Like a dog.'

The pain paralysed Tanner. He felt the crush of her hand through his lungs. The strength rushed out of his body with a gush of air that he could not call back. He struggled to inhale. Kei's grip loosened, and he sucked in a breath.

'Bark!'

The insulting command was a blow to Tanner's pride. He gritted his teeth and tried to push up with his arms, but Kei's grip only tightened again, even stronger now. He collapsed back onto the mat. 'Rowlf.' He managed the closest sound to a dog he could make.

'What?'

'Rowlf, rowlf.' His voice was louder now.

'You sound like a big dog, but you don't fight like a big dog. Bark like a chihuahua.' Kei squeezed and twisted as she spoke.

Tanner felt like he would pass out from the pain. 'Yip, yip, yip.' His voice was thin and high-pitched.

'Better.' Kei leaned forwards so Tanner could see her face. 'One more thing.' Kei pressed her thumb between his bottom cheeks and rammed it into his hole. She shouted a *kiai* and pushed hard against his prostate as she shoved him forwards on the mat. The rough canvas scraped away skin from his chest and face. She jerked out her thumb and stood, legs spread wide. A trickle of come ran along the inside of her thigh. She dipped a finger in her cleft and touched it to her lips, wet from the thrill of victory.

Tanner brought his knees to his chest and cupped his groin.

'Breathe, Dan.' Burke rolled Tanner onto his back. 'Breathe deep and straighten your legs.' He put his hands under Tanner's waist, lifted his hips in the air and bounced him slightly. 'Are you all right?'

Tanner shook his head.

'I guess this wasn't a good idea.'

'No. Five minutes.'

Burke pressed the heel of his hand down Tanner's lower abdomen.

'Five minutes for what?'

'Again.'

'Fight? I don't think . . .'

Tanner, realising that he wasn't going to escape so easily, sat up and tucked his legs under himself, Zen fashion. He closed his eyes and took slow breaths. He did not yet have the skill to draw power, but he did absorb a healing calm, and with it resolve. Okabe had said she created warriors. He now understood what that meant. With all his wrestling skill, he had been a sportsman, not a fighter. The difference was a mental threshold he would have to cross. With his eyes still closed, he spread his hand to indicate the number five.

Burke spoke to Okabe. She checked the clock and went to fetch Kei, who returned and knelt with her back to Tanner. When five minutes had elapsed, Okabe called them to their feet.

Tanner shifted his stance so his left side faced Kei. He kept his legs close together to protect his groin, but it made his stance less stable. His forwards leg was an easy target for a sweep. Kei kicked the inside of his shin. He staggered but stayed on his feet. A roundhouse kick flew to his groin. He twisted his hips, and the kick slammed into his arse cheek. His right hand had dropped to block, and his head was open. Kei punched a left hook at it. He ducked, but caught a grazing blow. She followed with a straight right, square on his nose. Tears welled up, beyond his control, blurring his vision. Kei swung the ridge of her left hand at his temple. Tanner blocked it with his forearm. She followed with a swarm of attacks, a front kick to the stomach, palm strike to the chin, punches, ridge hands, knife hands. She worked in close, an elbow to the head, knee to the ribs. She reached for Tanner's groin.

Her fingers had just touched his rod when he grabbed her wrist and forced her arm down, pushing her off balance. She tried to duck and roll free, but Tanner's grip held. She wrapped her free hand over Tanner's and pushed forwards with all her weight against his wrist. The move broke Tanner's hold, but before Kei could lock his elbow, he twisted down and wrapped his arm around her thigh. She struck the crown of his head once, twice, then aimed a third blow, but Tanner had worked his way behind her. He grabbed her around the hips with both arms and tried to lift her. She anticipated the move and lunged forwards on one leg, nearly breaking his hold. He followed her in a low stance and moved his arms higher around her waist. She shifted her hips, swung her leg out and hooked it back into the muscle of Tanner's side. The kick was a gamble – an inch higher would have brought victory, with a hard strike into his floating ribs and liver – but this time it wouldn't pay off. Before she could recover her stance, Tanner twisted her off her feet and onto the mat. She bicycled her legs to keep Tanner away from them, but he held onto her torso and worked his arms higher across her breasts. She grabbed for his little finger. Tanner jerked his hand away and forced it into her crotch to control her lower body. He worked his other arm up the inside of her shoulder and pressed his hand into the back of her neck in a half nelson. As he brought his leg over her, Kei reached back with her free hand in a desperate grab for his groin. Tanner guarded himself by pressing his cock and balls hard against Kei's buttocks. He forced his other leg between Kei's and, centimetre by centimetre, edged them farther apart.

Tanner's cock, wet from the sweat of Kei's body, grew hard as it pressed into her cheeks. Her shoulder lifted slightly off the mat as she reached back again. Tanner slipped his free hand under her breast and leaned the weight of his upper body into her back. He lifted his hips and probed the point of his prick into Kei's nether lips, drenched with her oil. He found her gate and pushed inside. As he did so, Kei gasped in anticipation, spread her legs wider and raised her hips to receive him. Despite his earlier abasement, he had no desire to humiliate this Amazon warrior. Still, where was the victory, if the vanquished relished her fate? He withdrew from her eager channel and guided his pole to the button above it. Kei grunted in protest. Tanner whispered, 'If I'm a doggie, I'll do you doggie-style. Yip, yip.' He punched through the outer sphincter of her anus. Kei scowled and tried to squirm forwards, but Tanner's half nelson held her firm. He slid the full length of his rod into her rectum. 'Rowlf!' He withdrew slowly and rammed his phallus home, slow–ram, slow–ram in a syncopated rhythm of lust.

Kei's protesting grunts turned to pants of pleasure. She reached between her legs and stroked her nub, bringing herself to the verge of release, then slid her fingers inside her sex. Waves of ecstasy shook her body as her fingers felt through her own tissue a man's piston thrusting inside her. She would not be denied. Her passions welled as she massaged her G-zone, her panting a long throaty growl, signalling orgasmic release.

Tanner sensed defeat in victory. Emptying himself in Kei's sated body would make him look like a fool, but he could not end this without achieving his own satisfaction. He released the half nelson and ran his fingers lightly along her spine as he withdrew his staff. 'Turn over.'

Kei was free to fight again or walk away or do as she was told. She rolled onto her back and lay there with her legs touching either side of Tanner's hips.

Their eyes met. In both shone the glint of a smile. They were free warriors, who knew defeat at the other's hand and victory at their own. Tanner stroked Kei's thighs and pressed his thumbs into her cleft and clit, then moved over her belly and kneaded her perfect breasts. As he leaned his body onto Kei, her arms welcomed him, her legs wrapping round his hips. Her face rose to meet his kiss as he entered her, sliding into her channel at an idle pace as though beginning an eternity of ravishment. It was not until Tanner came inside her that he noticed that Burke and Okabe had left.

He lay exhausted in Kei's embrace and slept. When he awoke, he was alone.

Thirteen

'The package has arrived.' Ishido clicked off his phone and checked the surveillance cameras before climbing the stairway and opening the door for two Scorpions and their unconscious captive. The Russian Potanin lifted Kharrazi, an Iranian diplomat, onto his shoulders and followed Ishido down two flights of stairs to his workroom. The underground chamber was expansive and soundproofed.

Potanin laid Kharrazi down in a tight plastic case and sealed the cover.

'What does he fear most?' Ishido addressed Bitaraf, who had replaced Mousavi as translator and interrogator.

'I don't know, not yet.'

'Potanin and I will work on him. When I think he's ready, I'll signal you.'

Through the ages, the Scorpions had developed the sophistication of their interrogation methods. Bitaraf would not ask the question directly. He had psychological quizzes that would tell him what he needed to know from answers to apparently innocuous questions. Often it wasn't necessary to find the greatest fear, but he knew Ishido by reputation. The Japanese was a methodical perfectionist. He would not feel he had done his job if he exacted anything less then a subject's ultimate terror.

Ishido stared into the face of the awakening Kharrazi, his new challenge. You could never tell what would break a man, he mused. He had once had a subject who endured days of pain and was apparently prepared for his death until Ishido discovered that he had an intense fear of a particular spectrum of light. His eyelids were braced open, and he was put into a cubicle painted the dark red of dried blood. In less than a minute he was ready to tell all, as soon as he'd finished screaming.

The first step was naturally the easiest. Still, Ishido took great care in its execution. He checked his stores for something to put into the plastic case with Kharrazi: rats, roaches, snakes, spiders, acids, vapours, even plain tap water.

What would make the Iranian most grateful to be rescued by his countryman? That was an important issue. A grateful subject would more readily, though unknowingly, reveal his ultimate fear.

Ishido preferred to concentrate on one matter at a time. Unfortunately, because of Mousavi's incompetence and Natsuko's disappearance, he had multiple issues to deal with. Natsuko must be found. He would send one more emissary, Risa, to the Excalibur to learn what she could of the building's interior and the routines of its people. Initially, he had wanted only to learn from Burke, but he was sure it was Burke who had bested Mousavi, and, if so, the Englishman had found out about the Scorpions. Ishido had to destroy Burke and everyone he had told. His own life might depend on it.

Risa appeared jovial as she sipped tea in Mai's office. She said she'd heard of the club from Yuri, who was on a long tour abroad. Ordinarily, Mai would not let a new guest past the front door unless she was accompanied by a current member. However it was Yuri who had asked Burke to train her acquaintance from the Bound Maiden. Mai wanted to know more about her. Either Risa was simply the sexually avant-garde woman she said she was, or she was a spy. Mai could not detect any mannerisms that indicated the woman was lying. If she was a spy, she was very good.

She was also an exotic beauty, with sharp angular features that Mai found bewitching in their contrasts. She was at once aloof, cool as carved ivory and approachable, with the promise of smouldering lust. Her hair was pulled back from her high forehead, accentuating unusually deep-set eyes. A graceful arc to her thin nose gave her a haughty air, offset by the earthy sensuousness of her pouting lower lip.

Mai was rarely drawn sexually to a woman, and she especially needed to keep her head clear with this one. She told herself that Risa must somehow be tested, but it was the twitch in her loins, rather than calculations of her mind, that caused her to leave her chair and sit next to Risa on a sofa. She traced her fingertips along Risa's thigh and kindled a fire in the woman's eyes that could not be faked. The look of passion thrilled Mai, but it also confused her. She had been ready to assume that Risa was a spy, but now she could not be so sure. She brushed the back of her hand across Risa's breast, finding the tip hard under the thin fabric of her silk blouse and bra.

At the touch, Risa pressed Mai's hand against her breast, leaned towards her and nuzzled her cheek in Mai's hair. Risa's hand caressed the inside of Mai's thighs. As they opened to her gentle touch, she reached for the moist lips of Mai's sex.

Mai's nostrils flared. She gripped Risa's hair, pulled her head back and kissed her mouth. As Mai straddled Risa's hips, she felt the woman's fingers fondle her sex, skilfully squeezing and stroking her throbbing nub. Her mind warned her to back away, but her body was too eager, pulling apart the buttons on Risa's blouse and forcing their way inside the flimsy fabric of her bra. The soft mounds yielded to her touch. Whatever else she needed to know about Risa in the future, right now she just needed to know her body. She stood and took Risa's hand, then pulled her to her feet. In seconds, she had stripped the woman nude.

Like her face, Risa's body was a mosaic of graceful curves and sharp lines. Her wide shoulders sloped gently above jutting collar-bones. The enticing mounds of her breasts stood soft but exquisitely formed, capped with pale-beige crowns. Below them, her ribs made hard lines against the rolling planes of her belly and the prominent mound that lay between the ridges of her hips. The light-brown hue of her pubic fleece indicated mixed ancestry.

Mai removed her own clothes. The women were about the same height, and their nipples met first as they embraced. Mai guided Risa to the sofa, but it was Risa who then took control. Her lips slid down Mai's body, teasing the pale-pink pips of her firm cones.

A tremor of delight ran through Mai's body as Risa's fingers entered her sex again, rhythmically stroking its liquid walls. Her mouth skimmed Mai's belly to her musky loins, wet with their own dew, then her tongue bore between the folds of Mai's sex and found her tiny nub. She pushed hard against it then relaxed and brushed it softly, then pushed hard again, building up a slow rhythm.

Mai grasped Risa's hair and pressed the woman's face to her sex as her hips bucked in short spasms, her quick peak taking her by surprise. Orgasmic tremors rolled through her loins and belly as the door to her office opened. Through the narrow slits of her eyelids, still contorted in ecstasy, she looked directly at Burke. His broad shoulders and wide stance filled the doorway; his presence filled the room. Mai's arousal quickly died down; Burke looked upset.

Risa lifted her head and looked back at him, then tensed in fear. It was only a prelude of what was to come. As he strode towards her, she stood, ineptly covering her breasts and mound with her arm and hand.

'Who is this?' he roared.

Burke's glowering countenance chilled Mai to her core, but she managed a façade of indignation.

'What is that to you? This is my club, my home!'

Risa reached for her clothes, but before she could touch them, Burke's hand lashed out and gripped her throat. With one arm, he marched her against a wall. 'Who are you?' He took a deep breath, drawing in the power of *chi*. It flowed from him into Risa's body and mind, making her mouth gape open in pain.

'You will tell no one of your encounter here with Mai. You will tell anyone who asks that the only person you met was me.'

'What are you doing?' Mai shoved Burke with all her strength. She had skill and power, and her assault would have felled most men. But with Burke, it was as though she had attacked a stone mountain.

He ignored her. 'Do you understand?' he asked Risa.

Her eyes were red with fear, but she couldn't speak. She sucked in air in short, shallow gasps and nodded her head.

'Tell whoever sent you not to touch you because of your failure. If you are harmed I will know, and I will find them. The truth is, I intend to find them anyway, but you don't have to say that, do you?' Burke released his grip.

Risa groped for her clothes. She pulled on her skirt and blouse, stuffed her underwear into her handbag and fled.

'You bastard!' Mai clawed at Burke's face.

He batted away her slashing hands, gripped her wrists and pinned her arms behind her. 'Why?' he asked.

Mai bared her teeth and aimed a bite at Burke's face.

He pulled away. 'You know the danger, yet you invite it into your home, the Excalibur.'

In the glare of her rage, Mai was silent.

'She could have harmed you. You can command anything you want. Why that woman? If you chose, you could command me.' In the time he had known her, Burke had never seen anything but cool composure in Mai's face; now there was mist in her eyes. 'If you were hurt, I have no idea what I would unleash. There are powers I've never tested, demons I'm not even sure I could control.' Burke crushed her naked body to him. 'Why?'

The fight flowed out of Mai, and along with it the toughness that had enabled her to use men in a man's world to achieve success. Her mouth was close to Burke's, her breath hot on his face. 'I never wanted to command you.'

'I know, Mai.' Burke tightened his hand in her hair and kissed her hard on the mouth. His tongue met hers, pushing, entwining. He held her face to his as he stripped off his clothes then impaled her, thrusting inside her, stabbing his cock into her sex.

Her arms tightened around his neck, both her legs wrapped around his waist. Her hips pounded against each plunge of his prick, ecstatic at being taken by a man strong enough to use her, a man who wanted her above anyone or anything else, a man who would risk all to protect her. 'James!' Her shout exploded with the cosmic violence of her orgasm. 'James.' She repeated his name, moaning her tribute as her body trembled in the aftermath of her peak. 'James.' She whispered the sound as she lay her face on his shoulder.

Burke gripped Mai's arse cheeks in his hands as his liquid fire rushed into her. It had been far more intense than he'd anticipated. They might each have known others physically – that was the way of their lives – but neither had given themselves as they had now to each other.

'Well, finally.' Mai pulled her head back and smiled. 'I've been waiting for that, James. Now, about those nasty Scorpions: you'll need my help. I can also train Tanner in *ninjutsu* weapons, as I trained you, but there isn't enough time. You know that.'

'I need an army, Mai. You won't make the difference.'

'Do you want to win or just die trying? I might be all the difference you need; besides, you can't stop me. I have as much at stake as you do. I can't afford for you to lose.'

'You, me and Tanner.' Burke laughed. 'If you can find a bookie who'll take the odds, I want to put a few quid on the villains.'

Mai nibbled Burke's ear. 'I'll take that bet personally.' She reached for his phallus. 'I'll even give you odds.' Burke began to stiffen in her hand. 'Let's say – two to one?'

Ishido watched Kharrazi's eyes as the diplomat listened to the sound of skittering legs from a hidden box. The sounds alone heightened the diplomat's imagination and fear in ways that the reality of sight could not. Ishido was pleased at the reaction. It was slight, but telling. Perhaps the man sensed what was in the box. Ishido showed him the tattoo on his hand and saw the pupils of the diplomat's eyes constrict. He smiled, with a sense of accomplishment.

He slid back a panel and dropped a few sandy-red scorpions onto Kharrazi's face. A few were enough. Ishido glanced at Bitaraf, who rushed forwards for the 'rescue'.

After a short time, Bitaraf found that Kharrazi had an even greater fear. With that information, Ishido led his team through the night and into the next day to learn the details of state secrets that Kharrazi had sold to Western intelligence agencies. When they were finished, they returned Kharrazi to his own people.

Ishido could now focus on the Scorpions' problems with Burke. Risa had returned. She had not learned much, but he believed that the simple fact that she had not run away proved that she had not told anyone who sent her. He could not imagine that she feared Burke more than she feared him. However, there was still the matter of Natsuko. Ishido encoded a message into a computer and sent it over a highly secret network. He would need reinforcements.

Fourteen

Tanner had found his own way home from Okabe's dojo. The next morning his body ached in unfamiliar places – deep in his shoulders, the muscles between his ribs, his lower abdomen, the backs of his thighs, even his feet. It had been a long time since he'd wrestled, and he'd never fought anyone like Kei. The side of his head was sore to the touch, but the soreness and aches were rejuvenating. He felt intensely alive, exhilarated by his rite of passage. Never again would he underestimate an opponent or take any threat lightly. Even though he had not fought a hundred per cent against Kei in their first match, he was still in awe that a woman he outweighed by at least fifteen to twenty kilograms could defeat him so easily. In the second match, he had scarcely avoided defeat.

His mental focus was sharper, warier. He easily cleared his mind as he practised *qi gong* breathing exercises. The flow of *chi* came readily now. He went to the Excalibur early, eager to meet Burke for more training. The first person he saw, however, was Sandra.

She flashed a coquettish smile. Her seductive charm was back, but she was less sassy. There was a new softness in her manner.

Tanner kissed her hand as though she were an Excalibur customer. 'Good afternoon.' He held her head, wrapped her silken hair through his fingers and kissed her forehead. 'My lovely.'

Sandra lowered her head. 'Save it for the paying clientele.' Her face touched Tanner's chest, her fingers digging into the sides of his waist. 'You're a pro now, aren't you? You won't get a quid from me.'

Tanner touched his finger to her chin and lifted her face. 'It's not your quid I'm after, Miss Callie.'

She pushed back. 'Work to do, Mr Tanner.' She looked back over her shoulder as she walked away, a slight blush brushing her cheeks.

Burke was practising t'ai chi in one of the private rooms when Tanner found him. His movements were deceptively slow and fluid, giving no hint of the power they carried. Burke finished the exercise before he spoke. 'You don't look badly damaged. I wasn't even sure you'd show up today.'

'How much can you teach me and how fast?'

'I could get you to an advanced level in, say, six or seven years. We're lucky to have that many days, so for the most part I won't be the one teaching you. That will be Mai's job.'

'Mai?'

'Have you heard of *ninjutsu*?'

'You mean like ninjas? Disappearing, levitating, magic powders?'

'No, I mean how to use a short sword; throwing knives; throwing stars; garrotte; sickle and chain; *sai*, a short trident with a long centre tine; and other *buki* – that means weapons.'

'Mai's a ninja?'

'Her ancestors were. Today there are no ninja, but there are still people skilled in the crafts. She is a master. I will continue to teach you the way of *chi*. That is integral to all the martial arts, but you had better learn weapons before empty-hand techniques. They will make you deadlier, faster.' Burke was a few paces away from

Tanner. He closed the gap and pushed his palm into Tanner's chest.

The movement was so subtle and smooth that Tanner hadn't even realised he was being attacked until he was on his back. 'How did you do that? You said Kei more than once nearly broke your elbow. Were you joking?'

'No. When I meet Kei, we practise aikido only. She is a powerful woman, and in that discipline she has much more experience than I do. If I didn't limit myself to aikido techniques, I don't think she would get close to my elbow. You did well against her. Now sit and breathe with me, about thirty seconds to inhale and the same to exhale. Clear your mind and focus here.' Burke touched a point below his navel.

As Tanner breathed, Burke instructed him to direct the flow of *chi* to specific parts of his body as a way to restore energy and to heal himself. 'Within an hour, your aches will be gone. In two or three days you will be able to use the energy to increase the power of your movements.'

There was a rap on the door before it opened. 'James.' Mai spoke softly and motioned for Burke to come to her. 'Have you invited a peasant girl to come here?'

'What?'

'There's one at the door now. She's wearing a T-shirt and jeans and is carrying a rucksack. She says she knows you.'

'I haven't invited anyone. Does she have a name?'

'Not one that I've heard before. She calls herself "Ping".'

Burke shook his head. 'Her father is Natsuko's caretaker. Let's see what this is about.'

'You go ahead.' Mai glanced towards Tanner. 'I think I'll get started with our young friend's training.'

Burke met Ping at the door. She grinned like a schoolgirl on a class picnic. 'The master sent me.'

'You mean your father; why do you call him "master"?'

'He is my master, my *sensei*. He's been teaching me the way of Tao since I was old enough to walk. Besides, if I call him "master", it makes him feel like he's too stern, so he dotes on me.'

Burke smiled. 'I expect he would dote no matter what you called him. Why did he send you? Is there trouble?'

'It's a long story. I'm also a bit thirsty, in case you forgot to ask.'

Burke apologised and led her to a private room. He asked one of the hosts to bring an array of drinks and delicacies that he expected would appear exotic to a country girl. When it arrived, the look in Ping's eyes told him he was correct.

'How is Koyanagi-san?' he asked as he watched Ping decide what to sample first.

'He's having a time of it with Natsuko. She's quite passionate, as you might know. She also talks when she's under the influence of the master's skill. He says that he does not have your ability to touch the mind, but he's quite adept at stimulating the body, or so I've been told.'

'He could have had my skill, if he had wanted it. I believe he called it a "damn nuisance". I expect he's right. If you've much of a conscience, there's the burden of deciding when and whether or not to use it.'

'And you . . .'

'Don't have much of a conscience, I'm afraid.'

'I'm glad to know that.' Ping held her head high and stared proudly into Burke's eyes. 'Neither do I.'

'Really? What about the bath? You were careful . . .'

'To lay the groundwork for what's coming.' She took Burke's hand, dipped his finger into a pâté of foie gras and licked the rich paste off slowly, taking his finger into her mouth. 'I had no intention of being only partially pleasured my first time, James. I haven't told you why father sent me.'

Burke cocked his head, but remained silent.

'Did you know that in China he was a leader of the resistance against the Imperial Army during the Great War, even though he is Japanese? My name is Chinese. He would have stayed there, but China betrayed its own destiny and allowed the communists to claim victory after the war, so he returned to Japan. He is a man of great character, and he knows what you are up against. You used him, James, without telling him everything, but he understands why. Natsuko doesn't know very much, but she told him enough for him to fill in the missing information. He knows about the Scorpions; so does Wei Xian-xi. Do you know why they know?'

'No.'

'In antiquity, it was a Scorpion of China who discovered the ultimate power of *chi*. With that discovery, the man also achieved *satori*, enlightenment. He held in his mind a double-edged sword of unthinkable pain or unimaginable pleasure – a "damn nuisance" for a man with a newly developed conscience. He fled China, and the Scorpions, into what is now Bhutan. Eventually, he made his way back to China and became the teacher of Lao Tsu himself.'

Burke scowled.

'The knowledge was lost for hundreds of years, until Wei rediscovered it. After what I've just told you about the Scorpions, do you still doubt me? The society of Scorpions has remained cloaked for millennia. The link to the masters of *chi* is a deep secret that father told me only before he sent me to help you. He agreed that I should tell you, so you would understand his decision to send me.'

'You won't be helping me, Ping. Go home and give my sincerest apologies to your father. Send Natsuko away. She can look after herself.'

Ping's hand gripped in a fist and shot to Burke's nose. In a blur of speed, she punched at his face three times as she rose to her feet. When Burke brought his forearms in front of his head, she hooked her knuckles into his left temple and threw a roundhouse kick to the right side of his head.

Burke blocked most of the attacks, but their force still jolted him.

Ping stepped back. 'The master sent me to fight. If he hadn't, I would have come on my own. I'll fight you, or I'll fight our mutual enemies at your side. If you try to send me away, you disrespect my father. In that case, by the time you get past me, you'll be in no condition to face the Scorpions.'

Burke held his hands up in supplication and laughed aloud. 'Whoa, princess. I need to talk to Koyanagi-san.'

'You can't. He's taken Natsuko into hiding. There's a trail that can be found, but not easily.'

'What do you mean?'

'A diversion. He sent me to you because he thought I'd be safer here. You cannot hide from them, but neither can he. The Scorpions will track down everyone who's seen their faces and knows who they are. As soon as you brought Natsuko, the master was implicated.' She touched Burke's face where she had hit him. 'I just wanted you to know that I'll be an asset when we fight. The only way we'll be safe is to defeat them.'

'I'm sorry about bringing Natsuko to him.' Burke's face was solemn. 'I didn't understand. Even so, are you certain you want to go through with it?'

'I have two conditions. First, you will show me the ultimate power of *chi*.'

'If you fight with us, and we win, agreed. The second condition?'

Ping stepped towards Burke and forced her leg between his knees. 'Haven't you guessed, James?' She took his face in her hands and kissed his lips. 'Father said he worried about me because I was nineteen and still a virgin. It's not good for Father to worry, is it?'

* * *

The blade nicked Tanner's ear as it flashed past his head.

'You're slow! The next one will sink between your eyes.' Mai picked up another throwing knife, feinted a throw at Tanner's head, flicked it back and threw it at his belly.

Tanner twisted to the side as the steel cut through his shirt.

Mai spun a razor-edged throwing star at Tanner's head. He ducked at the last instant. 'Better.' She tossed him a *sai* then attacked with a short sword.

Tanner caught the blade on the long tine, pushed up and twisted as the sword met the juncture of a long and short tine.

Mai was thrown briefly off balance and pulled back, ready for a counter-attack that didn't come. 'Why didn't you finish me off, Mr Tanner?'

He didn't respond.

'Are you afraid you'll hurt me?' Mai flung another throwing star at Tanner's thigh. It clipped the inner flesh of his leg. 'Two inches higher, one to the left, and you'd be singing soprano. You've learned nothing. Attack!'

Tanner thrust the point of the *sai* towards Mai's abdomen. He lunged into empty space as she spun away and cracked the flat of her blade against his head.

'Stop! That's better. First the spirit, then the objectives. Stand thus.' Mai placed her feet about shoulder-width apart, one in front of the other. Her weight was mostly on her back leg, and her feet were pointed forwards. Unlike Burke's subtle assault with t'ai chi, Mai attacked with explosive speed. She caught Tanner moving back too slowly, and stopped. 'To the side.' Mai pointed towards her nose, indicating that it was Tanner's move.

He rushed forwards, only to strike air. Mai shifted to the left and countered. 'Now the basics. Stand next to me. Match my speed.' Mai sprang forwards, leaving Tanner flat-footed.

'Are you sure about this?' Burke unfastened Ping's jeans and slid down the zip.

'Do I look like I don't know what I want?'

'You are a teenager, and you're still . . .'

Ping stabbed her hand towards Burke's throat but stopped short of contact. 'I may be a virgin, but I'm not naive. Do you think I've been saving myself for a randy country boy who will spend himself in ninety seconds?'

Burke twisted Ping's wrist away from his neck. 'All right, young tigress.'

'Spare nothing, James. The lash, the needles, I want it all. I want you, now.' She raised her arms, inviting him to strip her. She watched desire mount in his eyes as he lifted her T-shirt over her athletic torso. The rims of pink areolae peeked from beneath a bra that scarcely covered her tiny pips. She pressed against him as he reached back to unfasten the scanty garment, and anticipation welled within her when Burke unbuttoned her jeans and pushed them down her long, firm, finely tapered legs. 'Touch me,' she commanded in a voice thick with lust. Her hips bucked as Burke pressed the ridge of his hand into her cleft before removing the sheer film of her low-cut knickers.

Naked before Burke, she abandoned herself to his control. A quiet moan issued from her as the press of Burke's hands on her back pushed her face-forward against a wooden rack. Leather straps cinched her wrists and ankles, her helplessness freeing her mind from the distractions of choice. She had no need to think, only to feel the streaks of the lash across the taut muscles of her arse. The stings seared their way down her cheeks to her thighs, even reaching her calves. Not one inch of her lower body was denied the exquisite sensations. She looked back and a gasp caught in the throat when she saw the leather cat-o'-nine-tails in Burke's hand. Her back braced against her bonds when the lashes bit into the full of her torso, from shoulders to arse. 'Ahhh!' The groan was long as the cat raked her back from left to right then right to left and back again. Red striations criss-crossed her flesh before Burke put the cat aside.

'Enough?' Burke's question was a challenge.

Ping pulled back her lips and hissed through her teeth.

'Ayiiii!' The last thing she had expected was what came next. Burke's hands roved across her flesh, spreading peppermint oil over the raised welts. Her skin burned with an aromatic fire that cleared her nostrils and watered her eyes. She was weeping uncontrollably when Burke released her bonds, only to secure her face-up on the rack. Her vulnerability was complete as Burke adjusted the rack so her legs were spread wide. Through her watery vision, she saw a horsetail whisk in his hand. It lashed upwards between her legs, awakening her tender lips. 'Ungh!' She pressed her head against the rack and arched her breasts forwards, only for the whisk to slash across them. They grew red, along with her inner thighs, as the whisk moved from her loins to her breasts, one then the other, in a strong, steady rhythm.

Ping felt liquid gather in her core and flow to the gate of her channel. Her pubic floss became a damp, dark mass under the ministrations of the flashing whisk. With a clenched jaw, her head swayed from side to side as the whisk tormented the soft, yielding mountains of her chest. The hard press of Burke's thumb into her pink pearl sent a shudder through her entire body.

'Enough?' Burke asked again.

Ping didn't even try to answer, her eyes rolling back in unconscious abandon. The rack shifted under her, so she was parallel to the floor. Sweat covered her body, come drenching her loins. She felt the thin hard press of copper wire against her cleft, and the first flash of electricity swept over the surface of her skin, coursing through the salty liquid of her sweat. It was a tease of low amperage, and the amperage would remain low, but quickly became more focused. Her nipples grew erect in Burke's mouth, hard against his teeth. The acupuncture needle he twirled between his fingers gleamed in the light. Its prick began around her areola and moved inwards. Ping stared at the stabbing point in Burke's hand as it found the centre of her nipple and sank into her flesh; a second needle soon pierced her other breast.

Ping's breath came fast and shallow as she watched Burke connect wires from the needles to a transformer and turn on the power. The surge was light, but it made her body writhe. Her shoulders crunched forwards and rocked, her body bucking at the sensation of the electricity flowing through her most sensitive places. Sweat ran through the valleys of her torso, pooling at her pubic delta. Her eyes gleamed as she watched Burke, standing between her legs, strip off his clothes. Was he ready? The question cried out silently in her mind. Her hips twitched towards his erect rod, pushing her quim at him. She craved his sex inside her, but he stepped away, and her mind reeled as she wondered what would come next. The electric flow died as Burke cut the transformer's power.

'Now!' Ping's voice grated through clenched teeth, only for Burke to shake his head. His thumb pressing into her clit brought her to the verge of orgasm again, but he stopped before she achieved release. She felt the rapid pricks begin, her desire swelling with the rush of blood to her hard nub. Her mewing exploded in a shout as the needle bit into the tip of her clit, and her cry became a long scream of ecstasy as Burke turned on the power, and the low current ran into the core of her sensitivity. Of its own will, her body, driven by the hot rushing charges, thrashed against its bonds until her wrists and ankles grew red.

Burke cut the power and removed the needles.

Ping's body fell slack, her skin liquid with sweat. Rivulets of come trickled down her thighs.

'Drink.' Burke held a glass of water to her lips. When she had finished drinking, he released her from the rack.

Her eyes searched his, questioning what he had done. 'I still want you.' She took his hard staff in her hand, squeezed it and pressed herself against him.

'We met in a hot spring. Let's wash.' Burke led her to a large bathroom whose floor and tub were made of cedar. The wood's aromatic essence combined with lavender soap and herbal oils to produce a heady scent.

Ping shivered as though she were chilled, even though the water Burke poured onto her was hot, but the tremors soon subsided, and she felt calm and safe as his hands slid across her skin, cleaning away the perspiration and peppermint oil on her back. The fierce sting on her scourged flesh was eased by the herbal solutions Burke massaged into her flesh. As she stepped into the bath, each ripple of the water brought waves of sensations that were only intensified by the heightened sensitivity of her skin, but there was no more pain.

'Lie back, Ping.'

She rested her head on the edge of the bath and let Burke lift her to the surface. Her legs wrapped around his hips and drew him towards her, but his shaft slid under her arse cheeks, teasing her as she had teased him in the hot springs. A smile of amused irony played at the corners of her lips. As she watched Burke close his eyes and draw slow breaths, the smiled stayed, but now her gaze reflected eager anticipation, like a young girl picking out her first bike. Floating in the bath, Ping relaxed her mind and body, an empty vessel waiting to be filled by Burke.

The first wave of *chi* was a calm caress, and she felt a clear, clean sea of pleasure wash through her. Her hands strayed to Burke's arms, kneading his flesh, her psyche trying to bond to his physical being, bracing her for . . .

The second wave was a monster, crashing through Ping's defences an explosion of white heat so strong she feared she might pass out.

It was several minutes before Ping's sobs subsided to gentle moans. She opened her eyes, and met Burke's gentle gaze.

'How did we do, princess?'

Not yet composed, Ping took a few moments before she could answer. She smiled, then laughed softly. Her hands reached for Burke's steel rod. 'Correct me if I'm wrong, James, but do I not remain a virgin?'

'That correction is imminent, dear Ping.' Burke kissed her lips, nibbled her ear and traced his mouth along her neck, then sucked at her breasts, ran his tongue down her belly and lapped it against her nether lips, sweet and tangy to the taste. He parted the lips, swollen and greasy with her excitement, penetrated them, then moved up to her quivering nubbin. His tongue probed against it, his teeth raking it as Ping clutched his hair, pushing his face into her groin.

'You've given so much, James.' Ping shoved Burke's head away from her cleft. 'Even a woman has her limits. Take me now. Let me know that I have returned your gifts in some measure.'

Burke smiled and kissed Ping's palms and wrists before placing her hands on his hard staff. Together, they guided his rod into her, and he groaned as he slid in and out of her liquid core. She reached behind him, fascinated at the feeling of his cock inside her, and caressed his tight balls. 'Come inside me, James,' she whispered in his ear. 'Don't hold back, I want to feel it filling me.' She squeezed his balls, and with a long, low moan he let go and allowed himself to gush inside her.

The virgin Ping was no more.

Fifteen

'A diversion?' Mai sipped coffee in bed, her leg resting across Burke.

'That's what she said.' Burke stroked the inside of Mai's thigh.

'I can't see how Koyanagi can present a diversion that will be any good unless it's co-ordinated with our own plans.'

'When they find him, he'll try to get word to us. If we're ready, we could move then. If that doesn't work, I expect he'll try to make sure there are fewer Scorpions for us to face.'

'I'd feel a lot better if we knew how many there will be.'

'I've seen three of them. I doubt Mousavi is still around, but he was here for a reason, so there is probably a replacement for him. They might call in others to help find Natsuko and to come after me.'

'Come after *us*,' Mai corrected.

'*Us* probably means Tanner and me. He saw them with me. There's no reason for them to target anyone else.'

'One other.'

Burke paused. 'Sandra.'

'They saw her at the Bound Maiden, and they have no way of knowing whether or not she knows who they are. There are a lot of loose ends, which could mean a massacre.'

'I don't think we're talking about open war. They'd try to take us one or two at a time, which is why we have to take the fight to them. We can assume there are at least three Scorpions here now. Let's say they call in two more to find Natsuko.'

'Let's say they call in four, maybe five others. There are all those loose ends, remember. Five extras make a total of eight very bad actors.'

'Against four of us, plus Koyanagi?' Burke shrugged.

'Koyanagi's alone. We can't count much on that. Tanner's an asset, but . . .' Mai left her final evaluation unstated.

'I think he'll surprise you, Mai. What we need now is a detailed attack plan. I'm afraid we'll have to hit Ishido in his own lair, and we'll have to hit soon. Give me three hours to work out the strategy, then let's go over it together.'

'While you're at it, I'll work with Tanner and Ping together and see what she knows in the way of the arts.'

Mai had turned the lights in the training room down to a faint glow and placed obstacles at irregular positions throughout the room. 'We'll attack at night, and from what James has said, we'll be breaking into an underground room or rooms. We might find ourselves in an even darker spot than this. Are you scared yet, Mr Tanner?'

'Not yet, but I expect I will be.'

'Good, but you ought to be afraid now.' She kicked Tanner in the stomach lightly. 'You can use fear to make you alert to things like that. Hone your senses.' Mai shifted her shoulder towards Ping and punched at her head. Her fist moved too fast for Tanner to follow, but Ping had already slipped just outside the line of attack and stepped towards Mai.

Ping's open hand shot towards her throat. Mai deflected her wrist and with the same hand snapped a chop at Ping's face. Ping ducked low and leapt to the top of a gymnastics block that had been set as an obstacle. Mai swept a metal bar at Ping's legs. She dodged it as though she were skipping rope and jumped to the top of another block. Mai stopped attacking.

'I'm always afraid.' Ping smiled in the dark.

'Excellent.' Mai clapped her hands. 'There, Mr Tanner, see what fear can do?'

Tanner whistled under his breath. 'I think she's done this before.'

'I believe she has too. I also think she has as much to teach you as I do. I'm going to leave you to it and help James work out a few tactics. Ping, show our young warrior how to move in the dark, then how to defend himself, and finally how to attack. Don't expect too much.' Mai turned out the lights completely before she left.

'Ready, Mr Tanner?' said Ping.

'I'm ready, but call me Dan.'

Ping placed Tanner's hands on her thighs to show him how to keep his weight on one leg while he slid his other foot forwards. 'Always keep your weight on your back leg. That way you won't fall if you bump into something. It's easier than it sounds. Slide, then bring your weight to both feet. Slide again. It's like ballroom dancing.'

It wasn't long before Tanner was moving swiftly and surely in total darkness.

'Listen,' Ping said. 'Can you hear me breathe?'

'No.'

'I can hear you.' Ping tapped Tanner on the nose. 'Now learn silence. You've got to control your breath even when your heart's pounding.'

When Tanner had learned how to move, breathe silently and navigate obstacles, Ping taught him how to listen for an attacker, move aside and counter-attack. She trained him in bare-hand techniques and weapons, all the while wishing she had years instead of days to teach him. At least he had athletic skill from wrestling and a sense of combat. She taught him to attack without committing himself to forward lunges, always keeping his weight on both feet or his back leg. When she was satisfied, she said, 'Now you teach me.'

'What?'

'Wrestle, but first find me.' Ping became silent and moved away.

Tanner remembered his encounter with Kei and wondered whether he was ready for a match with someone with Ping's skills, but she seemed trained in strikes and weapons rather than grappling. That was Kei's speciality. In any case he had little choice. If he didn't find Ping, she would find him. He felt a tingle at his neck and dropped as either a punch or kick swept over his head. With an opponent at hand, he ignored what he had just been told and lunged forwards at Ping. She stepped to the side, but not before Tanner touched her. She was within his reach. A punch grazed his head. He wrapped his arm under hers and behind her neck, pulling her tightly against him. Ping clearly lacked Kei's grappling ability, but she was not without skill. It took Tanner several seconds to take her to the floor. Within a few minutes, he had immobilised her, face-down with one arm locked between her legs and the other around her throat. 'Enough?'

'Show me how you do that.'

During their bout, Tanner had thought of Ping only as an opponent. Now that their fight was over, he became keenly aware of his arm pressing into Ping's loins. He drew his hand slowly between her legs and pressed it against her mound and cleft and into her cheeks.

'My turn?' she asked.

Tanner showed her how to drive a leg or arm into an opponent's crotch to control the body's lateral axis.

Ping was a fast learner, and with Tanner putting up only partial resistance she soon had him pinned down. She laughed as she drew her arm between his legs. 'What's this?' She squeezed his hard rod.

'Too much excitement.' His hand found Ping's breast in the dark. 'Oops, excuse me.'

'Mmm, I think we've had enough training for today. You know what we need now?'

Tanner held his breath.

'What is it? Magic, mojo, is that the word?'

'If you mean something like a voodoo charm, that's the word.'

'Perfect. Those guys have scorpion tattoos, right? That's what we need, scorpion tattoos.'

'Are you serious? We couldn't fool them by pretending to be one of them.'

'No, I said magic. We'll get the tattoos on the bottoms of our feet. That way when we walk, we'll be squashing scorpions. My mother was Chinese, so I'm superstitious. I believe in mojo.'

Tanner laughed. 'All right. A little magic can't hurt.'

He was wrong.

'Are you sure?' The tattoo artist crossed her arms and stared at Tanner and Ping. 'What's the point of a tattoo if no one can see it?' She wore a *hapi* coat tied loosely at the front so elements of her full-body tattoo were visible.

'*Maho*,' Ping said, then whispered to Tanner. 'That's Japanese for "magic".'

'*Naruhodo*.' The artist said she understood, as though the odd request now made perfect sense. 'But there is something you should know. There are more nerves per square centimetre on the bottoms of your feet than anywhere else in your body. It will not be pleasant. Let me show you something.' The artist appeared to be in her early 30s. She was small, about 150 centimetres tall, and had a trim figure. 'Do you know the story of the Kaguya Hime?'

Ping nodded and told Tanner the Japanese fairy tale of a girl found in a bamboo grove and raised by an old couple who were childless. The girl was actually a moon princess, and when she had grown up she was taken back to the moon. It was a sad story about children's parting, she told him.

When she had finished, the artist untied the sash that held her coat in place. 'This tells the story.' She opened the coat and traced the length of a bamboo stalk from the waistband of her trousers to her collar-bone. She pulled the right side of the coat further back to reveal the second scene: a baby girl freed from inside the stalk. The girl's hand was drawn reaching for the artist's breast, her fingers etched into a nipple. 'The tattoo of the hand on the tip of my breast hurt more than I can describe.' The child's face was drawn on the contours of the artist's breast, the mouth open to suckle the nipple in her hand. 'Touch me here.' The artist put Tanner's finger to the tattooed arc of her areola. Then she touched it to the arc that was bare. 'Can you feel a difference?'

Tanner shook his head.

The artist picked up an emery board and sanded away dead skin from Tanner's fingertips. 'Touch me again.'

Tanner closed his eyes and concentrated on his fingertips as he pushed lightly against the artist's skin. He cupped the underside of her soft cone, then touched the upper, unpainted portion. 'Cooler.'

'Which?'

'The tattooed skin is cooler.'

'Very good. Would you like to see the complete story?'

Tanner and Ping both nodded.

The artist held her arms back and let the coat slide off. Her trousers were held up by an elastic band. She pushed them down and stepped out of them. A full moon was tattooed on her mound, giving the heavenly orb three-dimensional depth. She turned her back to let them see the tale of Kaguya Hime playing as a child on the right side of her back; growing to girlhood on the cheeks of her arse; making friends on the left side of her back; meeting emissaries from the moon on her left side and breast. On the inside of the artist's left thigh, a drawing showed Kaguya Hime being taken away from Earth. Her arm was extended towards the pubic-mound moon.

'The pain here was exquisite beyond dreams,' said the artist. She raised her leg and rested her thigh on the side of her tattooing table, then parted her nether lips. On the inside of her labia were etched the fingertips of Kaguya Hime. She looked at Ping. 'Can you imagine?'

Ping stared and shook her head. Surely not even Burke's lashings of the night before could match such agony.

'I can't speak with authority, because the bottoms of my feet are untouched. However, what you have asked for might be as bad as this.' She took Burke's hand and placed it against her quim. 'You feel how tender the flesh is? Even though you are a man, I think you can understand my experience. Once more, are you both sure?'

Tanner looked at Ping. '*Maho*, right?'

'*Maho* and mojo,' she answered.

Ping and Tanner nodded to each other.

The artist addressed Ping. 'I advise you to take off your clothes, everything, so you're as naked as I am.'

Ping frowned and cocked her head.

'I know it's only the bottom of your foot, but after I start, you'll understand why. If you have a callus, I'll need to sand it down to make sure the tattoo is applied evenly. That will make your skin even more sensitive. The scorpion will appear three-dimensional with fine red to brown shading. I will have to make multiple passes over the same area. It will take time.'

Ping disrobed, lay face-down on the table and rested her foot on a brace. The first stabs of the needle merely prickled, but as the artist applied shading along the same lines the pain became as gnawing as a dentist's drill without anaesthetic. For half an hour, Ping endured it, even though all she wanted to do was jerk her foot away and be done with it. She grabbed Tanner's hand and bit into the flesh as though it were a leather strop.

The artist ordered Tanner to strip. When he was naked, the artist pointed her chin towards Ping's nether zone and extended her tongue. 'It would make it more bearable.'

Ping sucked in a sharp breath as Tanner's fingers probed her, stroking her cleft and pressing into her tiny bud. At his touch, dew welled in her loins. She reached for Tanner's phallus and felt it grow hard in her hand. She looked back at him and, with her eyes, directed him to straddle her. Her liquid come ran freely down her thighs as Tanner penetrated her, and she pressed her face into a small pillow to last out the ordeal uttering small cries of ravishment.

'Done,' said the artist.

Tanner withdrew from Ping and checked the tattoo. 'It's good. The stinger is even scary.'

Ping nodded her approval when the artist showed her the design in a mirror.

It was Tanner's turn. He lay face-down, but the artist told him to turn over.

'I can work at this angle,' she said. 'You might need the same kind of help as Ping before I'm finished.'

Tanner turned over and lay still as the artist filed away a callus from his foot with fine sandpaper. On that tenderised skin, the darting needle stung like a swarm of hornets. Tanner gripped Ping's arse and pressed her mound to his face. Her odour and feel excited him in ways that transformed the needle into something arousing, something to quicken his sexual pleasure. He put his hands on Ping's hips and pushed in the direction he wanted her to go. She understood and swung her leg across him, straddling his hips. 'Inside.' His breath caught in the power of his desire. 'Take me inside you.' He put his fingers against Ping's nether lips as she guided his shaft into her. A fire of lust burned through his loins, soon indistinguishable from the agony of the piercing steel. He kept his hips still as Ping rocked against him, dipping her breasts to his mouth.

'Done,' said the artist at last, but Tanner had not finished yet. Free now to move, he drove his rod hard into Ping, once, twice, until the dam of his need burst inside her. He wrapped his arm around her neck and pressed her lips to his mouth as the spasms in Tanner's loins forced out the last of his white-hot seed.

'Come to the toilet with me,' Burke said.

'I didn't know it was that kind of place.' Mai smiled. 'I admit the Devil's Island theme is kinky, but I didn't think it might be competition.'

Burke had taken Mai to the mouth of the lion's den, the Devil's Island Café. They sat hidden behind burlap drapery. Burke had disguised himself as a South Asian, complete with a rebuilt nose, false eyebrows, a wig and grease paint. Mai was a short-haired brunette with a new nose.

'We're here for reconnaissance, not to check out the competition. You need to see this place, and I need to prove or disprove a theory I have about it.' Burke opened his satchel and showed Mai a drill bit, a torch and a periscope he had made out of cardboard tubes. 'We can go together. It's a unisex loo.'

They watched for waitresses and left the table unnoticed.

'Hear that?' Burke rapped the wall. 'It sounds thin. I think this panel is a wood façade with maybe something like sheetrock on the other side.' Burke began drilling a hole in the wall.

'And on the other side of the sheetrock?'

'My guess is it's a stairway.'

'It's too narrow.'

'We'll know one way or the other soon enough.' Burke broke through the first wall then the second, with a hole about two centimetres in diameter. 'Shine the torch inside as I slip this through.' Burke pushed the periscope into the holes. 'Mmm hmm. Take a look.'

Mai took a peek and shook her head. 'You're right; what's it for?'

Burke began filling in the small holes with putty. 'A private basement that probably doesn't exist on any architectural drawings. At least that's my guess. The construction industry here is hardly more than another branch of the mob. Payment to the right yakuza can get a lot done. Build a basement that isn't supposed to be there, then cover it over so the building inspectors don't see it. After completion, it would be easy enough to secretly take out the flooring over the stairs and hide it with a wall.'

He sanded down the putty on the inner hole. 'I'm done. Let's get out of here.'

At the Excalibur, Burke stood next to a scale model of the Devil's Island Café. He pointed to the narrow section of wall at the back of the toilet. 'That's the soft underbelly. Do you all understand your assignments?'

Mai and Ping nodded, but Tanner raised an issue that Burke had not fully covered. 'We're short of one person, aren't we?'

'Actually, we are short of two. To make sure we're inconspicuous, we need a couple, a man and a woman.

'You have several men to choose from. Who's the woman?' Tanner's voice had a hard edge.

Mai had helped Burke work out the details, and spoke up. 'I plan to ask Sandra. There's no danger, Dan.'

It was the first time since he'd started working at the Excalibur that Tanner had heard her use his first name. 'She's a kindergarten teacher, Mai. You can't bring her into this.'

'She's already in it,' said Burke. 'Just by being at the Bound Maiden with us. She's seen them and that makes her a primary target. Anyway, she's a good bit more than a kindergarten teacher. We need her. We'll send Rafael as her escort. He won't know anything except that he's entertaining Sandra. Apart from her role in it, Sandra won't know what we're doing. If everything goes to plan, she'll be out of the building before we engage.'

'That "if" rings loud.' Tanner folded his arms across his chest.

'The way you feel about Sandra has been obvious even before you were willing to admit it yourself,' Mai said. 'However, this isn't your choice. It's hers. I'm going to talk to her. If she says "yes", that's it. She's in. If you don't like that, maybe you need to think about your own commitment.'

'My commitment is solid. It's just that . . .'

'She'll be safer if we act,' Burke said. 'We're down to few options. We need to appear as normal as possible. A man and a woman go to the café, just a date. Who will notice? It isn't staffed by Scorpions. Sandra does her job and gets out with Rafael. They split up, and she goes home by train or taxi or the Yellow Brick Road. It doesn't matter. Her safety is in the Scorpions' defeat, the same as ours. If we lose, do you think they won't look for Sandra? She's implicated just by being seen with me. Whether or not you understand, I think she will. Anyway, like Mai said, it's her decision.'

Tanner nodded his head slowly. 'Is it OK if I talk to her first?'

'It's all right with me; just be straight with her,' Burke replied.

Tanner, Ping and Mai went back to their training, while Burke prepared an assortment of weapons and tools, including a battery-powered circular saw. By the time he was set up, Sandra had arrived at the Excalibur.

Tanner went to meet her. He felt a warm glow as she smiled in delight on seeing him.

'Why so serious?' She stepped inside.

'Burke has a request. We all have a request.'

Sandra's smile faded behind a cloud of self-doubt. 'I think I have an idea. After all, things haven't been normal for the last few days, have they? James hasn't shown his face; you neither, not much. Mai's preoccupied. I hear things. It doesn't take a genius to see trouble.' She looked down and spoke softly. 'You want me to leave, don't you?'

'What?' Tanner scowled. 'I wish it was that simple.'

Sandra snapped her head up, wide-eyed, as though she'd been slapped.

'I didn't mean it that way.' Tanner touched her hand. 'I didn't mean it at all. I don't want you to go. I just want you to be safe.'

'What are you talking about?' Sandra let Tanner take her hand and returned his light squeeze.

'When we met at the Bound Maiden, do you remember the man who paid for the woman James touched?' Tanner briefly explained who the man was and what the dangers were. 'Burke believes that if we don't act against these people, they will pick us off one by one. That's why I said I wished you could just walk away. I couldn't bear for you to be hurt.' Tanner ran his fingers along Sandra's temples and started to draw her towards him.

She pushed her hand against his chest. 'Don't, Dan. Not unless you mean it. I play, sure, but with you it wouldn't be play. I just . . . I know I've been bitchy.'

'Yeah, you sure have. You come on to me like a nymph of Eros, then you turn your back. During your dance, the way you looked at me, I thought, finally, this is it. But then you tried to humiliate me. Why?'

Sandra touched Tanner's hand to her cheek. 'I'm afraid.'

'Of what?'

'That's a long story. For now, let's just say I'm not quite what I seem. Not quite the playgirl of the Western, or Eastern, world. There's more than one way to get hurt.'

'You'd better tell me that story someday. If you want me, I'll be there to hear it. You said it wouldn't be play with me. I'm not playing.' Tanner embraced her and kissed her hair. 'No one wants you to leave, Sandra. James needs your help. As for me, I just need you.' He put his finger under her chin and lifted her face to his kiss. He felt her body stiffen only briefly before she put her arms around his waist and gave herself to his lips.

'Well done, Dan.' Sandra kissed him back lightly. 'I've been called a fool more times than I want to remember, and never falsely. Every accusation was correct. Never trust anyone again, I told myself, but here I go. Guess I'll just have to live with myself the way I am.'

'It's a lovely self to live with.'

'Let's go and find out what I can do for James.' Her hands dropped to Tanner's arse, and squeezed it. 'And for you, Mr Tanner.'

Tanner's hands pressed into the back of her neck. He kissed her again and felt himself grow harder against her belly. 'Oops.'

Sandra laughed. 'We'd better see to James first, hadn't we?'

Tanner led her to the war room.

Sandra bowed like a knight before a joust. 'At your service, Master Burke, Lady Mai.'

Burke returned the bow. 'Good.' He indicated the scale model of the restaurant. 'You'll go with Rafael. He won't know what you or we are planning, so don't say anything to him. If he thinks he's in danger, he won't go through with it. Be sure you sit in this area. It's close to an exit, and you'll have to pass near the kitchen on the way to the lavatory. You'll have a package to drop here.' He pointed to a corner near the kitchen. 'Continue to the lavatory, stay long enough to look like you've used it, then go out through an emergency exit here. That will set off an alarm, so get out fast and don't look back. Let Rafael get out on his own. Trust me, he won't go looking for you.'

'What will you be doing?' Sandra asked Burke the question, but she looked at Tanner as she spoke.

'There's no reason for you to know that. The less you know, the safer we all are. Remember, Rafael is not to know anything except that he's supposed to entertain you. If he knew there was any real risk, he wouldn't go. None of the escorts here would.'

'Sounds simple enough.' Sandra stuck her thumbs into her belt in a pose of bravado. 'When do I check out my toys?'

'They're right here.' Burke showed Sandra how to activate the devices. 'If you get out immediately, you'll be safe.'

'That's it, then. When do I invite Rafael to escort me to Devil's Island?'

'Don't know yet, but I'll take care of him,' said Burke. 'We should all stay here until the time comes. It won't be long, I expect three days at most. You know your way around, Sandra. Find a room. Any on the third floor should be unoccupied. Baths are at your disposal.'

'All right, I'll call in sick for my day job. Wouldn't mind some time off anyway.' On her way out, Sandra brushed past Tanner and pinched his arse. 'See you,' she whispered.

‘OK, let’s concentrate.’ Burke glanced at Tanner as he spoke. ‘We’ll sit in this section near the lavatory. I have a full-scale mock-up of the toilet. Let’s go and practise.’

It was tight, but all four of them fitted in the mock-up with just enough space to assemble their kits. They trained until they had got their kits ready in less than a minute and a half. ‘Good start,’ said Burke. They continued until the motions had become rote and their hands ached. Then he blindfolded them. ‘Again.’

When they had learned the procedure blindfolded, Burke called an end to the practice. ‘Let’s get some sleep.’ He noticed Ping’s glance at Tanner. ‘We need to stay alert. Ping, you can find a room on the third floor. Dan, why don’t you stay on the second floor? Ladies and gents separate tonight. And stay away from the first floor. Mai’s guests and hosts will have to get along without us for a bit longer. Get a good rest. I’ll be making a six o’clock wake-up call.’

Ping pulled her shirt away from her neck and sniffed at it. ‘I smell like a goat. Is there a bath upstairs?’

‘There’s a door with a hot-spring symbol on it. Towels and toiletries are available.’ Burke smiled at the memory of their encounter in the hot spring on her father’s land. ‘It isn’t quite one of the mountain pools you’re used to, but I think you’ll find it adequate. Good night.’

On her way up the stairs, Ping began unbuttoning her blouse, which was wet with perspiration. By the time she got to the bath she was naked from the waist up. She stepped out of her trousers and knickers and tossed her clothes into a corner. The bath was big enough to accommodate a small party, and it was full of steamy water. It was likely that Sandra had already used it. Ping dipped a pail into the water and splashed it over her face and shoulders. It would take several splashes to wash away her sticky saltiness so she could soak in the tub. The sweat from her upper body had accumulated in her quim and arse. She knelt with her knees spread and her cheeks resting on her heels as she rubbed water into the sparse thatch between her loins. She had just reached behind her to cup her hand against the bud between her cheeks when the door opened.

'Oh, excuse me.'

Ping looked back to see Sandra backing out of the door.

'It's OK.'

'Are you sure?'

'Of course, this is big enough for two. It's big enough for ten, if you don't mind sitting close. Anyway, it's your bath. You drew the water, didn't you?'

Sandra was wearing only a towel. She hung it on a wall peg.

'Wow!' Ping had her father's natural openness and was not shy about expressing her admiration. 'You're beautiful.'

'No, no, too much . . .' Sandra pinched the flesh at her waist.

'No, too much here.' Ping laughed and ran her hands over her breasts. She made an hourglass shape in the air. 'Glamour! I envy you.'

Sandra made a face. 'I sometimes feel fat in Japan. So many women here are very slender.'

'You mean too skinny. Men like . . .' Ping held her hands out in front of her chest.

'Some do, some don't. That doesn't matter so much, but all men like . . .' Sandra pointed to the rich thatch of her curly, strawberry-blonde V.

'Ha! Even that is beautiful. Look.' Ping stood and held out a few strands of her pubic floss. 'See? Almost straight and black – boooring.'

Sandra stepped close to Ping and touched the strands she held out. 'Your hair is lovely, dark and glossy. It doesn't get in the way when there's play.' She licked her lips. 'I've heard that the taste here –' Sandra briefly touched her finger to Ping's cleft '– is milder than the taste here.' She touched herself.

'Is that so? I think a rich taste might be interesting.' A wisp of a smile touched her lips. 'May I?' When Sandra nodded, Ping ran her palm across Sandra's light moss. 'It tickles, like a poodle's fur.'

'Hey!' Sandra grinned. 'Watch who you're comparing to a dog.'

'No, no, no.' Ping pushed her fingers through Sandra's fleece. 'It feels good. Sit down. Let me wash your back.' Ping soaped her bare hands and pressed them to Sandra's flesh. 'I like your skin, soft at the surface, firm beneath, and spotted. You are a pink panther.'

'You mean freckles. In school, I used to get teased because of them.'

'Freckles are rare for Japanese, and when we have them they are brown, not pink. Anyway, they are cute, no reason for *ijime*, teasing.' Ping rinsed Sandra's shoulders, then touched her lips to the other woman's neck and ran her mouth along the slope to her shoulder. 'You have a nice taste.'

'At the shoulder, I guess we all taste the same. Turn around, Ping.' Sandra soaped her own hands and ran them over the length of Ping's back. 'You are very strong.'

'Too much training. Since I was a little kid, the master, my father, taught me. I have muscles like a man.'

'Not like a man; like a lean, tough woman.'

'I'm not so tough, but James is as bad as my father. He worked us hard today. Sweat made me very sticky, and stinky. I'm afraid I'm too dirty to enter the bath. Could you make sure I'm clean enough to go into the water? I think I must be especially dirty down there.' Ping looked back into Sandra's eyes. 'Please.' The trace of Sandra's fingers down her spine sent a light spasm through her flesh. Her loins clenched in anticipation as

Sandra's finger pressed against her button then moved forwards between her nether lips. It sank into her sex for a moment, withdrew, found her nub and pressed hard. Ping released a quiet moan deep in her throat and leaned her body forwards to give Sandra better access, then sucked in a sharp breath as Sandra pushed the tip of her soapy wet thumb onto Ping's bumhole. At the same time a finger of her other hand sank into Ping's channel. Ping fell onto her hands and knees and raised her hips towards Sandra, her oil oozing from her quim. She pushed her hips back, forcing Sandra's fingers deep into her twin gates. 'Nnngh!' Ping's arousal began building as the rhythmic pace of Sandra's probing digits quickened. The thrust sped to a lively pace, driven by Ping's animal lust, already excited by the martial arts training. A groan that had begun deep in her belly rumbled out and erupted in a primal scream. Ping pitched forwards onto her belly, her body heaving in the throes of orgasm.

She turned face-up to look at Sandra, who straddled her hips and ground herself against Ping's mound.

'I want to taste you.' Ping hooked her hands around Sandra's thighs and pulled the other woman towards her face. The teenage girl could scarcely believe her good fortune. In only two days, she had been taken by James, a spiritual master of ecstasy; experienced the taboo rites of tattoo and sex simultaneously; and now savoured a Western beauty. She ran the flat of her tongue along the lips of Sandra's quim until the juices flowed freely into her mouth. The taste was pungent, alive with flavours Ping had never known, and she stabbed her tongue into Sandra's channel, savouring her completely.

Sandra gripped Ping's hair, slid away and kissed her mouth, tasting her own essence on the girl's lips. 'I want you too, Ping.' She turned and buried her face in the saddle of Ping's sex, lapping her tongue against Ping's scantly haired quim as Ping continued to lick her in turn. The stories were true: the aroma of the oriental girl's excitement was faint, the dainty bouquet giving no hint of her writhing passion. Sandra ground her nose into Ping's perineum, and her tongue dipped deep inside her quim. All the while, Ping's face in her own sex brought tremors of rapture shuddering through her body, until finally she came with a rushing discharge. Seconds later, she tasted an earthier, muskier essence as Ping bucked her hips in her own orgasmic spasm.

Sandra lifted her head and scooped water to wash herself and her new playmate. 'I think we're ready for the bath.' In the water, she slid the softness of her hourglass body over Ping's athletic physique. As she revelled in the girl's hard musculature, she laid her head against the rim of the tub and let Ping rest on top of her, the girl's face nestled against Sandra's shoulder. It wasn't long before Sandra realised the girl had fallen asleep. For a long time, she enjoyed Ping's body against her own, then nudged her awake. 'Best go now. Get a proper rest before tomorrow's training.'

Ping swayed in semi-consciousness as Sandra towelled her dry.

'Where are you sleeping?' Sandra asked.

'With you.' Ping kissed her on the lips.

Sandra led her above the third floor to the glass-walled room on the roof. Outside, the glitter of city lights, in league with dust and industrial vapours, masked the heavens' natural glow.

Sixteen

Three Scorpions closed in, cloaked in a darkness broken only by the silver sheen of a new moon, the ruby light of Mars and the diamond glow of Venus. They heard, more than saw, the old man and Natsuko in the hot-spring baths.

There was a rustle of water as Koyanagi's fingers slid along the muscles of Natsuko's back from her neck to her spine. Her sighs carried far in the night air. Sound was the problem for the invaders, who moved along the hillside gingerly, silently, two from above, one from below. Their convergence was a triangular pattern to block escapes.

Their briefing on Koyanagi had been extensive but hardly necessary. Among Scorpions, his story was a legend in the way that overwrought mothers put their children to bed with tales of trolls, ogres and other monsters. Koyanagi had been recruited by the Scorpions and was on the verge of joining them before he came under the influence of Wei. It was the master of *chi* who had turned Koyanagi away from the society of torture. During the Great War, he had hunted down Scorpions employed by the Japanese Imperial Army. As a reward, Wei had offered to teach him the final steps in his mastering of *chi*.

Koyanagi declined. His earlier readiness to leap into the abyss of his own dark nature had been seared into his consciousness. He feared himself.

And the Scorpions feared him too. Each of the three was armed with a gun that fired a narcotic dart. Koyanagi was to be brought back alive, as was Natsuko. They inched towards the sounds of water and Natsuko's mewing. One at a time they moved, stopped, and watched the areas where their comrades were supposed to be. They intended to co-ordinate their attack and surprise Koyanagi and Natsuko from three sides at point-blank range. It was too dark to aim from a distance.

A bird near the bath took flight into a sky where a nighthawk prowled. The raptor keened, then whooshed towards its prey. With scarcely a rustle of feathers, it gripped the bird in its talons. The victim's shrill cry was short, the sound of death blending in with the lapping ripples of the pool and Natsuko's 'ahs' of pleasure.

The Scorpion coming from below had the best cover. He crawled to within twenty metres of the bath then stopped. If Koyanagi detected the other two, his most sensible course would be to run towards the Scorpion positioned downhill. The man was ready. At a point ten o'clock from his position, a faint motion like a black bug in the dark indicated that a second Scorpion was closing in. Soon the third Scorpion was set at two o'clock.

The two Scorpions above the pool stood and walked swiftly towards the water, their dart guns aimed at their targets. The third Scorpion rose last, but all three stopped short when they reached the pool and saw Natsuko alone, rippling the water and sighing to herself. Their pause was a heartbeat too long. Koyanagi stepped behind the Scorpion below the pool and swung his arm in a powerful arc. The ridge of his hand slammed into the man's throat. The hyoid collapsed, choking off his breath. A second Scorpion leapt across the pool and pointed the gun towards Koyanagi.

The veteran fighter was back. In his mind, it was the Great War, and he, powerful in body and spirit, was battling the Scorpions who had almost claimed his soul. He used the man he'd attacked as a shield, letting the dying body absorb the fired dart. Koyanagi dropped the victim and struck the Scorpion before him with the heel of his hand. He snapped the ball of his foot into the man's groin, then stepped closer and kicked the other foot into his throat. Two Scorpions down and . . .

The third Scorpion shot Koyanagi in the side. The old man turned and stumbled forwards, unconscious.

Natsuko was out of the bath and sprinting downhill. The Scorpion picked up the last loaded dart gun and dashed after her. Her head start gave her a fifty-metre lead. She swerved onto a steep slope behind a rocky outcrop, lost her footing and slid down a grassy incline. The Scorpion saw her fall and slowed to avoid her error, but his caution was a miscalculation. Her drop was swift, and she reached level ground unharmed. Her lead had stretched to more than eighty metres. She was running again. A wood lay 200 metres ahead, a good place to hide or throw him off. Rough ground and rocks tore at her bare feet, and the pain seared her mind despite the adrenalin rush of fear. A river flowed just beyond the wood; if she could make it, she might be able to swim downstream unseen. She heard the Scorpion cry out a curse and dared to look back. He'd stumbled. She cut onto higher ground. It was a longer route to the wood but the land was grassy and smooth. An injured foot would be fatal. She was only fifty yards from the cover of the copse, and looked back again. The Scorpion had already taken to the higher ground and was running full speed, closing the distance between them. If she cut back to the rocky path she could reach the wood well ahead of him, if her feet held out. She took the chance, bounding in leaps to reduce the chance of stumbling. The first tree she reached was a sapling. She reached out for the truck and catapulted herself forwards into thick growth. Branches raked her bare shoulders and breasts. She assumed the Scorpion would expect her to continue away from him. Instead, she reversed direction and headed towards the river. If he stopped to listen, he would hear her, but that would give her more time. Her lungs and legs burned, phlegm raking through her throat. She held her arms to her chest to protect her tender breasts, but it was more difficult that way to keep balance, and her shoulder struck the trunk of a tree. She staggered sideways but kept on her feet, running towards the sound of the fast-flowing river, towards a dark shape that suddenly appeared in front of her. The shape held a gun and pointed it at her torso. She turned to flee and felt the dart pierce her buttock.

The Scorpion had studied the land before the attack, guessed the river was the best opportunity for escape, and run across open ground to the other side of the grove ahead of Natsuko. He easily lifted her naked form across his shoulders.

It would be evening of the following day before a maid found the robes of her master and Natsuko by the pool.

The brilliant light of an autumn sun warmed Sandra and Ping like a friendly smile. They snuggled in the drowsy afterglow of sleep and soothing dreams. Sandra traced her fingers along Ping's back, between her cheeks and into the dewy pillows of her sex. She pulled the covers off Ping and ran her hands down the teenager's legs.

'I've never seen anyone as sleek as you, slinky like a prowling cat.'

Ping made a growling sound in her throat. 'But no claws.' She held her hand out so Sandra could see her nails. They were clipped short, almost to the quick. 'They get in the way.'

Sandra caressed the graceful arch of Ping's foot. 'What's this?' She traced the outline of the scorpion tattoo.

'Oh! That tickles. It's still a bit tender. It's my magic to fight the Scorpions. I step on them.'

'Magic?'

'Just superstitious, but if I think I am crushing them underfoot like bugs, it might make me stronger. Dan has one too. We got them together after training.'

'Is Mr Tanner superstitious too?' Sandra's voice was abruptly crisp, as though suddenly exposed to a dry chill breeze.

'I don't think so. He just went with me.' Ping looked over her shoulder and saw a hardness around Sandra's eyes. She sat up and kissed Sandra on the neck. 'Why don't you get one too? We'll be the three musketeers, and James can be a sort of older d'Artagnan. What do you say?'

Sandra stroked the bottom of Ping's foot, her face wistful.

'It hurts, but the artist has a way to distract your mind from the pain.' She reached between Sandra's thighs. 'I'll go with you. It will be special.' She nibbled Sandra's ear as their breasts touched. 'Only three people in the world, I bet, with scorpions tattooed on the bottoms of their feet.'

Sandra smiled. 'How does the artist distract you from the pain?'

Ping pressed Sandra's nubbin and pushed her finger into the older woman's sex. 'Like that.'

Sandra's eyes widened, and her mouth formed an 'O' shape. 'It might be fun.'

'It might have been just as well to kill him.' Ishido stared into Koyanagi's eyes. The old man was secured with leather thongs to an oaken rack. 'He'll never tell us who else knows about the Scorpions. He fears nothing, not death or pain. There are no phobias. What do you do to a sack of flesh and bone? Nothing up here.' He rapped his knuckle on the side of Koyanagi's head.

Shakala, the surviving Scorpion from the raid, had carried Natsuko back to the hot spring, bound her and Koyanagi and loaded them into a van with the bodies of the other two Scorpions. When he returned to the Devil's Island Café, Ishido berated him for losing two men. Now they were down to eleven for their action against Burke and the others. 'Use her.' Shakala pointed to Natsuko, who was strapped nude and spread-eagled on the iron cross that had held Mousavi.

Ishido sneered. 'For what? He cares no more for her than you or I do.'

'He has a daughter.'

'Who you couldn't find. We don't know where she is.' Ishido walked to Natsuko and pressed his hand into her cleft. 'You wouldn't know, would you, lovely?'

In her fear, Natsuko scarcely managed to shake her head.

He walked back to Koyanagi. 'And you would never tell. Would you tell me who else besides your daughter knows, then?'

Koyanagi closed his eyes and centred his consciousness inside a private void.

'I didn't think so. I truly do not know what to do with this one.' Ishido selected a needle that was wired to a transformer. 'Still, one must try.'

Sandra flinched at the first prick of the tattoo artist's needle on the sole of her foot. She lay naked on her stomach with one leg bent back at the knee so the artist could straddle Sandra's hips as she worked.

'Not yet,' the artist cautioned Ping, who had reached for Sandra's quim. 'Let the pain build, otherwise the effect of the cure will be weak.'

In just moments, Sandra was gripping the small, thin pillow under her head. Sweat broke out on her forehead and along the nape of her neck. A short while later, she was biting the pillow to stifle her moans. Her mind's focus on the incessant stabs of the needle blurred as she felt the artist slide down her hips, to press her nubbin against the base of Sandra's spine. Sandra sensed the artist's pleasure as she rocked her hips slowly.

When Sandra's focus returned to the sharp assault on her delicate skin, the artist paused and pressed Sandra's other foot against her own naked breast. Sandra kneaded the soft mound with her toes, as the artist went over the same areas again and again to etch delicate gradations of tones. Under the torture of a biting, stabbing needle, Sandra could no longer contain her anguish. She pictured the artist having the inside of her nether lip tattooed and tried to imagine her pain. 'Mustn't be a coward,' she told herself. Still, her muted groans grew, to erupt in a cry between gritted teeth.

No sooner had the shout left her than she sucked in a sharp breath as Ping's fingers slid into her moist channel and massaged her nub. Her mind whirled at the sensations of pain and pleasure, each heightening the other, and she was powerless to resist as Ping massaged her clit, the first tremors quickly building up to a powerful head. Her anguished cry became a keening wail, stifled as she crushed her face into the pillow. Come flowed from her loins in a physical display of her arousal.

'Finished.' The tattoo artist showed the completed work to Ping, who nodded in approval.

Overwhelmed with emotion, Sandra sobbed into the pillow. She felt her back wet with oil where the artist had straddled her.

'I tried my best to complement your own beauty,' the artist whispered in Sandra's ear. 'I hope you will like it.'

Sandra turned and kissed the artist on the lips, wrapping her arms around the artist's neck. 'Thank you, and you too, Ping.'

The 'musketeers' smiled at each other, closer now, sharing the secret of their unique trial.

Sandra touched the artist's breast. 'Lie beside me. I want to see Kaguya Hime's fingers again.'

The artist stretched her small lithe body down next to Sandra, who caressed her partially tattooed nipple with her lips and tongue. 'How could you bear this?' She reached for the artist's quim. 'And this?'

'I'm a professional.'

'You're more than that. You're a silent poet. Your body is a living canvas, a visual tale of the loving sorrow of parting, of giving freedom to someone you adore above your own life.' Her finger slid along the sides of the artist's nether lips. 'Such pain.' Sandra traced her mouth along the artist's body to her shaved mound. She spread the lips of the artist's sex and touched her tongue to Kaguya Hime's fingers, tattooed on the inside. 'How could you suffer such astonishing pain, except for love? Your art would not be complete unless you had endured the ultimate agony. Even though it is hidden from the world, you know your own sacrifice. In that knowledge is your strength.' Sandra pushed her tongue deep into the artist's channel, then teased her perineum and the bud beyond. She lapped the tender tissue of the artist's labia and pierced through to her vibrant nub. It thrilled her to feel the woman respond in spasms to her caress as she dipped her fingers into the artist's sex while her teeth raked the woman's nub. In moments, the artist's body thrashed in rapture.

'Will it really make us stronger?' Sandra teased Ping as they walked along the street. She was enthralled with her experience and could scarcely stop herself from kissing her new friend in front of everyone.

'Sure, that's why I brought you. We're tough gals now, right?' Ping looked around before she pinched Sandra's arse.

'Tougher than any Scorpion, I'd say.' Sandra stamped her foot against the pavement.

They walked together, brushing against one another, pressing briefly, reinforcing their affection with casual physical contact. They were in Roppongi, near the Excalibur, when Ping pushed Sandra towards the window display of a restaurant. 'Someone's watching us.'

'Who?'

'I saw a man take our picture.'

'Could be a tourist, hobbyist.'

'Maybe, but I suspect he's not. If he is, maybe we can trick him. Walk slowly as though we're looking for a place to eat.'

They strolled together past cafés, bars and restaurants. Ping nudged Sandra into a dead-end alley. 'I want to draw him out, but I need a lure.'

'Me?'

Ping nodded. 'Are you afraid?'

'Of course.'

'Good. Will you do it anyway?'

Sandra's heart sped and a taste of bile rose in her mouth. 'Yes.'

Ping gripped Sandra's hand. 'Wait five minutes then take off your shoe and lift your foot so he can see the tattoo. I think it will confuse him, rouse his curiosity, and he'll come near you. I'll be here, trust me.'

Sandra nodded as she watched Ping slip into an alley between two cafés and walk down the narrow path behind them. She looked at her watch and counted each minute, wondering who could possibly come at midday to attack her, then realised that there was little traffic down the alley. Who would notice? Four and a half minutes later, she took off her shoe. Thirty seconds after that, she raised her foot at the knee, so anyone behind her could see the tattoo. Despite the chill autumn air, perspiration welled beneath her clothes, giving off an acrid odour of fear. Seconds passed and nothing happened. She put down her foot then picked it up again.

'What's this?' A man gripped her ankle and jerked her leg up, almost toppling her off balance. His other hand gripped her throat. 'Are you playing a game with me? Where's your friend?'

Ping cracked the heel of her hand into the back of the man's head. 'Right behind you,' she said as he dropped to his knees. A kick to the side of his head rendered him unconscious. She broke each of his arms at the elbow, then above and below each elbow. She broke his wrists and his hands, his shins and the bones in his ankles. For spite, she broke his jaw and nose. He would heal, but he would not join the fight against them.

'Let's go,' said Ping. She and Sandra made their way back to the Excalibur.

'You're sure he's down?' Burke paced the room with his arms folded across his chest.

'The only way I could be more sure is if I had driven a stake through his heart.' Ping sniffed at Burke's doubt. 'He has breaks here.' She tapped her own arm in five places. 'Here.' She struck her legs and ankles. 'And here.' She hit her jaw and nose. 'You aren't fighting phantoms. They're men, and that one is out of this fight, all right?'

Mai, Tanner and Sandra watched the interchange between Burke and Ping, but remained silent.

'Sorry, Ping. I didn't care about your verification. I just . . .'

'Just what?'

'We got news that I wanted to delay telling you.'

Ping fell silent. Her eyes misted before she spoke. 'Papa?'

Burke nodded. 'One of your father's maids called. She found his *yukata* with Natsuko's next to a hot spring. There were tyre tracks leading up to it, but no sign of your father or Natsuko. We have to assume the worst.'

'No we don't.' Ping shook her head. 'The worst is that he's dead, but they might be holding him. That's what they do, isn't it? Capture people and torture them. We have to go now.'

'We can't get in until the restaurant opens. That isn't for another three hours.'

'Before that, they might come here,' Ping said. 'They know Sandra. The Scorpion who I put down took our pictures. With a wireless transfer of data, he could have immediately sent the photos to whoever's in charge of this. They're probably looking for me. I was a loose end until now. They know I'm here, so there's no reason for them to delay.'

Burke stopped pacing. 'I doubt they will attack in daylight. If they come at night, you'll have some surprised customers, but as for us, we'll be at their house.'

'If the Excalibur is being watched, they'll see us leave.'

'There is an exit through the third floor obscured by trees. It leads to a path that runs between homes. It goes uphill and meanders for blocks until it intersects a thoroughfare. We'll leave one by one. I'll draw a map to a meeting point. We'll also need a bit of makeup to throw them off the scent when we do arrive. Are there any questions?'

Tanner spoke first. 'What do we do for the next three hours?'

Burke glanced at Sandra and Tanner. 'No one can guarantee your safety, whether you go or not. Take thirty minutes to gather your thoughts. Prepare yourself mentally, and then come back here. We'll have a weapons check and apply makeup for disguises. Go.'

Ping left the room and closed the door behind her.

Tanner looked at Burke and an understanding passed between them. The young apprentice would not spend 30 minutes in mental preparation. Tanner walked out of the room and waited for Sandra to follow. When she did, he didn't speak. He simply took her hand and led her to the glass-walled room at the top of the building.

He kissed her mouth, the tip of her nose and her eyes, then silently nuzzled her neck and ear. 'I've known you only a little while, Sandra, but I feel like I've wanted you all my life.' Tanner's groin tightened as he kissed her deeply.

'Me too, Dan. Take me, quickly.' Her whispers aroused a passion in his spirit as real as the throbbing lust that stiffened his cock. He pressed his fingers into the back of Sandra's neck and pushed down her spine to the marvellous globes at its base. He kneaded those fleshly mounds and pushed his fingers between them, forcing Sandra's quim against his hard rod. Her groans of passion burned his ear as she pushed herself against him. He seemed to have desired her for an eternity. He would gladly have spent an age sucking on one breast, another savouring the aroma of her sex and yet another teasing her gate before entry. Their lives, however, were not measured by ages, but by moments, and they had few left before the attack. Tanner gripped her blouse in his hands and ripped it open, then tore away her skirt, bra and knickers. He fell to his knees and buried his face in her silky, strawberry-blonde bush. His tongue pushed through her fur to the musky oil of her sex. He savoured her taste, lapping at the tender doorways to her gate, then thrust his tongue inside. Her whimpers and her hands on the back of his head urged him on to the pearl of her sex, and he teased her gem with his tongue and teeth until it seemed that her whole body would melt in the heat of her passion.

Tanner removed his clothes as Sandra reclined on the bed, then lay on top of her and at long last eased his shaft into her hot quim. At last he was fucking her, this temptress who had teased him so unmercifully, but he held no grudge, and felt only joy as he looked into her eyes, sparkling with desire and gratitude for his forgiveness. He kissed her with his lips still wet from the dew of her passion, his tongue entwining with hers as his shaft slid inside her liquid channel. He moved within her at a languid pace, as though they had all the time in the world.

It was a sweet illusion.

His tempo quickened, and he burst inside her. In the seconds that followed, his rod remained hard, he continued thrusting until Sandra came too, squeezing his softening phallus in the walls of her sex. He withdrew and lay beside her, kissing her neck and stroking her body. It was only moments before there was a knock on the door and they heard Burke's voice.

'Time to move, people.'

Burke, Mai and Ping were applying makeup when Tanner and Sandra entered Mai's office.

'Welcome, Dan, Sandra. Take seats. Mai will fix you up.'

An hour later, Burke and Tanner could pass for moustachioed Pakistanis. Sandra was a brunette with an olive complexion and an aquiline nose, while Ping and Mai were blondes.

Burke laid out their kits. Mai and Sandra would carry shopping bags from premier department stores. Ping had her own stock of weapons, including a *nunchaku*, in a leather satchel. Burke and Tanner would carry canvas sports bags, each big enough to hold supplies for a month's march. One last time, Burke briefed Sandra on how to set her devices, then reviewed a diagram of the Devil's Island Café with her. She would need to be precise. For everyone else as well, timing was the vital factor.

Ping had scarcely spoken a word since learning that the Scorpions had taken her father. She seemed to look through people instead of at them, even when she was addressed directly. Her hands clenched and unclenched. Every few moments, she shoved her tattooed foot against the floor. Mai had tried to console her, but she didn't respond. It was as though she had already engaged in battle mentally and could not take her focus off the enemy.

Tanner stayed as close to Sandra as he could and told her more than a few times to be sure to get out of the café quickly. She told him just as often that she'd be waiting for him when it was over.

Mai rechecked everyone's face, and applied finishing touches of grease paint to disguises that were already perfect.

Burke checked his watch for the tenth time in five minutes. 'Let's go.'

Seventeen

Like troops headed for a war zone, they were united by fear, camaraderie, obligation and trust. The night-time scents and sounds of everyday life rose up about them but were not part of their world, as they traversed what was for them an alien land of families, friends, petty quarrels and laughs. They walked in the midst of people clinging to the moment, anticipating tomorrow or savouring a memory. Lives around them were being lived, not put at risk by the unnatural law of soldiers and marines – attack or die.

The path they took from the Excalibur was well hidden, meandering along beside the walled gardens of multi-storey homes. Mai led the way and Burke followed as a rear guard until they reached a main thoroughfare. Giovanni was waiting at a corner for Sandra. He knew nothing of their plans. After complimenting her new look as a brunette, he escorted her to a taxi. Mai, Burke, Tanner and Ping passed by unrecognised. They took a different car through the fancifully dressed crowds of Roppongi and along broad avenues to central Tokyo, then got out of the car well away from the café and walked the remaining distance. A man near the door looked into their faces. His mouth smiled, but his eyes were the empty slate-black of a shark.

The café had opened only minutes earlier, and was just beginning to receive a few customers. Mai asked for a table in an area near the toilet. Once they were seated and had ordered, Burke walked past the table where Sandra and Giovanni were supposed to be. He heard their voices and went back to his table. No one among the staff looked out of place. There might be Scorpions at some of the tables, but what would be the point? The man outside was probably taking care of surveillance. Burke went to the toilet and checked the wall. There was no evidence that the hole he had drilled and puttied over had been discovered.

Nothing was left for them to do but wait.

Wait and watch Ping clench and unclench her jaw in anger and resolve.

It was Sandra's move. She was not as cavalier about Giovanni's well-being as Burke had been. To get him out of harm's way, she told him that she had forgotten to buy cigarettes. There must be a shop near the café that sold them. Would he be a dear? His instructions from Mai were to take Sandra out and treat her as he would a paying client. Of course he would go.

Sandra did not use tobacco, but she did have two smoke devices. Her heart racing, she set their timers to three minutes, pushed aside the burlap curtain in front of her table and headed towards the toilet. Burke had shown her where to plant the mini-bombs in his drawing of the café. One went near the kitchen, a natural source of fire, and one near an air vent, to spread the vapours quickly through the café. She walked past Burke's table, put her hand through the curtain and made a victory sign. After ten seconds of washing her hands, she went back to her table.

The bombs went off with muted bangs and rapidly expanding clouds of smoke.

When Sandra had passed their table on the way back to her own, Burke, Mai, Tanner and Ping began strapping their weapons to their belts. As the smoke drifted through the café, they went towards the toilet.

Burke taped a homemade explosive to the wall, then connected it to a twisted-wire cable, which he ran under the door. He closed the door and waited.

Sandra watched the smoke and the café's staff. When she saw a waitress hurry towards the kitchen, she walked to an emergency exit and shoved open the door. It automatically tripped a fire alarm.

At its sound, Burke touched two strands of the cable to the poles of a torch battery. The current set off an explosion that blew open the toilet wall and sent a rush of customers and staff alike fleeing for the exits. Burke rushed in first and leaned through the hole. The stairwell was a short drop below him. He held a ceramic globe in one hand and watched the door. When the first Scorpion stepped through, Burke hurled the globe at him. A thick cloud of smoke enveloped the man. Burke leapt towards the stairs and struck the Scorpion with a steel bar. The man staggered back. Mai jumped to the stairs behind Burke. Another Scorpion stormed through the smoke. He was huge, and slammed into Burke, knocking him against Mai. All three fell. Tanner leapt onto the man's back and met another Scorpion, then twisted away from a punch and wrestled his enemy to the floor.

The bull of a Scorpion that had felled Burke and Mai raised his fist to smash Burke's head when a scream ripped through the air. Ping jumped down to the stairs with her *nunchaku* swinging. She slung one end of the hardwood bar at the giant's head as her feet landed on his back. The blow glanced off the side of his temple, but it stunned the giant enough for Burke and Mai to get to their feet. They stepped over Tanner and rushed into the room beyond. Tanner freed himself from the Scorpion he had taken down and followed them. The four formed a square, back against back. There were three Scorpions in front of them and three behind, as the ones who had attacked them at the door followed them inside.

'Papa!' Ping shouted and almost rushed towards her father. Burke stopped her with a touch of his hand.

Ishido stood next to Koyanagi, scraping away patches of the old man's skin with fine sandpaper. He glanced at a Scorpion standing next to an open cabinet containing an array of vials.

The Scorpion who had been watching the café entrance had rushed downstairs when he heard the alarm. He stepped into the room, making four Scorpions at the entrance. None held weapons. Burke had his steel bar, Ping swished her *nunchaku*, Tanner gripped a *sai* and Mai held a throwing knife, with several more in her belt. Given their advantage in arms, Burke calculated their chances as good, until three more Scorpions stepped out from a hidden corner of the room and advanced towards them. They held quarter-staves and increased the number of Scorpions to ten, against four of Burke's team.

The Scorpion next to the cabinet grabbed a vial and flung it at Mai. She ducked and threw a knife into his abdomen. But the vial struck Tanner in the side of the head and burst. An acrid, blinding powder forced his eyes shut. Mai looked towards him and was also temporarily blinded. Her knife-throwing skill was now useless.

The big Scorpion rushed in but stopped short when Tanner swung the *sai* wildly and cut him across the face. The Scorpion who Tanner had wrestled to the ground dived low to take him down at the knees.

The other two who had stood behind them rushed Ping. The first raised his arm to block her *nunchaku*. The bones of his arm shattered, but the heel of his other hand was already driving towards her jaw. She staggered back into Burke as the hand slammed into her.

Ishido and another Scorpion moved cautiously towards Burke. With the defences at his back falling, they did not need to risk a direct attack against his steel bar.

Burke felt Ping falter. 'Attack or die,' he told himself and took one step towards the Scorpion next to Ishido. He leapt off his forward foot and kicked at his opponent's head. The man bobbed and evaded the kick, but left himself open to the bar. Burke struck his temple full-force. The man fell unconscious.

Ping retreated into the space behind her. She had to help better their odds. The flashing *nunchaku* swished over the head of the Scorpion in front of her, and the man ducked low enough for her to step on his shoulder and jump behind him. The room was built for extraordinary purposes, but by ordinary means. As in most rooms, the light switches were by the door. Ping reached them and turned them off. She spun away but stayed close enough to guard the switches. She heard someone come near and swung the *nunchaku* into flesh. 'The lights are out!' Ping alerted Mai and Tanner to their new advantage.

The reddish glow of light that had penetrated Mai's closed eyelids turned black, confirming the darkness. In a crouch, she slid silently out of her position, held a knife in a stabbing grip and listened. She heard Tanner struggling on the floor with two Scorpions. Something brushed her hair, and she sensed or heard someone pass by where she had just stood; not close enough to have touched her with his body, but it could have been a quarter-staff held horizontally. She measured the distance, moved behind him and crept forwards, her arm extended. When her hand touched his arse, she swung the knife up into his groin. The man gasped in pain and fell. Almost immediately, she felt another staff swish past her head. She somersaulted backwards, landing behind the attacker, and rolled to the side.

Burke heard the sound of Tanner's scuffling grow quieter. There were now four distinct voices among the fighters on the floor. One made a choking sound. It must be Tanner. In a low stance, he slid towards the noise. His foot made contact. He couldn't tell who he'd touched, but he assumed Tanner would be on the bottom. He slashed down with the bar and heard the 'thunk' of steel against bone. But he was not the only one drawn towards the sounds. A Scorpion's quarter-staff slammed into his upper arm, and Burke felt as though the arm had shattered, the power of the blow reverberating through his spine to his knees. He dropped as the staff swished past his head from the opposite direction. From the floor, Burke slung the bar again and judged by the sound and feel of the impact that he had struck an arm or leg. He heard a sharp gasp for air. The strike had most likely loosened the hold on Tanner's throat. An instant later, the quarter-staff slammed home, but not into Burke. He silently thanked his attacker for taking out his own ally. The noise of scuffling grew louder. Tanner was now one-on-one with a Scorpion. Burke again heard the sound of choking, but this time he doubted it came from his young friend.

Mai had backed into the table where Koyanagi was strapped. She felt along his body to the bonds and cut them. The old man rolled off the table in her direction and kissed her head. He was in the fight.

Like an anaconda, Tanner had worked his way towards the neck of the Scorpion who had helped hold him down while he was choked. He slipped his arm around the man's neck and squeezed off the blood flow through the carotid arteries. In seconds, his enemy was weakening, but he still made a noise, a noise that attracted a man with a quarter-staff. Tanner felt the tip of the 'weapon of weapons' smash into his side, cracking into his ribs. Air gushed out of his lungs, but still he tightened his grip on the Scorpion's neck. He felt the enemy in his grasp go limp just before a kick struck the back of his head, and he fell unconscious.

Ishido had every item in his workshop committed to memory. He knew the location of each rat, each spider and each vial of chemical substances. The cabinet was behind him, and he felt along its rim to the third row from the top, the seventh compartment from the left. The vial inside held magnesium and a catalyst to light it. He took it out, and quickly decided to throw it at the empty wall near the light switches. Ishido hurled the vial and it smashed against the wall, bursting and filling the room with a brilliant, eye-searing glare.

In the flash of light, Ping saw in front of her the Scorpion whose arm she had broken. He reacted first. His foot seemed to leap from the floor at the speed of thought and slam into her solar plexus. When she doubled over, the Scorpion punched his good arm into the side of her head. Ping slumped unconscious to the floor.

A bellow erupted from Koyanagi. He was naked and weakened from hours of abuse, but his youngest child had been assaulted. He strode towards the injured Scorpion, intent on finishing his daughter's work. Through the corner of his eyes, he sensed a quarter-staff slashing towards his head. He raised his hands and caught the wood in his palms, then quickly drew his hand to his shoulders, dissipating the power of the blow over distance. He raised his foot and stamped into the knee of the Scorpion. The man stumbled but remained standing, fighting for control of the weapon. Koyanagi ran his hands along the length of the staff to the enemy grip that held it. He wrested it away and struck the man who had wielded it on the crown of his head.

Mai's vision was gradually returning. She saw the blurred shape of the other staff-wielding Scorpion move towards Koyanagi, and threw a knife that just grazed the man's leg. She drew another knife as he turned towards her.

Burke started towards Mai's attacker, but was stopped by Ishido. The master torturer grabbed his injured arm just below the shoulder and twisted. His grip was steel. A white flash of pain seared Burke's mind, but his body continued to struggle. He raked his thumb across Ishido's eye and hooked his foot behind the Scorpion's knee. They both went down.

Mai threw another knife, this time sinking it into the muscle of the Scorpion's left side. The wound scarcely slowed him. Mai's vision was returning quickly. She drew two knives and crossed them in front of her to block the quarter-staff slashing towards her head. She stepped in and kicked her attacker in the groin. He stopped cold, but did not fall. In a fluid motion, Mai kicked her other foot into his chin. This time he went down, and Mai took his quarter-staff. She saw Koyanagi fighting two Scorpions and swung the staff at the head of the one nearest to her. His body crumpled.

Koyanagi now faced the Scorpion with the broken arm, the one who had knocked out his daughter. He snapped his fist into the bridge of the man's nose, then blocked a desperate counterpunch and hit the Scorpion in the throat, not hard enough to break the hyoid but enough to leave him helplessly gasping for air. Koyanagi quickly broke the elbow of the Scorpion's good arm. He had intended to inflict more injury but stopped at the sounds of thuds against the outer door.

Firemen responding to the alarm had not risked jumping through the hole in the toilet's wall. Instead, they had found the steel outer door and begun hacking at the hinges with fire axes.

Ishido wrested himself free from Burke, ran across the room and slid back a false wall panel. On the other side was a door. He looked once behind him then escaped.

'Will you be all right?' Burke asked Mai as he headed towards the door.

'I'll take care of them.' She pointed to his limp, swollen arm. 'You can't go after him. Another time, James.'

Burke's left arm dangled uselessly at his side. 'If I find

him, I won't need it.' He raised his right arm in an arc, breathed in the power of *chi* and rushed out.

Mai unshackled Natsuko, and helped Tanner to his feet. Koyanagi had lifted Ping in his arms. 'You need clothes,' she told him.

'I'll do it.' Tanner stripped the shirt and trousers off an unconscious Scorpion and gave them to the older man. 'What about her?' He nodded towards Natsuko, who was trying to cover herself with her hands.

'We'll make do. Let's go.' They all entered the tunnel and Mai pulled the false panel back into place as she heard the sound of the firemen breaking through the front entrance. Carefully, she closed the door and led them down a black corridor, into the unknown.

Eighteen

Hurried footsteps echoed through the tunnel. Burke followed as fast as he dared, his healthy arm extended in the dark. Ahead of him the sound grew dim, and came from the left. He gauged the distance and slowed before he reached a wall, then turned towards the sound, louder now. He wasn't gaining, but he was keeping pace, guided by the click-tap of leather on concrete. In the black maze, he turned again and again, wondering, fearing, if an ambush or booby-trap lay ahead. Suddenly, the floor seemed to drop away from under him. He almost fell as he stepped onto a steep decline, careening into a wall and slamming his damaged arm against concrete. Scarcely able to keep his balance, he stumbled downwards, deeper into the man-made cavern, until he was stopped by another wall.

He stood still and listened, but heard only silence. The sound of footsteps was gone. To his front and both sides was solid wall. He was at a dead end, a cul-de-sac. Ishido had either taken a turn off the main tunnel earlier, or was waiting in the dark behind him. The first one to move would give his position away, but it was a chance Burke had to take. He started back up the slope, feeling the walls for an opening, when the rumble of a train grew suddenly loud for one, two, three seconds, then dimmed. No light shone through, but the sound told him that somewhere above him a door had opened and closed quickly. He moved in the direction he thought it might be, but precious seconds passed before he found the door and pushed it open. He found himself in a storm drain.

Dim light filtered through grates overhead. Water dripped from the walls and ran fast along the floor. A splash sounded in the distance. Holding his injured arm against his side, Burke sprinted through the wet cavern, towards the sound of Ishido's footfalls. He sensed he was gaining ground but he could not be sure, as his own heart, lungs and pounding feet resounded in his ears. He could see now. There were no side paths for escape. His quarry was in front of him. Through pain and exhaustion, he pushed towards it.

A scraping of metal against ferro-concrete scratched through his mind. It came from a point just ahead. He ran to the next grate, stopped and listened, to hear only the sound of the next train coming. But the grate was askew, so Burke reached up and pushed it aside. He jumped to give himself momentum and grabbed the rim of the opening with his good hand. With one arm, he managed to pull himself shoulder-high and press the back of his head against the outer edge of the opening. He used his neck muscles to raise himself far enough to bring his elbows over the rim. A cascade of pain swept through him as he brought his body higher. His shoulders were on the level of the train tracks. He arched his back and pushed with his good arm to bring himself out of the pit.

A train rolled in front of him, easing to a stop to his left. Ishido would not have been able to run in the same direction as the train; he would have been crushed at the platform. Burke turned to his right and dashed along the tracks. There was no indication of the path Ishido had taken. Burke watched for side routes that would lead to escape, but found none. He pushed forwards as the grade of the subway train's track took an upward slope. He reached another platform. The light of a train lit the subway tunnel 100 metres or more in front of him. There was no sign of Ishido. He vaulted onto the platform, jumped the ticket barriers and ran up the nearest stairway to the street.

It was no more than a shadow at the corner of his vision, seeming to flit into the trees and shrubs of a park surrounding the Emperor's palace. The palace covered a vast area in midtown Tokyo, and at one time, its real-estate value had been estimated at the same level as the entire state of California. It was an absurdity of Japanese hubris, but still a lot of space for a desperate man to find cover. Burke ran towards the shadow, but the vision was gone. He breathed in slowly and deeply and listened with his sharpened sensations – to the paddle of swans' feet in the moats, to the ripple of water along the back of an imperial carp, to the rasping breath of a Scorpion. Burke focused on that sound, eleven o'clock from his position, and ran towards it. It was moving again, shifting direction to ten o'clock, nine o'clock. Burke gained ground, until he saw the fleeing shadow. There would be no escape now, for the Scorpion or for him.

Ishido must have sensed the inevitable. He turned and sneered at Burke's left arm, dangling limp at his side. When they closed to fighting distance, he circled towards Burke's weak side.

Burke followed the Scorpion with his eyes, calmed himself and opened his spirit to receive *chi*. He turned his body, keeping his injured arm towards Ishido, giving him a target he was not likely to refuse. The torturer sought out weakness as naturally as other men sought beauty or wealth. When Burke sensed Ishido was poised to attack, he shifted his strong side towards him. His enemy paused and circled again. Burke feigned weariness and let Ishido circle to his weak side, as he charged his being with the universal power.

Ishido sprang forwards and punched at Burke's head. It was only a feint that Burke easily evaded. The Scorpion's real target was the injured arm. He grabbed the limb and twisted, without realising the arm was merely bait.

Burke gripped Ishido's wrist and released the power into him. He held his grip as the Scorpion's mouth and eyes opened wide in shock, as he slumped to the ground, as his body quavered. Through sheer force of will, Burke made himself an empty vessel, then placed both hands on Ishido and breathed in, absorbing the Scorpion's foul spirit, melding it with the universal power. A cold, terrifying darkness filled him, a tempest of evil tearing at his soul, threatening to destroy his own humanity. Yet still he held it inside, letting it grow stronger. He stared into Ishido's eyes. In their reflection he saw himself fulfilling Ishido's ambition, becoming a malevolence possessing the ultimate power of *chi*. In those eyes, he saw a gleam brightening. He read Ishido's thoughts. Whether the Scorpion's body lived or died, his spirit was on the verge of conquest. Burke threw his head back. He saw the face of Master Wei and the smile of Ling-shau. With a shout that broke the clutch of Ishido's dark spirit, Burke sent the storm raging back into the Scorpion. He stood and watched Ishido's body writhe in the pain of his victims, in the cumulative horror wrought by the society of torturers. He backed away slowly, until he had enough distance to be able to turn and leave Ishido to an eternity of madness.

Nineteen

'You could have called!' Mai had rushed to the front door of the Excalibur when she heard Burke's voice on the intercom.

He was standing in the foyer with his arm bound in a sling. 'I did call, twice, from a private clinic. You weren't here.'

'I'm sorry, you're right. We got back only a little while ago.' Mai stepped back from the doorway. 'It took us a while to get through the tunnels. We stole clothes for Koyanagi, but Natsuko was a problem. Dan donated his undershirt, but that was about all we had: no knickers, no trousers, no skirt, no shoes. She got some admiring glances on the way here, I must say. Let's go to my office before any clients see you. You might scare them away.' She led Burke down the hall. 'Did you catch our man?'

'Yes.'

'And did you best him?'

'I'm here, aren't I?'

'All right, James, either you tell me what happened in detail or I toss you out on your ear.'

'There isn't much to tell, really. I followed him through the tunnel. There was only one logical path for him to take, so it wasn't difficult to keep up.' Burke paused.

'And –' Mai nipped his ear '– you found him, and you did what, James?'

'I gambled with *chi*, Mai. I'd never done that before. For an instant, I was afraid I'd lost. I let his soul into me at the same time as the power.'

'But you didn't lose.'

Burke shook his head. 'I sent it back, I think at the last possible moment, before it consumed me. He was laughing at me. I could feel it.'

'You sent what back?' Mai stroked his hair.

'I sent his own self back into his black soul, magnified by the horrors that he and the Scorpions have inflicted on their victims through the ages.' Burke buried his face in Mai's hair. 'I don't expect he'll recover from that, not ever.'

Mai grew solemn. 'Not that Scorpion, maybe, but others might come, right?'

'They probably will. The war isn't over, but the battle is. Let's just think about that for now. Are you all right?' Burke asked as Mai poured out two glasses of wine.

'Except for a scary period when I thought I might be blinded for life, I came through it well enough.'

'I saw you get hit with the powder, Tanner too.'

'Tanner got the worst of it, I expect.' Mai smiled and pointed to Burke's arm. 'Except for you, obviously. Ping has a sore jaw, a big bruise right here.' She pointed to the side of her head. 'Then there's Koyanagi. That old man's amazing. After half a day on the rack, he moved like a gazelle with the power of a five-hundred-pound gorilla out to rescue its young. He took out two of them.'

'I'm not surprised. As for my arm, the doctor said it's not so bad. There's a hairline fracture that doesn't go all the way through the bone. You were the star tonight, Mai. In terms of numbers, I think you beat everyone, and blind to boot.'

'We all got our share, didn't we? If Ping hadn't cut the lights, we might not be standing here talking to one another. There was an act of courage, skill and quick thinking.'

'It was that, wasn't it? Where are they?'

'Are you bored with me so soon?' Mai ran her fingers along Burke's arm and pressed his hand into her lower belly.

'Hardly.' Burke smiled. 'There's something about surviving combat, isn't there?' He pushed his hand lower, pressing against Mia's cleft. 'You can still taste that rush of adrenalin. There's a tingle in your being and you think you'll live forever, because you're alive now. The only reality of time is this instant. In the eternity of the moment, we do live forever, don't we? We beat them, Mai, this time. Life itself means victory, but we got a bonus. We thrashed some truly vile bastards.'

Mai smiled and nodded. 'That's the past, though, isn't it, James? Mustn't live there.' She kissed him, working her tongue into the warmth of his mouth and finding it dry with desire. Her hand cupped his loins. She felt him grow hard in her touch, and unzipped his trousers. 'Carpe diem, carpe this,' she said as she seized his steely rod.

Burke lifted his sling-bound arm. 'I'm afraid, Mai, that you will have to do most of the work.'

Mai flicked her tongue into his ear. 'Not a problem,' she whispered. Her breath was hot against him. 'Lie down.' She pulled off his trousers and briefs, delighted by the sight of his burgeoning cock. She opened his shirt and traced her mouth along the hard muscles of his chest and belly, nipping his flesh as she went. Skirting his shaft, Mai pushed her face against Burke's inner thigh and nuzzled his ball sac. Her tongue played with his balls and brought them into her mouth, warming them, teasing them, until she heard his sharp breaths and felt his hand on the back of her head, urging her higher. She pressed her soft lips along the sensitive underside of his shaft, then pushed her tongue into the tiny slit at the tip of his cock. Her lips wrapped round the tender glans, and she took him deep into her mouth, stroking his ready organ with her warm, wet tongue. When she sensed he was on the verge of release, she stopped.

'I'll do all the work, but you will not have all the pleasure, James.'

Mai stripped and straddled Burke, then took him inside her and rode his pole with languid strokes, lifting herself off him then sinking back down on his cock. The rhythm of her hips was a smooth pounding that quickly brought Burke to the edge of release. But she wasn't about to let him come yet; she relished controlling his urges too much. Her pace quickened until she saw a grimace tighten around his mouth and eyes, then withdrew to let his passion ebb, while she pressed her nub against his hip-bone, rocking back and forth until she brought herself to a shuddering orgasm. Come flowed onto Burke's skin as she slid along his thigh.

She pressed her lips against the underside of his shaft, teasing him again to a fevered need for release. She was a master at riding the razor's edge. Her fingers probed Burke's perineum and pushed into his arse, pressing against his prostate gland. Her mouth covering his prick, she delighted in his bucking hips as he thrust himself into her throat, his arse cheeks squeezing her fingers. At last she let his shaft have its will, sucking hard on the end as she bobbed her head furiously up and down. He gushed inside her, and she swallowed the hot seed that erupted from his loins. Her hand squeezed around his softening rod, milking the last of his flow into her mouth, then she lay down beside him, her thigh across his hips, and stroked his chest and belly.

'Well, love,' Mai whispered in Burke's ear. 'In a minute or two, would you like to go and see the gang?'

Mai and Burke dressed in *yukata* and went to the glass-walled room. He was greeted by a chorus of

'James!' Ping was the first to hug and kiss him, followed by Sandra and Natsuko. Tanner shook his hand and then embraced him. Koyanagi simply bowed.

'Well done,' Burke said. 'We have a victory to celebrate, but it might be short-lived. I have no idea what the Scorpions will do.'

'I expect you'd better leave that to me then, hadn't you?'

Everyone looked at Koyanagi.

'I think I might be able to put an end to this, but I'll need to use someone's phone.'

'How?' Mai's face scrunched up in doubt.

'If you give me a phone, I'll tell you after it's done.' Koyanagi was not used to having his word questioned.

'A minute.' Mai went back to her office and returned with a remote handset. 'Call anyone you want.'

Koyanagi smiled. 'When I finish, James, you might want to say hello to Master Wei.' As Koyanagi lapsed into Mandarin Chinese, only Ping and Burke could follow what he said. When he hung up, Ping's face glowed in admiration at the strength of her father. Burke bowed deeply in respect.

'We have an ally, if we need one,' Koyanagi said as he cupped his hand over the receiver. 'He has a network of friends, friends with extraordinary power, as James knows. For a brief time, Wei was once a Scorpion. He achieved an enlightenment and broke from them. In his own way, he has spent the rest of his life in atonement.' Koyanagi's mind peered through time to his own past, and his close brush with joining the Scorpions. It was a past he preferred not to speak of. 'Do you want to talk to him, James?'

Burke nodded. 'I would be most grateful.'

When Burke had finished speaking, he shook his head in admiration of both Wei and Koyanagi.

'It's done, then,' Koyanagi said. 'Master Wei will help us even if it means going to the Scorpions' nest.'

'If he can do that, why hasn't he taken them out before?' Tanner folded his arms across his chest.

Koyanagi wagged his head as a wry smile crossed his lips. 'It would not be easy, Mr Tanner. I said I hope we can end our problems. That is a very different matter from "taking them out", as you say. If that were our objective, I expect we would need more than Master Wei to carry it out.' Koyanagi nodded towards Burke and his battered arm. 'In any case, what would be gained by a victory? Even if all the Scorpions were to die, others would take over their work. It is an economic problem, you see. If there is demand, there will be supply. People with less skill would simply exercise harsher brutality. Who benefits? This way, if we can intimidate them with the threat of the master's power, we can exert some influence over the society. They might prefer to avoid a fight, even if they could win. Power unused can be stronger than power exerted. Do you follow me?'

Tanner nodded.

'Very good.' Koyanagi grinned and took Natsuko's hand. 'No one would object, then, if I eased this lady's strain in a very hot bath?'

'Let me guide you.' Mai smiled as she led the pair to the second floor.

'You'll do all right without me, I suppose,' said Burke. When no one objected, he nodded to the remaining trio and left.

Ping giggled and looked at Tanner. 'Did you see Sandra's tattoo?'

Sandra blushed and raised her foot so Tanner could see the image on its sole.

'What's this?' Tanner took her foot in his hands and kissed it. He ran his lips across her sole to her toes, pushed his tongue between them and sucked on them, each one in turn.

'I'm not much of a fighter, but we're the three musketeers, aren't we, Ping?'

'Nonsense! Of course you're a fighter. Without your smoke bombs, we would never have got inside, would we, Dan?' Ping kissed Sandra on the lips.

'That's right.' Tanner kissed Sandra and Ping in turn. 'I hope your father is right about Master Wei, Ping, but what if we do have to face the Scorpions again?'

'In that case, we'd better "make hay while the sun shines". Isn't that your American expression?'

'It's one of them.' Tanner pressed his lips against Ping's. As his tongue entered her mouth, he let his hand stray to Sandra's thigh. Spasms of lust stirred in his loins as she gripped his hand and pushed it between her legs. Tanner had experienced three-way sex before, with Natsuko and Reina. It had been thrilling in its wanton spontaneity, but this was a new, more profound encounter. This time he was with two women with whom he shared deep emotions. Ping was a hard warrior who had taught him how to survive battle in darkness. Sandra was a fighter in her own right, who had hidden her emotional desires behind a teasing façade, but she had come to trust him with her heart as well as her body. Two strong, sensuous women wanted him without jealousy or pretence.

Tanner turned to Sandra and kissed her mouth as Ping took his hand and pressed it to her breast. His rod grew stiff when Ping opened her blouse and guided his hand under her bra to the bare skin below, soft and supple. The pip at the apex of her mound was hard between his fingers. Someone unfastened his trousers, he didn't know who, and fingers probed his shaft and balls. He feared he would explode before he had satisfied even one of his lovers.

Sandra had stripped from the waist up and offered a firm, lush breast to Tanner's kiss. He sucked on her marvellous globe as Ping slid his trousers down and removed them. His prick throbbed as Ping's fingers pushed under his briefs and probed the flesh of his cock, balls and arse. He felt Sandra stiffen as he sucked harder at her nipple.

Tanner's passions swelled as Ping's finger pushed between his arse cheeks. He bit down on Sandra's sweet breast, feeling the fleshy mound push into his face as her back arched in response to his teasing teeth. He reached between her legs to find dew flowing from her crotch.

When Sandra pulled away, Ping pushed her small warrior's breast to Tanner's face. He unfastened her blouse and bra and removed them, his hips twitching all the while as Sandra's lips played along his shaft and nipped at its tip.

In the throes of passion, Tanner sat up and tore off his shirt, then removed the remaining clothes from Sandra and Ping. He pushed Sandra onto her back and buried his face in her quim, then rolled his hips to the side to give Ping access to his painfully hard staff. Spasms rippled through his belly as Ping's lips enfolded its tip.

Tanner pushed his tongue into Sandra's channel, tasting her rich oil. His face was wet with her spicy essence as she rolled her hips over, turning him onto his back. She switched positions to straddle his face, and he pushed his tongue between her lush bottom cheeks to taste her sap once more. Two pairs of lips played along his shaft, teasing its base and tip at the same time. A tongue pushed between his arse cheeks, as teeth nipped at his ball sac and inner thighs. Fingers, lips, tongues and teeth probed, teased, stroked and nipped at his flesh. He wrapped his arms around Sandra's hips and crushed her to him, craving all her tastes, his tongue seeking out the pink rosette closeted between her bottom cheeks. She squealed as his finger probed at its centre, and his lips moved along her cleft to her nub. He nipped it lightly until Sandra's hips gyrated in tight circles and her quiet mewing gave way to throaty moans.

Her breasts pressed against Tanner as contractions of ecstasy rolled through her belly, and her moans became an orgasmic growl. She turned and kissed Tanner's lips, wet with her own juices, her tongue probing his mouth and savouring their combined essence. Her hand reached for his staff and held it erect, and she looked into Ping's eyes, inviting her to take it inside her sheath.

The young warrior straddled Tanner's hips and slowly lowered herself onto the offered pole, until her nether lips rested on top of Sandra's hand.

Sandra followed Ping's rise and fall along Tanner's moist phallus, feeling her friend's inner labia push in and pull out. She shared the passions that welled between Tanner and Ping, and thrilled in their mutual pleasure, sucking on the tiny pips at Tanner's chest and caressing his balls as Ping rode his rod.

Ping bent forwards to kiss Tanner and Sandra in a three-way union. Her hips quickened as Sandra's finger pushed deep into the forbidden hole between her bottom cheeks.

Tanner's hand found Sandra's quim and pushed inside it, massaging her G-zone as his hips pushed upwards to meet Ping's driving thrusts. He arched his back and came with a guttural cry, but continued pounding inside Ping, sensing her need, as his white lava erupted from him and flowed out of Ping's hot channel. He pressed his thumb hard against her nub as he thrust again and again into her body, until her teeth bared in a grimace and her muscles stiffened in rapture.

Afterwards, the three musketeers lay entwined like puppies, enjoying the warmth of each others' bodies and friendship. Their eyes closed and the rise and fall of their chests slowed until they fell, one by one, into a gentle sleep.

Natsuko had certainly had more handsome men, but despite the youth and muscular strength of many of her lovers, none had the staying power of Koyanagi. None, equally, had his incredibly sensuous touch, which came only from experience, or his knowledge of the body. Nor had anyone been as tender, or cared so much for her needs. The young Adonises she had known had been more infatuated with their own beauty than with her, while the dapper middle-aged men she had known had been in love with their wealth. They had all used her as a prop to bolster their egos, and expected her to be grateful that she had been chosen for one night in a penthouse or a week in Paris, Rome or Madrid. She could tell from the structure of Koyanagi's face that he had never been handsome, even in his youth. In his long life, he had surely acquired money, but no more than he needed to provide a pastoral home for himself and Ping. Her encounter with Burke had been more intense than anything she had ever experienced before, but he had brought her terror as well as rapture. She feared him. Intuitively, she knew that men who evoked fear were weaker than those who earned trust.

Burke had sought the infinite power of *chi*, which Koyanagi had declined even though it had been offered to him. Surely the old warrior, who fought with his own power, had the stronger spirit. In the short time she had known him, she felt she had become a central figure in his life. The Scorpion who had said she meant nothing to him had been wrong. She realised Koyanagi did not need her to make his life full. She wasn't even sure he wanted her with the same passion that she felt when he touched her. However, there was no doubt in her mind that he cared for her deeply, without a desire to possess her. She found great comfort in that, and always enjoyed pleasing him. She was eager to do so now after Mai had left them alone in the bath.

All she wore was Tanner's undershirt. She crossed her arms in front of her and slowly pulled the shirt up past her mound, her slim waist and her modest firm breasts.

She smiled at the admiration and affection in Koyanagi's face as she removed from him the clothes they had stolen from the Scorpion.

'Let's burn those,' he said.

Natsuko wadded the clothes together and threw them into a corner. She sat on a small stool behind Koyanagi and washed his hair and back. He turned to face her and she ran a sponge over his chest, arms and legs, then used her bare hand to lave his phallus, sac and arse. She put the sponge into Koyanagi's outstretched hand and relaxed as he returned the favour by running the rough, soapy fibre over her body. The heat of the water as he splashed it over her pricked her skin, sensitised by his scrubbing. They entered the bath and sank into the water up to their chins, facing one another. Koyanagi's hands, pushing into nerve centres and axes in the flow of *chi*, evoked a calming relaxation at the same time as he stirred her sexual desire. She arched her back so her breasts jutted from the water, droplets running down from their pink crests. Her lean chest and belly also rose as she felt Koyanagi's strong hands along her back, lifting her, moving under the taut globes of her hips, pushing her mound out of the water. Pulses of erotic pleasure coursed through her loins as Koyanagi's face pressed between her thighs.

His broad tongue lapped against her nether lips. Playfully, he filled his mouth with water from the bath, pushed his lips to her gate and forced the liquid into her channel. He chuckled with pleasure then opened his mouth to receive the water again. It passed between them once, twice, three times. With each exchange its pure taste grew tangier with Natsuko's essence. Koyanagi spouted the water inside her again and pressed his thumb against her gate to stop its outflow, then filled his mouth from the bath and forced more liquid into her.

Her eyes and mouth widened as her channel filled. She drew in a breath to take as much as she could hold, and when she could bear it no longer let the mouth-to-quim douche spew out onto Koyanagi's face.

The old man laughed aloud as Natsuko's geyser washed over him. 'Look what you've done to me.' He stood and displayed his proud staff, hard as iron. 'You've a lot to atone for, girl.'

Natsuko gripped the hard phallus and kissed its tip. 'Then I guess I had better get on with it.' She took the rod into her mouth and sucked hard.

Koyanagi pulled away and stepped out of the bath. 'Let's go to bed.' He reached for her hand. 'You and I have had an extraordinary time, haven't we? This night, I think, will be long. It will be a very –' he held Natsuko's tender fingers around his engorged pole '– very long night, Natsuko.'

They walked naked to their bedroom and spread out the futon. Natsuko lay on her back and opened her tender thighs to Koyanagi, who entered her slowly. Scarcely had his shaft sunk to its hilt when the phone rang. Koyanagi answered.

Natsuko could not follow his conversation, in Mandarin Chinese. 'Who was it?' she asked when he had hung up.

'It was Master Wei, with another response to my query. He has contacted all his disciples, just in case. He also knows where the Scorpions keep their headquarters.'

Natsuko's forehead wrinkled.

Koyanagi kissed her. 'That isn't your worry. This, however, is your responsibility.' He placed Natsuko's hand on his rod before he pierced her again. He sank to her depths and pulled out as, in his mind, he heard Mozart's Flute Concerto No. 1 in G. The first movement, Allegro Maestoso, 8 minutes and 42 seconds; the second, Adagio Ma Non Troppo, 8 minutes and 41 seconds; the third movement, Rondo Tempo Di Minuetto, 7 minutes and 9 seconds. He flowed with the maestro's genius for 32 minutes and 8 seconds. A change was due. He heard jazz, Jimmy Smith pouring his spirit into an organ, playing 'The Sermon', twenty minutes long and full of sin. Music was a vital essence of Koyanagi's eclectic spirit. After jazz, he might top off with the Flamenco vigour of the traditional Carlos Montoya or the modern Vicente Amigo. There was much to choose from as he slid in and out of Natsuko's channel.

It would be a very long night indeed.

Twenty

Burke scowled as Koyanagi told him about his late-night phone call from Wei. 'Where's Bukhara?'

'About three hundred miles south-west of Tashkent.'

'Right, that would be somewhere in Central Asia, wouldn't it? Tajikistan?'

'That inhospitable swathe of rock and sand? Hardly. Uzbekistan is also a bit rocky and dusty, but quite a different experience, a cultural Mecca by contrast.'

'You've been there?'

Koyanagi nodded.

Burke sat silent as he thought over the proposition.

'You stirred up these poisonous bugs,' said Koyanagi, 'but you didn't mean to. We aren't planning to invade them, just bring them a message. You don't have to go.'

Burke looked up at Koyanagi. 'I'd rather not go, to be honest. It sounds too dangerous to me. In any case, I'd like to know what the plan is before we set out.'

'The way I understand it,' Koyanagi said, grinning, 'we walk into their headquarters with Master Wei and ask them to leave us alone.'

Burke shook his head. 'I was hoping for more detail. Besides we can't be sure they'll bother us again. Taking the fight further might just make some people who didn't really care about what we did angry. Maybe Ishido wasn't such a popular guy.'

‘Think it over. If you still don’t want to go, then don’t, but remember, Wei said he is willing to take us to the heart of their organisation. He’s the only one who can do it. We wouldn’t be going to fight, only to let them know that *if* they continue to harass any of Wei’s disciples, they will have a war on their hands. Before you went after Ishido, you felt the safest course was action. I believe that’s how Master Wei feels now: not to attack, but to show strength. If the Scorpions sense weakness, they might try to go after every disciple of his they can track down.’

‘Let me think for a while. I want to talk it over with Mai as well.’

‘She can’t go, James. Only those who know Master Wei.’

‘I wouldn’t allow it anyway. I only want her advice.’

‘Let me talk to her. I believe I know more about Wei and what he’s capable of than you do. Even though he’s taken you further in training, I’ve known him from an earlier time. While I’m at it, why don’t you visit Natsuko? Do you know she is afraid of you?’

Burke looked away and frowned. ‘I needed information quickly.’

‘Um hmm.’ Koyanagi crossed his arms over his chest. ‘I understand, but I think you might try to atone for that session you had with her, anyway. She’s been handled by some rough hands in her life, but yours were the worst.’

‘I’m not sure what I can do to make her feel any differently. I know from experience that the memory of a session like that remains strong.’

‘I said your hands were the worst.’ The old man leaned forwards and patted Burke’s arm. ‘I expect they were also the best. You’ll find a way.’

‘I’ve been here nearly a week, and I still haven’t seen the main room that Sandra keeps telling me about.’ Ping scrunched her nose in an exaggerated pout.

Tanner waved off her disappointment. 'Without Mai orchestrating the shows, I doubt there's much to see. When she's ready, I expect she'll come up with a doozy to celebrate our victory.'

'I just want to see the room. Are there really ropes and chains in there?'

'There certainly are. If that's all you want to see, I can take you now. You'd better wait until Mai says it's OK before you go at night though.' He patted Sandra's rump. 'Are you coming?'

'Un-uh, I'm going to lie in until noon. If I fall asleep, wake me for lunch.'

Tanner gave Ping a tour of the stage and showed her the pulleys and rafters above it. 'If you have an idea for a show, Mai might let you act it out. Sandra did the dance of Salome. Do you know the story?'

'Sure.' Ping slid her finger across her throat. 'John the Baptist, right?'

Tanner winced at the memory of Sandra's ridicule. 'Yeah, that's right. Let's go back.'

'Do you mind if I stay a while? I want to look around some more. I might get an idea for an act. Sounds fun.' Ping found a thick rope hanging from an overhead beam and secured to the wall. She freed it and climbed up. The beams were wide and provided good footing for daring stunts. She pulled herself onto one beam and then leapt to another before grabbing a rope and swinging to the ground like a monkey on a vine.

When she alighted, a young man she hadn't seen watching applauded her performance.

'Bravo! You must do a show for us.'

Ping blushed. 'I didn't think anyone was here. Are you a host?'

The man bowed and gestured towards another man, who smiled and stepped towards her. 'You have very strong arms,' he said, 'especially for a woman.' He reached out as though to feel her muscles, but Ping stepped back.

'Isn't it early for the hosts to be here?'

The man who had applauded smiled gently. 'The early cock bird, as they say, catches the young hen.'

Ping's eyes widened in fear as they sprang upon her. One pinned her arms down as the other pressed a damp cloth over her mouth and nose. She wanted to fight and shout, but before she had drawn a full breath she was unconscious.

Mai served tea and sat next to Koyanagi on the sofa in her office. 'I wouldn't try to stop James, if he decides to go. Though we've never met, from what I know of Wei, he would not undertake anything rashly. Besides, if he's the man who taught James –' she leaned her shoulder against the old man and squeezed his thigh '– and you, Koyanagi-san, well . . .' She raised her eyebrows and cocked her head to the side.

Koyanagi covered Mai's hand with his own. 'Someday, I want to hear your story. How did you learn to handle the knives? That's an old art.'

Mai held her lips close to Koyanagi's ear. 'I know many ancient skills. Would you like to hear my story now?'

'Perhaps when there is more time. Burke is making up with Natsuko. I asked him to.' The rasp in Koyanagi's voice grew huskier. 'I expect he will be back soon.'

'He has a lot to make up for, doesn't he?' Mai pushed her hand up Koyanagi's leg. 'He'll probably take a while.'

'Unn.' Koyanagi pressed his thumb into the inside of Mai's thigh, just above her knee, and stimulated the flow of *chi* on a physical level.

A tingle raced through Mai's loins and spine. 'That was nice. You know a few ancient arts yourself.'

'That's true, but when I learned them, they were new.' Koyanagi chuckled. 'I'm an ancient man.'

'Who fights like a young tiger.' Mai was not one to tease for long. She straddled Koyanagi's lap, facing him.

'Try another *tsubo*. I want to know your technique.' Mai felt her channel moisten as Koyanagi pressed his fingers to the back of her neck and her shoulders. She leaned forwards, her cheek against his as he worked his way down her spine. His hands burrowed under her skirt then pushed it up as he began kneading her taut bottom.

'I believe this technique is even older,' Koyanagi said as he reached down and brushed his fingers lightly along the inside of Mai's thighs.

She nipped his shoulder with her teeth as his hand slipped inside her knickers and pushed into her cleft. Her hands went to his shirt and pulled it over his head. Never had she felt musculature like that of the old man's chest and shoulders. The finely defined striations of sinew were as tough as oak. She unfastened his trousers and pushed them down his hard belly, exposing his even harder rod. Mai removed her own clothes and sat astride him, taking his staff into her. She was already stimulated to the edge of ecstasy by the novelty of this encounter, revelling in the passion of this warrior who had driven himself to ageless power. Her hips slapped against him in a quick rhythm.

She gasped at the ease with which Koyanagi gripped her shoulders and threw her to her back. She wrapped her legs around his hips as he pierced her.

'Faster!' In only seconds, tremors of pre-orgasm wracked Mai's body. She pulled away, mirroring his movements. His cock withdrew completely and re-entered her as she bucked her hips to meet him, hungry for the full length of his shaft, sliding in and out of her now at a frenzied pace. 'Harder!' She felt as though her body would be torn asunder by his ravishing thrusts. An orgasmic rapture charged through her, but she continued pounding against him, craving more. She bit into the hard muscle of his shoulder and sucked the sweat that oozed from his skin. The ages of his wars, his struggles, his victories and his power surged through his loins into hers. Her back arched, and a groan rumbled out of her as Koyanagi erupted with a final savage plunge of his phallus.

They moved together slowly. Koyanagi's cream ebbed to drops, then nothing. He withdrew and kissed Mai's mouth for the first time, then pressed his lips to her eyelids and the tip of her nose.

'You're a strong woman, Mai.'

She merely shook her head, took his head in her hands and kissed him back.

Burke had allowed Natsuko to shackle his wrists and ankles to a rack. 'Whale away, Natsuko.' He nodded to a quirt she held loosely in her hand. 'Purge the demons I inflicted on you. Your tormentor becomes your whipping boy. Even the score so you will neither fear me nor hate me. Don't let me poison your spirit. Get it out.'

Natsuko did fear him, but she didn't hate him. She understood why he had used the mental torture on her, yet still fear eroded her spirit.

Burke braced himself for the lash that didn't fall. He looked over his shoulder. 'Do it!' he snarled.

She pictured Koyanagi in her mind. He had made her feel safe and stronger than she really was. He was here. His spirit would protect her. Her arm swirled the quirt in the air and slashed it into Burke's arse. Despite her reluctance to inflict pain, she felt empowered at the cringe on Burke's face, the jerk of his body as the quirt struck home.

She felt good.

Pleased with herself, she struck again and again. Her eyes widened at the sight of the red welts scourged on Burke's muscular cheeks. She gripped the quirt in both hands and swung with all the power of her hips and shoulders. The smack of the quirt rent the air and left an angry red streak across his back. She put down the quirt and took up a cat-o'-nine-tails. A shout erupted from her as she whipped the cat across his flesh. Burke's back arching, his head tossing, his groan filling her ears, all thrilled her with her own power. She slashed at his sides and felt a liquid ooze from her channel and trickle down her leg. Her nostrils flared as she paused to examine her work. Burke's head hung down. He breathed in gasps. She was ready to face her demon.

Natsuko put slack in the chains holding Burke's wrists. 'Kneel.'

Burke sank to his knees.

She stepped in front of him, looked down and saw that his shaft was nearly erect. That state could be enhanced. The ball of her foot teased his pole until he was as hard as ironwood. She kicked it lightly and watched his stiff phallus wobble from side to side like a compass point.

'Look at me,' she demanded. Burke's eyes rose to her face. Natsuko unfastened her skirt, pushed it down her legs and kicked it away. Her thumbs hooked inside her knickers and pulled them down. 'Lick.' She thrust her mound to Burke's face and her eyes closed as she enjoyed the feel of his tongue lapping at her sweat and the effluence of her loins. Her hands gripped his hair and pushed his face harder against her. The ridge of his nose pressed against her nub, opening her cleft in front of his probing tongue.

She pushed down on his shoulders so that his arse sank to rest on his heels. She turned her back to him and fell to her hands and knees, her hips thrust towards his face. 'Kiss me.'

Burke put his mouth to her nether lips.

'Lick me.'

Burke lapped her oily labia and continued upwards to the pearl hidden within her slit.

She reached between his legs, gripped his shaft and lowered her hips to his, oiling his rod in her juices, but she didn't guide him into the channel to her womb. Instead she pushed his tender tip to the painfully tight pucker between her cheeks. She eased herself against him, pushing back inch by inch until the full length of his phallus had penetrated her. Her mouth opened to ease the entry. 'Do it!' she ordered, looking back into Burke's eyes and holding her hips rigid as he slid slowly in and out of her.

His pace quickened, lust surging through his groin.

Natsuko's head dropped and wagged from side to side. In moments, she felt Burke gush inside her. She pulled away and rested until the spasms of her inner and outer sphincters had ebbed away. When she was ready, she turned and released Burke from his chains. She had tamed her demon. When he stood, she clasped her arms around his neck and kissed him.

'Not so scary now?' he asked.

She smiled and shook her head.

'Let's go and see Mai.'

Mai and Koyanagi had just showered and were wrapped in towels.

'Did you purge the dragon?' Mai asked Natsuko, but it was Burke who answered.

'I believe she did.' He took off his shirt and showed his back. 'I could use some of your lotions.'

Mai clapped her hands. 'Well done, Natsuko.'

A blush tinged Natsuko's cheeks. 'I hadn't expected ...'

'Expected what?' Koyanagi held out his hand.

Natsuko stepped towards him and brought his fingers to her lips. 'I hadn't expected to ...' Her blush deepened.

'Enjoy it?' Koyanagi smiled gently. 'Of course you would. I imagine James did as well.' He looked at Burke, who winked and grinned back. 'The urges to dominate and to submit are two sides of a coin spinning in our souls. It falls heads; it falls tails. Which way it lands depends on a mood, a circumstance.'

Natsuko frowned. 'Not with us, you and me. You make me feel safe. You protect me.'

'The stronger protect the weaker. Isn't that a type of dominance? At my age, every day that I still have my strength is a blessing. If I became feeble, would you care for me?'

She turned his hand and kissed his palm. 'Of course.'

'At that time I would gladly submit to your gentle dominance. There is never equality in a relationship between people who in some way want to share a part of their lives. There is only balance in submission and control. What happened after you spent your wrath on Master Burke?'

Natsuko's face grew crimson.

Koyanagi pulled her to sit beside him. He caressed her hair. 'I'll be feeble any day now. Are you sure about what you said? There are witnesses.'

She nuzzled his ear and whispered, 'Yes, I'm sure.'

A knock stopped Koyanagi's response.

Burke opened the door for Tanner and Sandra.

'Has anyone seen Ping?'

'I thought she was with you.' A scowl crossed Mai's face.

'She wanted to see the main room, so I showed her and left her there. She said she wanted to explore, but she didn't come back for a long time. I went looking. She wasn't there.'

'Go to the top floor, Mr Tanner,' Mai ordered. 'Work your way down. Don't miss an inch. James, you start here and work up. Sandra, come with me.' Mai led the way to the main room.

Koyanagi's face was grim. 'I'm going with James.'

There was no sign of Ping in the main room, but when Sandra looked along the bar, she gave a terrified gasp. Her hand trembled as she pointed.

Mai's lips curled down in disgust. On the bar lay a patch of human skin with a scorpion tattoo.

'We got tattoos, Ping and Dan and I.' Sandra's voice quavered.

'Where?'

Sandra showed Mai the sole of her foot.

'The design is different, and this patch didn't come from the bottom of a foot. Look at the hair on it. Ask everyone to come here when they've finished checking all the rooms.'

Mai was handling the skin with a pair of chopsticks when the group filed in.

'The "hidden" third-floor door was open,' Burke said.

'I'd like to know how they found it.' Mai's face grew red in anger. 'From the outside it looks like part of the wall. There was no warning. They must have disabled the alarm system. How did they do that? How did they know the layout of rooms?'

'They might have bribed a bureaucrat. The building plans have to be on file somewhere. This is their modus operandi, isn't it? Study a location and strike where they see weakness. Or at least where they think they see weakness. When they tried it with Koyanagi-san, they got a surprise. We relied too much on technology. We thought we had won, at least for a while. They got us with our pants down, didn't they?' Burke took the chopsticks from Mai and looked at the tattoo.

Koyanagi was not as squeamish. He snatched away the patch of skin with his bare hand. 'This is probably from one of the men who came after Natsuko and me. Two of the three didn't survive. I need to use your phone.'

'Wei?' Burke asked.

Koyanagi nodded.

'There is no way to know where they've taken Ping, but if we strike at the head of the Scorpions, I think we can find out. Tell Master Wei I'm going with you.'

Twenty-one

The dying days of summer in Japan were the beginning of two months of temperate weather on the steppes of central Asia, seared by scorching heat in summer and cursed by numbing cold in winter. Howling winds and dust storms announced each change of season. It was here at the core of the massive continent that monsoons were born, the great winds that brought flooding rain and choking drought to the lands that lay along the Pacific and Indian oceans. The people of those areas lived at the mercy of the wind, but seldom did the wind show any mercy. It was, instead, a torture of dust or deluge.

The birthplace of the monsoon was the home of the Scorpions.

Wei accepted few disciples, but many of those he chose went on to become men and women of power. Among his followers was a woman from India who had great influence with the Uzbekistan ambassador to Tokyo. Oleg Gabidova expedited visas for Koyanagi and Burke. Seven hours later they were on an ANA flight to Seoul. They changed planes for the leg to Tashkent and there changed again for Bukhara, a pearl of a city on the ancient Silk Road to China.

Wei was waiting for them at the Lyabi House Hotel, in the old-town section of Bukhara. Despite the perilous nature of their meeting, they were each warmed by the reunion. Wei heartily embraced Koyanagi, and gripped Burke's shoulder in greeting. 'What have you got us into, James?' He smiled when he spoke.

Burke opened his mouth, but no words came. He was grateful when Wei raised his hand to his face to indicate that none were necessary.

'It isn't your doing,' Wei said. 'This is my fate, and it has been too long in coming. After the Great War ended in 1945, I lost contact with my few *qi gong* disciples. I had not yet discovered the ultimate way. For the next four years of China's civil war, both the Nationalists and the Communists used the Scorpions. What was the point of fighting, then, if evil was on both sides? I retreated into the countryside. It took me a long time to understand that my fight was personal. Your actions have taught me that, James. I was once one of them. And now –' he gestured towards Koyanagi '– it is very personal indeed.'

'What do we do?' Burke asked.

'First, I need a private talk with Koyanagi-san. If we agree on tactics, I'll explain the plan. In the meantime, why don't you go to this room?' He handed Burke a slip of paper. 'There's someone there you might want to see.'

Although Burke didn't like being left out of the planning session, there was little he could do but respect Master Wei's decision. He went to the room number Wei had given him and knocked on the door.

'I've been waiting for you, James.' A Chinese woman opened the door and stood back to invite Burke inside. She wore a loose tunic that fell to mid-thigh. Her legs were bare.

'Ling-shau!' Burke lost his normally stoic demeanour at the sight of his first mentor in the way of *chi*. He was hit by a rush of memories of the summer night when he'd had his first experience with electricity and then his first orgasms through *chi*. He stepped into the room and held Ling-shau in a tight embrace. At her touch to the back of his neck, he felt tremors course through his body. He grew hard as he returned the favour. A sharp gust of her breath struck his ear, and he felt her belly flex in waves of passion. Burke reached under her tunic to test his effect on this *chi* master. She wore nothing underneath and her sparsely furred cleft was already wet, with come trickling down her thighs. Her nether lips made a small wet gateway to her tight channel, already contracting around Burke's probing finger.

'Better than a handshake.' He smiled. 'I wasn't sure I would ever see you again.'

'I don't know how much time we have.' She unfastened his trousers and pulled off his shirt.

Burke loosened the sash that held her tunic. Her light-beige skin was still flawlessly smooth and her body trim and firm, except for the soft breasts that just filled Burke's hand. He kissed her neck and sucked on the pale-brown tips of her cushiony mounds before lifting her up. No sooner had he laid her on the bed than she sat up.

'I'm still your senior, James.' Ling-shau took Burke's cock in her mouth briefly before pushing him onto the bed and kneeling beside him to feast on his erect pole. Between her legs, his hand teased tremors of delight from her loins, then lifted her hips high. She opened her legs as she was lowered to straddle Burke's face. All the while, she sucked and nipped at his iron staff. As she took his rod deep into her throat, she thrilled at the sensation of Burke's tongue pushing into the button between her silky, smooth cheeks. She pushed back to drive him deeper inside, and Burke's obliging probe forced its way past her outer sphincter as his fingers stimulated her oiled nub and slid into her taut liquid channel, massaging her core.

The ancient ways of woman and man could still incite a *chi* master to electric passions. Fires of ecstasy burned through her body at the physical entry of Burke's tongue and fingers. She turned to kiss his mouth, pressing her tongue against his.

She reached for his staff and pressed its head against her narrow gate. The entry of that massive pole into her tight but pliant body forced a grimace across her face, but she plunged herself against him. Her hips lifted and fell as her channel expanded to accommodate Burke's length and width. He was big, almost too big for Ling-shau, who had a moment of fear that he would sunder her. But still she craved him. Her eyes glowed in lust as she stared into his face and plunged her cunt against his glorious cock. In minutes, she had milked him dry, and eased herself off his phallus. Both of them lay back, panting in rapture.

'There are seven of us, plus Koyanagi. That makes eight, a lucky number.'

'Who is "us"?'

'Disciples of Master Wei who have gone to the ultimate level.'

Burke's mouth curved in a thin smile. His eyes were grim. 'Should be quite a show. Still, I wouldn't mind going in with a few more than eight.'

'That's everyone. The master takes only one disciple at a time. The training is long and not everyone succeeds. If we fail here, it's the end of our Tao.'

Burke caressed Ling-shau's silken black hair. 'Chances are, all we'll have to do is keep out of Koyanagi's way. I think he could defeat an army to either save or avenge Ping. I know only you and Master Wei. Who are the others?'

'I'll tell you only their fighting names. It will be easier to remember. The master's first disciple is named for a fantastical beast that you would call Griffin. He is Chinese and even older than Master Wei. There is Badger, a Chinese man, and a Nepalese Gurkha called Cloud.' Ling-shau traced her finger along Burke's lips. 'You will like Mongoose from the northern Indian city of Jaipur. She is very beautiful.'

'And there is you,' Burke said, 'the Raven. The most clever of birds.'

'And you, Jaguar, mystical and powerful.'

Her fingers wrapped around Burke's staff and had just coaxed it to life again when there was a knock at the door.

It was Badger. He was a rectangular block of brawn, medium height but wide across the torso. His thighs had nearly the girth of Burke's waist. He nodded to Burke and addressed Ling-shau. 'Master Wei is ready.'

Badger led them to a small meeting room. Bright tapestries hung from the walls, and straight-back chairs were arranged around a table with a mosaic inlay of tiles. The five others had already arrived.

Griffin was tall and lean. He had a high forehead and long hair that gave him an ascetic appearance. Despite his age, his face was scarcely lined. Cloud, the Gurkha, seemed almost fragile with his short, wiry frame. However, his easygoing manner belied the confidence of a giant. Mongoose had exquisite beauty and an aloof aura that challenged a man's desire for her body. Her skin was pale, her eyes black coals shimmering on the edge of fire. She captured Burke in their gleam. Her tunic opened to show a prodigious cleavage, her trousers hugging the slight protrusion of her lower belly, her mound and her firm thighs.

Heat welled within Burke, and was clearly sensed by Mongoose. She smiled and narrowed her eyes. Burke bowed in reply.

Wei called the assembled warriors to attention. 'We have a strategy.' He looked at Koyanagi, who nodded.

Koyanagi's eyes were narrow, grim and determined. For him, the strategy was quite simple.

'I go first. You follow.'

The old man in search of his daughter strode alone across the desolate plains just beyond Bukhara. He walked towards a complex of buildings that he knew to be a nest of bugs with stings in their tails. The edifices were aeons old, built of stone and clay bricks that over the centuries had survived searing heat and numbing cold. They had been built to last as noble testament to ancient industry. The main building stood before him, majestic, certainly, but its majesty was nothing compared to Koyanagi's rage over Ping's fate.

In his peripheral vision, he sensed a furtive figure flitting towards the main building. He paid no heed as he walked with the focus of a wild boar to the door and flung it open. He was in a cavernous hall. The ceilings were three metres high, arched and inlaid with tile mosaic. Great tapestries illustrating epic tales of the Scorpions' history hung from the walls. There were secrets here that demanded the death of outsiders who learned them.

Koyanagi sneered and walked to the centre of the room. 'Ping!' His deep, rasping voice resounded through the hall.

'Papa!' Ping's cry echoed from a far room. Its shrill timbre chilled Koyanagi's soul. He sensed fear in the heart of his child. He walked towards the source of the sound and threw open a door. The way before him was a dark narrow hall. From within he heard a fearsome growl. Wisdom tempered his rage, and he stepped back into the light.

A great hound advanced towards him from the darkness. It stood as high as Koyanagi's shoulder. Slather dripped from its maw as threats rumbled from its belly. Koyanagi crouched slightly at the knees, his arms hanging loose at his sides. He committed his body to nothing but potential for movement. He would let the hound strike, then he would counter.

To the massive hound, Koyanagi was a meal, a fawn frozen in fear. It sprang at his throat, jaws agape, fangs flashing. Koyanagi dived forwards and rolled under the attack. He was back on his feet in a second and spun around as the hound recovered for another go. The animal was intelligent and would not repeat its mistake. It crouched low, snapping at Koyanagi's limbs.

The old man aimed a kick at the hound's throat, but the beast evaded the blow with astonishing speed. It realised its reflexes were its advantage, and moved in cautiously. Koyanagi aimed a punch at its muzzle, then tried to grab its ear. The hound slipped away easily at each attack, gauging its opportunity. It saw an opening and snapped Koyanagi's knee in its jaws, then loosened its grip and bit into his thigh. The next move would take the ravaging teeth into Koyanagi's groin. The old man forced his hand into the animal's maw and pushed back. He felt the hound bite down with razor teeth and thousands of pounds of pressure. Bones in Koyanagi's hand snapped, yet still he fought back. He wrapped his legs around the hound's midsection and squeezed, cutting into the animal's body with a scissor hold, squirming and wrestling the hound onto its back. If the animal had the experience of a human warrior, it might have used its weight and strength to right itself, but it did not. Instead it only bit harder, and thrashed its head and legs. As it did so, Koyanagi drew back his free hand and slammed his fist into the beast's throat, again and again, until the bones of its neck were crushed.

Koyanagi withdrew his mangled hand from the animal's teeth and stood. Scorpions of the human kind seemed to materialise from the walls. He was surrounded. They closed in around him.

'You've killed my pet.' A man, more than a head taller than Koyanagi, strode towards him. He stopped just beyond a distance that would allow immediate attack, as though the giant feared the ancient man with a maimed hand. 'I expect you'll have to be punished for that.'

'Where is Ping?'

'What is that, the sound of a bell? A small young bell?'

'My daughter!' A terrible rasping sound emerged from Koyanagi's throat as he turned, counting Scorpions. There were 21. 'Ping!' He heard only echoes. There was no repeat of the earlier cry for 'Papa'.

'I don't think she can hear you now, Koyanagi.' The giant folded his arms across his massive chest. 'Before we came to greet you, we placed her in a special room. We've already finished a physical examination. We were quite thorough. I'd have to say there is nothing, nothing at all that we do not know about her most lovely body. We, that is, all of us here –' the giant swept his arm in an arc to indicate the assembled Scorpions '– have participated in the, um, examination.' He leered down at Koyanagi. 'Her endurance would have made you very, very proud.'

Koyanagi felt his blood rush through his body, reddening his face. 'Anger is the first step to defeat.' He repeated that mantra in his mind until it took hold, and his cold need for revenge quelled the rage in his breast. His left hand was destroyed, but he still had weapons – and allies.

'I think we ought to examine her again under your supervision, of course. After that, we'll see to your –' the giant sniggered '– to your punishment.'

'Perhaps not.' Wei reached out and touched the base of a Scorpion's spine. The Raven, Ling-shau, and Mongoose also touched men they were near. While the Scorpions had closed in, focused on Koyanagi, Wei and the others had entered the great room and moved to the periphery of the group.

The effect of *chi* was not instant. Scorpions rushed to protect their allies. Burke met the first and, with an aikido twist, redirected his enemy's momentum back into the throng behind him. Scorpions stumbled over each other. Cloud leapt high and kneed an adversary in the head. His victim fell unconscious. With a kick, Griffin swept the leg from under a man attacking him. He spun and swept again, his long limbs whirling like the blades of a windmill. Badger punched with two fists at once to the head and solar plexus of a Scorpion, driving him back, then ploughed forwards on pile-driver legs.

The giant in front of Koyanagi looked towards the attack. The old man took advantage of the distraction by turning, stepping in low and thrusting a back kick waist-high. The giant shifted his posture at the last instant and caught the blow in the thick muscle of his side. He retreated from the force but was unharmed as he had tensed against the impact. At the sound of their master's grunt, the standing Scorpions halted. Except for the man Cloud had knocked out, the fallen men recovered and formed a wall between the invaders and their master. They watched as the three Scorpions under the power of Wei, Ling-shau and Mongoose writhed to the floor in torment.

The Scorpions knew then that the legends they had thought myth were true. Their adversaries had extraordinary powers, but then so too did the Scorpions. Unseen, unheard, another twenty men entered the great room. Their numbers now were 37 against 7, plus Koyanagi, a cripple after his fight with the hound.

Koyanagi was isolated. Burke saw the danger. He glanced at Cloud and Badger, then flashed a fist into the face of the Scorpion nearest to him. The adversary fell unconscious. A series of kicks and punches brought him to Koyanagi. He glared into the giant's eyes as he gripped the old man's collar and dragged him backwards. Cloud and Badger guarded his flanks. Soon the old man was within a ring of the *chi* masters.

'Attack!' The giant bellowed an order to his followers. As they advanced on the ring, he spun away and strode towards a far door.

'Get Ping.' Koyanagi gripped Burke's shoulder. 'Go after him.'

Wei pulled Burke into the centre of the ring. 'Do what he says. We will give you an opening, but I don't know how long we can hold.'

The *chi* masters stood shoulder to shoulder, their power flowing from one to another. The air about them was charged, as though electricity danced in the ether. In a great shout of unison, the six released a *kiai* that stunned the attackers where they stood. Burke dived between the legs of the Griffin. The twenty Scorpions who had joined the fray late carried weapons. Burke paused to snatch away seven of them from the momentarily stunned adversaries, and tossed them to Koyanagi.

'Hurry!' the old man snarled as he caught staves, steel bars and scythes.

Burke grabbed a short staff for himself and slammed it into two prone Scorpions as he rushed towards the far door. Before it closed behind him, he felt the electricity dying in the air and heard the sound of wood and metal slamming against human flesh and bone.

The way before him was a dark silent hall. He rushed along it, brushing his hand against one wall, feeling for doors and crossways. There were none. The hall ended, blocked by a bolted gateway. Burke spun and kicked his heel into the thick wood. It splintered on impact. He whirled again and the door flew open. Three Scorpions stood before him. Burke flashed the point of the short staff into the throat of the man closest to him. At the same instant, he whirled and swept a kick into the head of the man to his right. One Scorpion remained. Burke snapped a front kick into his groin and slapped the short staff into his collar-bone, breaking it. The Scorpion stumbled to his knees. Burke breathed in the power of *chi* and inflicted more pain than the torturer could have delivered in a lifetime.

'Where?'

The Scorpion's eyes rolled in his head.

Burke eased the pressure. 'Where is she?'

Saliva frothed from the Scorpion's mouth like foam in the muzzle of an overworked steed. 'To Muynak.'

'Where is Muynak?'

'Aral Sea . . .' The Scorpion struggled against the pain to speak. 'Fishing port . . . salt desert . . . sea dying.'

Burke squinted in incomprehension.

'Ask . . . anyone.' The veins of the Scorpion's face and neck were fat worms throbbing under his skin.

Burke let go and escaped from the building. He ran to the hotel and demanded a car. He wanted it now, not in the standard of Bukhara time, but in the time of Tokyo, where office clerks trotted from their desks to the copy machine; old men, weeks from retirement, ran to catch trains that left platforms every five minutes; and 'office ladies' jabbed 'close-door' buttons on elevators to save seconds. He snarled. He wanted the car yesterday. He pressed cash into the hand of the concierge. A car arrived quickly. Its driver was young, and spoke English. He was hungry for a fare, but Muynak was far, 200 kilometres away. It was a hard trip and costly. Burke flashed a handful of 10,000-yen notes and shoved them into the man's shirt pocket. It was hard currency equivalent to months of the driver's normal earnings.

Burke brushed past him, striding towards the hotel door, desperate to make up the time he had already lost.

'Do you have a bag, sir?' the driver asked.

There was no reply. Burke stood silently dismayed as he looked at the car. Rust pockmarked the body. A crack ran along the windscreen. The Scorpion had about a 30-minute head start, and he would be driving a fast car. He looked back at the driver, who shrugged.

'Just get me there,' Burke snarled.

* * *

The late-afternoon sun was still brilliant in the autumn sky. Its angle was low, its light inescapable, as it dispersed in haze across the horizon. Burke shut his eyes. They'd travelled for hours over rutted roads in a car with bad suspension. He felt the pounding low in his back, where his spine protested with a dull ache that spread through his body. The car slowed and stopped. When Burke got out, the ache wasn't the only thing he felt. Winds whipped swirls of salt and pollutants up from the great desert that was once the Aral Sea. The poisoned dust stung his face and neck and burned into his throat with each breath. Shanties and clapboard shops made up the town of Muynak. A fleet of fishing boats rested, rusting and rotting, on the barren soil. They, like the town itself, had been abandoned by the retreating sea.

The driver tried to hide his anxiety. He was tough himself, he said, but he thought Burke should know about the odd ailments that afflicted the people here. Few were left from a population that had reached 60,000. Unemployment ran to 50 per cent or more. You could buy the entire town for a penny and song, if you wanted it. No one did. The young man rambled on while Burke walked towards a shop. It was a grocery of sorts, selling a few canned goods, powdered milk and some sacks of rice. There were no vegetables or fresh meat – or fish of any kind.

An old man smiled and welcomed them. 'What would you like? You are thirsty? We have juice, beer, vodka.'

Burke bought bottles of fruit juice for himself and the driver.

'Are you a reporter?'

Burke shook his head.

'A scientist, come to see what happens when water turns to salt. If every reporter and scientist who visits here brought a pail of water, we would still have the Aral with us.' The old man laughed at his retelling of a local joke.

'Has a very tall man visited here today?' Burke held his hand several inches above his head.

The old storekeeper's expression changed slightly, briefly. He'd given himself away with a widening of his eyes, a catch in his throat, but he recovered quickly. He smiled gently, his voice smoky, as smooth as a gull on the wing. 'You're my only customers today.' He waved his arm. 'As you see, I have no help. If something happens outside my shop, then . . .' He cocked his head and shrugged.

Burke held the man's eyes in a hard stare. 'Where is he?'

'Who?' The catch had returned to the shopkeeper's voice.

Burke stepped towards him, his hand over his head again. 'Tell me of your own accord and forget you saw me. Whether you volunteer the information or not, you will tell me.'

The driver stood nervously to the side. He was eager for the return fare and perhaps a generous tip, but still the shopkeeper was his countryman, and his customer was a foreigner. He reached to grip Burke's shoulders and pull him back.

Burke swept his arm in an arc and pinned the driver's elbows against his side. 'You know the man. Where is he?' He addressed the shopkeeper as he held the struggling driver helpless, a puppy in its mother's jaw. 'There would be a woman with him, East Asian. I won't ask again, and I won't wait long for an answer.'

The shopkeeper's face blanched. 'Outside, among the boats. I don't know exactly where.'

Burke released the driver and walked towards the door. 'Wait for me,' he said to the driver. 'Double the fare back.'

The driver nodded. If his customer kept his word, he would earn nearly half a year's wages in a single day. It was worth the risk.

'The man you seek, the tall man . . .'

Burke spun on his heel and gazed at the shopkeeper's sneer.

The man squared his shoulders in false courage. 'He is our benefactor. He supplies a bit of money to everyone in the town in exchange for little more than a hidden retreat. We would not like anything to happen to him. There is not much work for us now. His gifts are important. He told us you would be coming. We are ready for you.'

The warning had not prepared Burke for what he faced when he walked towards the boats lying idle in the salt desert. A throng of people, a thousand or more, was forming a ring around the giant. He gripped a rope bound around Ping's waist and with one hand lifted her over his head. His eyes met Burke's, taunting him. The ring of citizens protecting him grew to at least twenty people deep, shoulder to shoulder.

In an instant, Burke's mind evoked Mai's face. She was the anchor to his being. She was the one memory he sought, if he did not survive Muynak. He could not leave Ping, but if he did not, how could he rescue her from the Scorpions? If he rushed the horde, he might be able to take out one or two, perhaps three, even four. But what was the point? He could not prevail, and the people were not his enemy. They protected their livelihood, nothing more.

A great shout rolled over the flat, poisoned land. The giant had taken Ping's bonds in both hands and pumped her over his head like a pom-pom, urging his legion forwards. The crowd began to re-form, the people behind the Scorpion coming forwards along the flanks to encircle Burke.

When they attacked, they would become the enemy, and Burke would take down as many as possible. He cleared his mind and breathed deeply to his core, filling his body with the power of *chi*. Perhaps he could strike one of the citizens with *chi* and scare the rest. If the individuals composing the mob cowered long enough for him to reach the giant, then he might defeat his foe and carry away Ping. He steeled his resolve and pushed to the back of his mind his knowledge that the plan was unfeasible. It was all he had. He drew a second breath, and as he did so, he felt the air sundered by an electric charge. Muted screams sounded across the desert.

Burke looked around. Apparitions of the six *chi* masters swept through the crowd. People fell in agony. Discharges of power crackled away from the ghostly images as they cut a swathe through the horde. A path towards the giant opened, and Burke seized his chance.

The torturer dropped Ping and focused on Burke, breathing in deeply and unleashing a wave of energy.

Burke nearly stumbled to the salty earth. Somehow the giant had gained the knowledge of *chi*. Burke had been caught off guard by the most dangerous mistake a fighter can make, underestimating his opponent's strength. Wei's apparition drew next to Burke, its aura protecting him from the next wave. The man from the Excalibur recovered and struck the giant in kind.

The Scorpion staggered back, and retreated still further when Wei's apparition struck. Burke stepped in front of Wei's ghost and moved in for hand-to-hand combat. No power from the ether would come into play now, just muscle, bone and a fighter's wiles. The giant stood splay-legged, reaching for the sky to make himself appear even more formidable, as Burke advanced with his arms tucked tight, ready to spring forwards, jump to the right or left or roll to the ground. As he closed in, he scooped a handful of salt and dirt and flung it at the giant's eyes.

It was an obvious ploy. The Scorpion blinked away the minor irritation and stepped back, then grinned, mockingly swept his hand above the earth and flicked his fingers towards Burke. The taunt was followed by a kick towards Burke's belly, a punch to the head, a vicious back-fist, a chop, a ridge hand.

Burke evaded or blocked each attack. The giant was moving, advancing towards him, committing himself in ways that Burke could anticipate.

The Scorpion punched at Burke's head and midsection with both fists at once.

Burke ducked low and to the side. He caught the Scorpion's wrist and slammed the heel of his hand into his enemy's elbow. At the same time he spun, redirecting the monster's energy towards the ground.

The giant hit the ground face-first. He rolled to the side and blocked a kick flashing towards his head.

Burke was poised to attack again when Wei's phantom glared at him and glanced at Ping's bound body. The horde of Muynak citizens was beginning to re-form as the apparitions of Wei's disciples were fading. Burke stepped back, hoisted Ping across his shoulders and ran for the car. The Uzbekistani who had brought him had already started the engine. Burke threw open the back door and pushed Ping inside. He tossed 10,000-yen notes into the front seat. The energy that had charged the air was dying, and the Scorpion was on his feet.

'Drive!'

Twenty-two

'A little higher!' the newly confident and cheerful Kazuko ordered the hosts outside the Excalibur, precisely calibrating the hoisting of a drum so it would fit through the big bay window on the club's second floor. It was a tight fit. Other hosts were bringing smaller drums in through the front door.

Mai smiled at her. Kazuko had been transformed by her session with Dan. Since she'd accepted her plump body as desirable, she'd ironically started getting thinner. 'I'll leave it with you.' Mai patted her shoulder and walked slowly down the hall to the bathroom. The anxiety that had consumed her over the last few days was finally easing. Burke was back, and he'd brought along a crew of fascinating guests. She knew that if he hadn't returned she would have coped, but she would never again have felt whole. Not to worry; he was waiting for her in the tub. She kept her eyes on his as she inched out of her dress, revealing her perfect skin in delicious stages. She slipped her thumbs into the waistband of her knickers, pushed down to the fringe of black strands and paused. Moving even slower, she slipped the white cloth past her darkening foliage, beyond her cleft and down her finely tapered legs, then turned to give Burke a view of her back and high round cheeks as she unfastened her bra. She turned again, grinned and flung away her last garment with a girlish giggle. She put one foot into the water and ran the sole over Burke's phallus. It was hard as oak.

'You're back.'

Burke grunted. He'd just returned yesterday, and they'd spent their first night back together with nothing more than a gentle embrace, grateful that fate had granted them more time as a couple. They had talked a little, but mostly explored their own thoughts of what they meant to each other.

Mai pushed harder and turned Burke's grunt into a guttural moan. She entered the bath, lay across him and slid her body over his through water slightly slick with bath oil.

'Do you think you'll ever know what happened at Bukhara?'

Burke shook his head. 'Wei says there's no need for me to give it thought. That sounds final. None of the others will say anything unless Wei speaks first. Besides, I haven't even figured out what happened at Muynak, and I was there.'

'I guess it doesn't matter. You're here now.'

'We all are. Ping is one tough girl, her father's daughter in spades. Too bad the old man's in hospital.'

'Maybe it's just as well. I don't think the show today will be a family affair. Now, about last night . . .' Mai straddled Burke's hips. 'Cuddling has its place . . .' She gripped his rod. 'But I wouldn't want to overdo it.' Her eyes narrowed as she sank the shaft slowly inside her.

Clack, clack . . . clack, boom.

The lead drummer struck her thick wooden sticks together twice, paused, struck them again on the up beat, then slammed one into the leather head of a drum that was almost as tall as she was. As the second stick thundered home another drummer hit a smaller drum twice for each sounding of the massive bass. A third drummer filled in the off beats. Two others joined until a complex rhythm reverberated in the spines of the audience and seemed to vibrate the building itself.

The drummers wore *hapi* coats, tunics that fell to mid-thigh and were secured by a single sash. With each beat, the breasts of the women drummers jiggled unencumbered beneath the thin fabric. The bass drummer swung her arms in wide arcs, pulling her garment open to the cusp of the pips growing brownish red in her body's heat. Below the sash, the tunic opened to show flashes of inner thigh with each twist of her body.

'Quite a show, Mai.' Burke put his mouth against Mai's ear so he could be heard above the throbbing, resounding drums.

'Quite a reason to celebrate, wouldn't you say? Look.' Mai pointed towards Natsuko. 'She seems to have developed a taste for older men.'

Natsuko had caught the Griffin's eyes. She bit her lower lip as she looked coyly over her shoulder.

'And there.' Burke nodded towards Kazuko, who was brushing her ample hips across the Badger's groin. They both grinned at the same time, as though they shared a secret; perhaps Badger had risen to the occasion. She pushed the soft globes of her chest against him, and he responded with a thrust of his pelvis.

The *chi* masters were prize partners and were likely to be shared by many guests before the night was over.

The hairless Aya, not to be denied, stood on a table and leapt in front of Cloud, who stood a few centimetres shorter than the Japanese Amazon. She flung off her wig, gave a shout of laughter and crushed him to her bosom. Cloud roared, clasped Aya's arse in both hands and lifted her off the ground.

The drummers responded with a frenzied beat. Salty dew beaded on their skin.

'I believe your master needs attention.' Mai squeezed Burke's hand.

'I expect he does.'

'I might not be sufficient.'

'You're enough for any man, Mai.'

Mai shifted her eyes towards Sandra, who had been glancing at Wei.

Burke laughed. 'He would be delighted, trust me. So will you two. Go to him.'

'Not two, Sir James.' Mai gestured for Ping to join them.

Sandra was seated next to Dan. When she whispered in his ear, he grinned and spanked her arse to send her on her way. He then looked back at Burke.

Rafael had approached Ling-shau, who graciously evaded him and smiled at Dan.

He quickly seized the opportunity and walked to the Chinese *chi* master.

Her eyes glistened. 'James has told me a bit about you.' The back of her hand brushed against Dan's groin. 'He said you had a warrior's instincts.' She stood so her breasts pressed against his arm. 'You wrestle.' Her hand pushed hard against the front of his trousers. 'Show me.'

Three hosts surrounded the Mongoose, who looked past them at Burke as he strode towards her. She merely had to push against the chest of one of the men, and all three withdrew to mingle with the usual clientele. She wore a long dress whose filmy material draped her body, revealing the outline of generous breasts and wide hips. Her waist was narrow, her belly flat and firm. The fluffy down of her pubis stood out against the translucent fabric clinging to her thighs as she strode towards Burke.

'You brought her back.' Mongoose glanced at Ping.

'I expect I had the easiest of it. You defeated those demons, and there's not a mark on you.'

'Not true.' Mongoose lifted her dress along her left leg. Her slender limb swelled to a full but firmly muscled thigh. She pulled the dress higher. 'See here.' She pointed to a scratch on the outside of her hip. 'And here.' She turned her leg out to show a bruise that ran across the front of her thigh. Her dress opened on her lower belly, exposing the fringe of her black, curly moss.

'If that's all, I'd say you came out of it quite well. I've seen worse from training.'

'But it's not all, James. My back too.' She turned around and looked over her shoulder. Her black eyes teased Burke. Each feature of her face was distinguished, from her proud nose to the ripe puff of her lips, which curled at the corners in a coy smile.

Burke reached down and slipped his hands under the hem of the dress, brushing her legs as he lifted it past her hips. The sight of her taut cheeks and the sound of the frenzied drums roused his lust. He pressed his bulging groin against her as he lifted the dress to her shoulders and kissed a bruise that marked her upper back.

She bent forwards pushing her hips against him. Her hand closed over the back of his as he gripped her breast in a hard squeeze.

'With or without the power?' she asked.

'Without. I want to savour your essence, pure, raw and musky.' Burke pushed the dress over her head and let it fall to the floor.

Fully nude, she turned to face Burke. She was dancing, inching towards him until his arms were around her, then she pressed her hands against the back of his neck and head, forcing his lips against hers. She opened her mouth to take in his tongue, then guided his mouth across her creamy, latté-hued skin to the tender tips of her delicious mounds. His mouth warmed her and brought a rush of blood to her now-swollen pips. He lingered there then moved to suck the other breast. She responded with a shiver, her hips pushing up towards him. She pressed his head, lightly urging him lower, towards the mossy thatch growing damp with her musky oil. His fingers ran through her moss, parting a path to the bud that lay beneath. The tiny clutches of her stomach that came from the shivers of ecstasy running through her body grew to pronounced spasms as Burke's tongue stroked her nub. Her hands gripped his hair and pushed his head hard against her sex, until his tongue entered her channel and his teeth raked her nether lips. She flung one leg over Burke's shoulder and clamped his head between her legs, rubbing herself against his face as she came in a rush of viscous oil.

Burke pulled off his shirt and trousers. His staff pressed hard against his briefs as he pushed Mongoose onto a sofa. He watched her eyes widen as he slipped off his last garment and let his cock stand free and tall. Her gasp as he entered her felt hot against his ear. His hips rose and fell with the beat of the drums. First he followed the slow resounding base, then quickened to the counter beats. Mongoose writhed beneath him and matched his pace alternately with her loins and with her arching back and thrusting chest. Burke felt her shudder with another tremor, and still the drums rolled on.

The women drummers pounding out lust on leather skins watched Burke take Mongoose in front of them. They saw Cloud strip Aya bare and bind her wrists to chains hanging from the ceiling. He applied a horsehair lash to her back and bottom as he touched her, projecting into her the ecstasy of *chi*. Aya grimaced and gasped, her head thrown back in the floods of sensation ravishing her body and mind.

At another table, Kazuko was bent at the waist, impaled by Badger, in which orifice only they knew.

The drummers had broken into a sweat that caused the tunics to cling to their skin and creep open revealing cleavage and bellies and flashes of black floss between their loins. The wooden sticks chafed their callused hands and their shoulders ached as they pressed on, driving the passion of the orgy before them.

* * *

Rafael was the first host to go to the stage. He stood behind a drummer, carefully unfastened her sash and pulled her tunic open. From behind, he reached between her legs and eased two fingers into her sex.

The drummer did not hesitate or miss a beat, but merely shifted her stance wider, inviting Rafael deeper inside her.

Instead he withdrew. He stripped himself, lay on his back and, feet first, inched between the drummer's legs.

Deftly, still keeping the beat, the drummer lowered her hips to Rafael's steely rod. She glided down it, slick with sweat and passion. With each strike on the leather head, her hips twisted, gyrating her sheath around the host's staff. Her knees were on the floor. She raised herself and let her body plunge in time to the unstoppable throb of the bass drum.

Other hosts followed and challenged the drummers with their fingers, tongues and pricks. None of the women lost her concentration, yet all yielded readily to the men of the Excalibur.

Among those in the audience, no one but Dan himself noticed Ling-shau send a wave of *chi* rolling through him. He nearly fell to his knees. He checked to see if he had soiled his trousers with come, but he had not. Another orgasmic undulation wracked his frame, then another and yet another. He gripped Ling-shau's shoulders. 'Enough.'

'You take it well. I've seen some lose consciousness.' Ling-shau reached inside Dan's trousers, ran her hand down his staff and fondled his balls.

'I nearly did pass out.'

'After the fourth time.' She smiled, stroked his pole and pushed her thumbnail into the tiny lips at its head. 'What's the longest time you've stayed this hard during sex?'

Dan shrugged. 'Fifteen, maybe twenty minutes, but that was with two condoms, and I had to think about baiting fish hooks most of that time.'

'You're about to break that record a few times over, and I want you to think about Ling-shau every second that you are inside me. You won't come until I let you or until you tell me you've had enough.' She pulled her blouse over her head and saw Dan's eyes widen at the definition of her slender musculature. She turned her back and bent at the waist as she slid her trousers and knickers down her legs. When she turned back, Dan had begun unbuttoning his shirt. 'No, let me.' As she lifted his shirt off his shoulders, her breasts pushed against his chest. Her fingers slid inside his trousers, unfastened them and lowered the zip, pressing into his swollen cock. He wore no underwear and his prick sprang from his trousers. She noticed a slight blush on Dan's face and sensed the reason for his shyness. 'That's a nice size, Dan.' Ling-shau smiled and stroked him lightly. 'You know James is quite well endowed. At first it is thrilling, but I can't endure more than fifteen minutes or so. With you –' Ling-shau nipped Dan's ear '– I expect a long, very long pleasuring.' She put one arm behind Dan's neck and lifted herself as she wrapped her legs around his hips and guided his shaft to her gate.

As Natsuko's eyes met Griffin's across the room, he sensed that she had experienced the art of *chi*, probably at Burke's hand. Her beauty was stunning. She dropped her skirt where she stood and pulled off her blouse as she walked towards him. Next, her bra dropped to the floor. Griffin removed his own clothes as he watched her approach. When she reached him, she stepped out of her knickers and looked up expectantly. He would not disappoint her. Without touching her, he enclosed her in a circle made by his arms. His hands were open, and his fingers were held just a short space apart from each other. He breathed deeply and let the universal power flow through him. The air between him and Natsuko became charged.

She closed her eyes halfway and made a humming sound in her throat as the energy tingled across her skin, firing impulses that gathered and grew in intensity as they flowed like liquid fire into her spirit. She felt Griffin's fingers on the back of her neck and a surge of power lanced the sex of her mind and body. Her back arched, and she thrust her breasts against Griffin's belly, then slammed her head forwards and bit into the muscles of his chest. Her fingernails dug into the cleft of his arse and clawed at his sac.

Griffin's eyes narrowed and his lips contorted in a grim smirk. He clasped his hands to the sides of Natsuko's head and directed a wave of *chi* to her pain centres. Her body shuddered in his hands, her face grimacing. The ancient *chi* master let go and stimulated her pleasure zones. Tears ran freely down Natsuko's cheeks even as rivulets of come oozed from her loins. Griffin again changed the sensations to pain, then back to pleasure. The intervals from one to the other grew ever shorter until the dualities melded as one, Griffin simultaneously projecting pain from one hand and pleasure from the other.

Natsuko's head thrashed from side to side, her jaws clamped tight as an eerie keen came from her throat. She pushed one hand hard into her sex and with the other gripped Griffin's proud shaft. The trickles of come had become a free-flowing stream down her thighs. With a shout, she grabbed Griffin's cock with both hands and yanked as though to wrench it from his body. The *chi* master let the power ease, and Natsuko slammed her fists into his chest. She grabbed a short bamboo lash and flailed it against his rock-hard torso, her eyes gleaming as the lash etched thin red hash marks across his skin. She stepped back and swung at Griffin's stiff rod, then slowed her pace and took heavier strokes against him, grunting with each slash, now against his back, now his buttocks and legs.

Griffin stood stoically, his eyes black coals of passion. His nostrils flared, his mouth set in a fearsome leer. A lash into his tender ball sac forced a short grunt from him, and he whirled around, clasped Natsuko's wrist in a steely grip and dragged her to a table.

She fell onto it face-down, her breasts crushed as Griffin's powerful hand pressed against her back. Her perfect cheeks were exposed, unguarded, vulnerable to his bare palm slamming against them. His hand was callused from practice with sword and quarter-staff, but still he could feel the sting through his thick skin. Natsuko's velvety cheeks were quickly growing hot and red under his assault. He lowered his aim and slapped her thighs and the lips that peeked between them, until his hand was sopping with her lust. He rubbed her liquid into the welts she had lashed into his cock. When he had lubricated himself, he pushed her legs wider. Easily, smoothly, he impaled her, sinking into the lush grip of her sex. As he withdrew, his shaft shone in the light that glinted off Natsuko's oil. He drove into her fiercely, then wet one finger and pushed it into the pucker between her cheeks, turning it and easing it in and out until the tight, pink bud was supple and ready to yield. He pulled himself free of her sex and pushed his oaken prick into the taut, round eye that opened above it. Griffin eased the head of his cock inside her slowly, then rammed it home. His rhythm grew steady, matching the accented beats of the savage drums.

'Your hair is as fine as gossamer.' Wei ran his fingers through Sandra's strawberry-blonde tresses and touched them to his lips. He was surrounded by Sandra, Mai and Ping, each of whom he praised for their special qualities: Sandra's hair, Mai's skin and Ping's athletic physique. As he charged his core with *chi*, the women slowly stripped themselves bare, letting their garments fall to the floor at their feet.

Sandra unbuttoned his shirt as Ping stood behind him and lifted it off his shoulders. Mai untied the drawstring that held his trousers up, then let them drop down his legs.

'I've never tried this before,' Wei said.

'You've never had three women at once?' Mai teased.

'Of course I have. What I mean is I've never done what I'm about to try. We did things in Uzbekistan, all of us together, that I had never dreamed of. I'm still learning, testing myself.'

'Am I going to like it?' Sandra pressed the swell of her tender breasts against his chest as she whispered the words close to his ear.

Wei ran his fingers through the curls of Sandra's V. 'We will have to see.'

'Well, you're going to like this, I'll wager.' Sandra flashed her tongue into his ear, then bit into its pulpy lobe. Mai sank to her knees and took his stiff rod between her full lips, taunting its head and sensitive underside with her skilled tongue. Ping pushed her breasts against his back and probed his cheeks with her fingers, dampened with her own oil. Sandra's hand went to his sac, gently massaging it as she ran her lips along his neck. Ping spread his cheeks and pushed her tongue to the pucker between them.

The old man's pole swelled larger and harder from the rush of sensation. Tongues and lips teased his nether zones, teeth nipped at his neck and arse, fingers and nails stroked and scraped at his legs, back and chest. Mai stood and took his cock inside her, stroking it with her internal muscles for a few moments then pulling away, to be replaced by Sandra, then Ping, the channels of each woman caressing his staff with their own unique qualities.

Long ago, Wei had learned to draw universal power from the ether and to project it in selected ways. Now he used the physical union with the women to draw the power through them. As it filled Wei's spirit, it was amplified by their lusts, imbued with their personal strengths and coloured by their wildly different characters. The Tao flowing into him overwhelmed the vessel of his spirit and flowed back to the women, each excited by the passions of the other. A dimly visible aura emerged around them, glowing golden, with spikes of red, yellow and bright bluish white.

The aura swelled slightly and brightened. Spikes of light flashed through the room. A drummer dropped her sticks as a bolt stabbed through her. The host between her legs cried out as his liquid essence gushed from his cock. The lightning spikes stopped and the aura withdrew into itself, growing brighter, hotter, until it exploded throughout the room. Couples, trios and quartets were engulfed in a universal passion rendered into pure energy. The drums died, to be replaced by shouts, moans and gasps. The orgy in the Excalibur ended in an explosion of lust none had foreseen.

Their passions spent, the customers, guests and hosts lay gasping, sated beyond their most carnally savage fantasies – except for one pair, over whom the aura's warm glow had settled.

Ling-shau was on her back now, and Dan, pounding away to his own internal drummer, was bound for a record that few mortals could hope to challenge.

Twenty-three

The drums were gone, but the echo of their throbbing passion lingered along with the odours of their wood and leather, mingling with the scents of human lust and sweat. Most of the *chi* masters had left to catch planes to their homelands. Only Wei and Ling-shau remained, and they had little time left.

Burke, Wei and Ling-shau chatted about trivialities of their past, but their communication ran much deeper. Even in training, Wei never explained the Tao. He showed it. Words would have been an obstruction to attaining knowledge.

Mai, Dan and Sandra sat with them in the main room, but mostly they just listened, until Mai announced it was time to leave for the airport.

'If you can, I hope you will come back,' she said. 'I promise not to tell the customers. That way you can relax.'

Wei laughed. 'That was the most fun I've had in a good while. Next time send out fliers to your customers that we are coming.'

'I'd need a bigger club. I might need one anyway once word gets around about last night.'

'In that case, we'll come back for certain. What do you say, Ling-shau?'

'Yes, but what about . . .?'

'Our discussion?'

Ling-shau nodded.

Wei smiled, put his hand on Tanner's shoulder and looked Burke in the eye.

Burke grimaced. 'That was too easy.'

Ling-shau whispered in Burke's ear.

'Does he know?'

'What are you talking about?' Dan sensed they were talking about him, but he had no idea why.

Burke ignored him. 'But you require that anyone accepted must first increase your knowledge.'

'He already has.'

'How?' Burke put his hands on his hips.

'A trick to control a physical reaction through mental concentration. It has to do with thinking about fish-hooks and bait. Actually, I learned it through Ling-shau, but he was the source.'

Burke looked at Tanner. 'She says you have natural talent.'

'For what?' Tanner was growing irritated at being left on the fringe of the conversation.

Wei continued talking about him in the third person. 'Let us know what he says. You're driving us, right, James? Goodbye Mai, Sandra, Dan.'

'See you again,' said Ling-shau. 'Especially you, Dan.'

'Wha –'

'Later.' Burke held an index finger in front of his mouth and led Wei and Ling-shau to the car.

'Do you know what they're talking about?' Dan scowled after the door closed.

'The lad's a bit thick, isn't he, Mai?' The two women watched Tanner's expression change as the understanding of what Wei was considering sank in.

'It's quite an honour,' said Mai. 'He's getting old, and the training is rigorous for him as well as for the disciple. You might be the last.'

Tanner opened and closed his mouth, but no words came. He tried again. 'When?'

'I guess that's up to you, but I wouldn't wait long to answer.'

Dan's mouth widened in a boyish grin of anticipation and adventure. Then he realised what leaving might mean. 'Sandra?'

'You won't be rid of me that easily, Dan Tanner. I'll be around when you get back. And when you do, I'll expect a long demonstration that you learned your lessons well.' Sandra hooked her leg behind Tanner's knee and pushed him onto his back on the floor. 'You'll need all the skills you can get.' She picked up a quirt and slapped it into Tanner's thigh. 'If you expect to tame –' she slapped him again and held her bare foot over his face '– this lass . . .'

Her tattoo was inches from his eyes.

'The Lady Scorpion.'

nexus

The leading publisher of fetish and adult fiction

TELL US WHAT YOU THINK!

Readers' ideas and opinions matter to us. Take a few minutes to fill in the questionnaire below and you'll be entered into a prize draw to win a year's worth of Nexus books (36 titles)

Terms and conditions apply – see end of questionnaire.

1. **Sex:** Are you male ☐ female ☐ a couple ☐?

2. **Age:** Under 21 ☐ 21–30 ☐ 31–40 ☐ 41–50 ☐ 51–60 ☐ over 60 ☐

3. **Where do you buy your Nexus books from?**

☐ A chain book shop. If so, which one(s)?

____

☐ An independent book shop. If so, which one(s)?

____

☐ A used book shop/charity shop
☐ Online book store. If so, which one(s)?

____

4. **How did you find out about Nexus Books?**

☐ Browsing in a book shop
☐ A review in a magazine
☐ Online
☐ Recommendation
☐ Other _______________________________________

5. **In terms of settings which do you prefer? (Tick as many as you like)**

☐ Down to earth and as realistic as possible
☐ Historical settings. If so, which period do you prefer?

____

☐ Fantasy settings – barbarian worlds

☐ Completely escapist/surreal fantasy
☐ Institutional or secret academy
☐ Futuristic/sci fi
☐ Escapist but still believable
☐ Any settings you dislike?

____

☐ Where would you like to see an adult novel set?

____

6. In terms of storylines, would you prefer:

☐ Simple stories that concentrate on adult interests?
☐ More plot and character-driven stories with less explicit adult activity?
☐ We value your ideas, so give us your opinion of this book:

____

____

____

7. In terms of your adult interests, what do you like to read about? (Tick as many as you like)

☐ Traditional corporal punishment (CP)
☐ Modern corporal punishment
☐ Spanking
☐ Restraint/bondage
☐ Rope bondage
☐ Latex/rubber
☐ Leather
☐ Female domination and male submission
☐ Female domination and female submission
☐ Male domination and female submission
☐ Willing captivity
☐ Uniforms
☐ Lingerie/underwear/hosiery/footwear (boots and high heels)
☐ Sex rituals
☐ Vanilla sex
☐ Swinging

☐ Cross-dressing/TV
☐ Enforced feminisation
☐ Others – tell us what you don't see enough of in adult fiction:

8. **Would you prefer books with a more specialised approach to your interests, i.e. a novel specifically about uniforms? If so, which subject(s) would you like to read a Nexus novel about?**

9. **Would you like to read true stories in Nexus books? For instance, the true story of a submissive woman, or a male slave? Tell us which true revelations you would most like to read about:**

10. **What do you like best about Nexus books?**

11. **What do you like least about Nexus books?**

12. **Which are your favourite titles?**

13. **Who are your favourite authors?**

14. **Which covers do you prefer? Those featuring: (tick as many as you like)**

- ☐ Fetish outfits
- ☐ More nudity
- ☐ Two models
- ☐ Unusual models or settings
- ☐ Classic erotic photography
- ☐ More contemporary images and poses
- ☐ A blank/non-erotic cover
- ☐ What would your ideal cover look like?

___

15. **Describe your ideal Nexus novel in the space provided:**

___

___

___

___

16. **Which celebrity would feature in one of your Nexus-style fantasies? We'll post the best suggestions on our website – anonymously!**

___

THANKS FOR YOUR TIME

Now simply write the title of this book in the space below and cut out the questionnaire pages. Post to: Nexus, Marketing Dept., Thames Wharf Studios, Rainville Rd, London W6 9HA

Book title: ___

TERMS AND CONDITIONS

1. The competition is open to UK residents only, excluding employees of Nexus and Virgin, their families, agents and anyone connected with the promotion of the competition. 2. Entrants must be aged 18 years or over. 3. Closing date for receipt of entries is 31 December 2006. 4. The first entry drawn on 7 January 2007 will be declared the winner and notified by Nexus. 5. The decision of the judges is final. No correspondence will be entered into. 6. No purchase necessary. Entries restricted to one per household. 7. The prize is non-transferable and non-refundable and no alternatives can be substituted. 8. Nexus reserves the right to amend or terminate any part of the promotion without prior notice. 9. No responsibility is accepted for fraudulent, damaged, illegible or incomplete entries. Proof of sending is not proof of receipt. 10. The winner's name will be available from the above address from 9 January 2007.

Promoter: Nexus, Thames Wharf Studios, Rainville Road, London, W6 9HA

NEXUS NEW BOOKS

To be published in March 2006

FORBIDDEN READING
Lisette Ashton

Librarian Justine is given a chance to acquire La Coste: an unpublished story that is supposedly the most disturbing work written by the Marquis de Sade. Alleged to contain details of his most twisted indulgences, La Coste is being put up for sale to anyone who can prove themselves worthy of owning this long lost catalogue of excess and depravity. Justine's quest will bring her face to face with extremes of punishment and pleasure. Certain to face sacrilege, sadism and subversion she knows there are no limits in the pursuit of forbidden reading.

£6.99 ISBN 0 352 34022 3

DICE WITH DOMINATION
P. S. Brett

Having taken up the reins of river-side casino The Paddle-Boat, the dazzlingly sexy and wickedly imaginative Valerie McKnight is determined to bring a new service to her thrill-seeking gambling public. Her beautiful and libidinous croupiers are re-trained to provide a profitable sideline in Domination and Fantasy in the newly appointed cellar of the grand casino building. Rumours of the activities in that subterranean den of iniquity soon attract the attention of many curious local gents.

£6.99 ISBN 0 352 34023 1

DERRIERE
Julius Culdrose

Julius Culdrose has spent over four decades delighting in every aspect of the female bottom – the different shapes and sizes, the possibilities for presentation, the aesthetics, the uses – and now reveals his explicit experiences and frank thoughts.

This is not only an epic journey to the extremities of bottom adoration, but the second book in the new Nexus Enthusiast imprint: an original series that will explore, reveal and tantalise the reader with the most highly detailed fetish literature actually written by genuine enthusiasts for genuine enthusiasts. As kinky as fiction can get!

£6.99 ISBN 0 352 34024 X

NEXUS BACKLIST

This information is correct at time of printing. For up-to-date information, please visit our website at www.nexus-books.co.uk

All books are priced at £6.99 unless another price is given.

ABANDONED ALICE	Adriana Arden	0 352 33969 1	☐
ALICE IN CHAINS	Adriana Arden	0 352 33908 X	☐
AMAZON SLAVE	Lisette Ashton	0 352 33916 0	☐
ANGEL	Lindsay Gordon	0 352 34009 6	☐
THE ANIMAL HOUSE	Cat Scarlett	0 352 33877 6	☐
THE ART OF CORRECTION	Tara Black	0 352 33895 4	☐
THE ART OF SURRENDER	Madeline Bastinado	0 352 34013 4	☐
AT THE END OF HER TETHER	G.C. Scott	0 352 33857 1	☐
BARE BEHIND	Penny Birch	0 352 33721 4	☐
BELINDA BARES UP	Yolanda Celbridge	0 352 33926 8	☐
BENCH MARKS	Tara Black	0 352 33797 4	☐
BINDING PROMISES	G.C. Scott	0 352 34014 2	☐
THE BLACK GARTER	Lisette Ashton	0 352 33919 5	☐
THE BLACK MASQUE	Lisette Ashton	0 352 33977 2	☐
THE BLACK ROOM	Lisette Ashton	0 352 33914 4	☐

THE BLACK WIDOW	Lisette Ashton 0 352 33973 X	☐
THE BOOK OF PUNISHMENT	Cat Scarlett 0 352 33975 6	☐
THE BOND	Lindsay Gordon 0 352 33996 9	☐
CAGED [£5.99]	Yolanda Celbridge 0 352 33650 1	☐
CHERRI CHASTISED	Yolanda Celbridge 0 352 33707 9	☐
COLLEGE GIRLS	Cat Scarlett 0 352 33942 X	☐
COMPANY OF SLAVES	Christina Shelly 0 352 33887 3	☐
CONCEIT AND CONSEQUENCE	Aishling Morgan 0 352 33965 9	☐
CONFESSIONS OF AN ENGLISH SLAVE	Yolanda Celbridge 0 352 33861 X	☐
CORRECTIVE THERAPY	Jacqueline Masterson 0 352 33917 9	☐
CRUEL SHADOW	Aishling Morgan 0 352 33886 5	☐
DARK MISCHIEF	Lady Alice McCloud 0 352 33998 5	☐
DICE WITH DOMINATION	P.S. Brett 0 352 34023 1	☐
DEMONIC CONGRESS	Aishling Morgan 0 352 33762 1	☐
DEPTHS OF DEPRAVATION	Ray Gordon 0 352 33995 0	☐
DISCIPLINE OF THE PRIVATE HOUSE	Esme Ombreux 0 352 33709 5	☐
DISCIPLINED SKIN [£5.99]	Wendy Swanscombe 0 352 33541 6	☐
DOMINATION DOLLS	Lindsay Gordon 0 352 33891 1	☐
EMMA ENSLAVED	Hilary James 0 352 33883 0	☐
EMMA'S HUMILIATION	Hilary James 0 352 33910 1	☐

EMMA'S SECRET WORLD	Hilary James	0 352 33879 2	☐
EMMA'S SECRET DOMINATION	Hilary James	0 352 34000 2	☐
EMMA'S SUBMISSION	Hilary James	0 352 33906 3	☐
EROTICON 1 [£5.99]	Various	0 352 33593 9	☐
FAIRGROUND ATTRACTION	Lisette Ashton	0 352 33927 6	☐
FORBIDDEN READING	Lisette Ashton	0 352 34022 3	☐
THE GOVERNESS ABROAD	Yolanda Celbridge	0 352 33735 4	☐
HOT PURSUIT	Lisette Ashton	0 352 33878 4	☐
IN DISGRACE	Penny Birch	0 352 33922 5	☐
IN HER SERVICE	Lindsay Gordon	0 352 33968 3	☐
THE INDECENCIES OF ISABELLE	Penny Birch (writing as Cruella)	0 352 33989 6	☐
THE INDIGNITIES OF ISABELLE	Penny Birch (writing as Cruella)	0 352 33696 X	☐
THE INDISCRETIONS OF ISABELLE	Penny Birch (writing as Cruella)	0 352 33882 2	☐
INNOCENT	Aishling Morgan	0 352 33699 4	☐
THE INSTITUTE	Maria Del Rey	0 352 33352 9	☐
JULIA C	Laura Bowen	0 352 33852 0	☐
KNICKERS AND BOOTS	Penny Birch	0 352 33853 9	☐
LACING LISBETH	Yolanda Celbridge	0 352 33912 8	☐

NON FICTION: LESBIAN SEX SECRETS FOR MEN	Jamie Goddard and Kurt Brungard	0 352 33724 9	☐
LESSONS IN OBEDIENCE	Lucy Golden	0 352 33892 X	☐
LETTERS TO CHLOE [£5.99]	Stephan Gerrard	0 352 33632 3	☐
LICKED CLEAN	Yolanda Celbridge	0 352 33999 3	☐
LOVE JUICE	Donna Exeter	0 352 33913 6	☐
THE MASTER OF CASTLELEIGH [£5.99]	Jacqueline Bellevois	0 352 33644 7	☐
MISS RATAN'S LESSON	Yolanda Celbridge	0 352 33791 5	☐
NAUGHTY NAUGHTY	Penny Birch	0 352 33974 4	☐
NEW EROTICA 6	Various	0 352 33751 6	☐
NIGHTS IN WHITE COTTON	Penny Birch	0 352 34008 8	☐
NO PAIN, NO GAIN	James Baron	0 352 33966 7	☐
NURSE'S ORDERS	Penny Birch	0 352 33739 7	☐
THE OLD PERVERSITY SHOP	Aishling Morgan	0 352 34007 X	☐
ONE WEEK IN THE PRIVATE HOUSE	Esme Ombreux	0 352 33706 0	☐
ORIGINAL SINS	Lisette Ashton	0 352 33804 0	☐
THE PALACE OF PLEASURES	Christobel Coleridge	0 352 33801 6	☐
PALE PLEASURES	Wendy Swanscombe	0 352 33702 8	☐
PARADISE BAY [£5.99]	Maria Del Rey	0 352 33645 5	☐
PENNY PIECES [£5.99]	Penny Birch	0 352 33631 5	☐

PET TRAINING IN THE PRIVATE HOUSE [£5.99]	Esme Ombreux 0 352 33655 2	☐
PETTING GIRLS	Penny Birch 0 352 33957 8	☐
THE PLAYER	Cat Scarlett 0 352 33894 6	☐
PLAYTHING	Penny Birch 0 352 33967 5	☐
PLEASING THEM	William Doughty 0 352 34015 0	☐
THE PRIESTESS	Jacqueline Bellevois 0 352 33905 5	☐
PRINCESS	Aishling Morgan 0 352 33871 7	☐
PRIVATE MEMOIRS OF A KENTISH HEADMISTRESS	Yolanda Celbridge 0 352 33763 X	☐
PRIZE OF PAIN	Wendy Swanscombe 0 352 33890 3	☐
THE PUNISHMENT CAMP	Jacqueline Masterton 0 352 33940 3	☐
PUNISHED IN PINK	Yolanda Celbridge 0 352 34003 7	☐
THE PUNISHMENT CLUB	Jacqueline Masterson 0 352 33862 8	☐
RITES OF OBEDIENCE	Lindsay Gordon 0 352 34005 3	☐
SCARLET VICE	Aishling Morgan 0 352 33988 8	☐
SCHOOLED FOR SERVICE	Lady Alice McCloud 0 352 33918 7	☐
SCHOOL FOR STINGERS	Yolanda Celbridge 0 352 33994 2	☐
THE SCHOOLING OF STELLA	Yolanda Celbridge 0 352 33803 2	☐
SERVING TIME	Sarah Veitch 0 352 33509 2	☐
SEXUAL HEELING	Wendy Swanscombe 0 352 33921 7	☐
SILKEN SERVITUDE	Christina Shelly 0 352 34004 5	☐

SILKEN SLAVERY	Christina Shelly 0 352 33708 7	☐
SINS APPRENTICE	Aishling Morgan 0 352 33909 8	☐
SLAVE ACTS	Jennifer Jane Pope 0 352 33665 X	☐
SLAVE GENESIS [£5.99]	Jennifer Jane Pope 0 352 33503 3	☐
SLAVE REVELATIONS [£5.99]	Jennifer Jane Pope 0 352 33627 7	☐
THE SMARTING OF SELINA	Yolanda Celbridge 0 352 33872 5	☐
STRIPING KAYLA	Yvonne Marshall 0 352 33881 4	☐
STRIPPED BARE	Angel Blake 0 352 33971 3	☐
THE SUBMISSION GALLERY [£5.99]	Lindsay Gordon 0 352 33370 7	☐
THE SUBMISSION OF STELLA	Yolanda Celbridge 0 352 33854 7	☐
THE TAMING OF TRUDI	Yolanda Celbridge 0 352 33673 0	☐
TASTING CANDY	Ray Gordon 0 352 33925 X	☐
TEASING CHARLOTTE	Yvonne Marshall 0 352 33681 1	☐
TEMPTING THE GODDESS	Aishling Morgan 0 352 33972 1	☐
TICKLE TORTURE	Penny Birch 0 352 33904 7	☐
TIE AND TEASE	Penny Birch 0 352 33987 X	☐
TORMENT INCORPORATED	Murilee Martin 0 352 33943 8	☐
THE TRAINING GROUNDS	Sarah Veitch 0 352 33526 2	☐
UNIFORM DOLL	Penny Birch 0 352 33698 6	☐
VELVET SKIN [£5.99]	Aishling Morgan 0 352 33660 9	☐

WENCHES WITCHES AND STRUMPETS	Aishling Morgan 0 352 33733 8	☐
WHEN SHE WAS BAD	Penny Birch 0 352 33859 8	☐
WHIP HAND	G.C. Scott 0 352 33694 3	☐
WHIPPING GIRL	Aishling Morgan 0 352 33789 3	☐

- - - - - - ✂ -

Please send me the books I have ticked above.

Name ....

Address ....

....

....

.... Post code ....

Send to: **Virgin Books Cash Sales, Thames Wharf Studios, Rainville Road, London W6 9HA**

US customers: for prices and details of how to order books for delivery by mail, call 1-800-343-4499.

Please enclose a cheque or postal order, made payable to **Nexus Books Ltd**, to the value of the books you have ordered plus postage and packing costs as follows:

UK and BFPO – £1.00 for the first book, 50p for each subsequent book.

Overseas (including Republic of Ireland) – £2.00 for the first book, £1.00 for each subsequent book.

If you would prefer to pay by VISA, ACCESS/MASTERCARD, AMEX, DINERS CLUB or SWITCH, please write your card number and expiry date here:

....

Please allow up to 28 days for delivery.

Signature ....

Our privacy policy

We will not disclose information you supply us to any other parties. We will not disclose any information which identifies you personally to any person without your express consent.

From time to time we may send out information about Nexus books and special offers. Please tick here if you do *not* wish to receive Nexus information. ☐

- - - - - - ✂ -